The Crooked God Machine

Autumn Christian

First Published December 2011 by
Never Sleep Again Press

Cover Design by CL Smith of
www.goonwrite.com

Part One

One

BEFORE DADDY STARTED stuffing road kill in the living room, I almost thought everything would turn out all right.

My Daddy's hands were like burnt maps. He said if we wanted to learn how to conquer the world, all we needed to do was look at his hands. He came home from the factory and sat at the kitchen table with a glass of whiskey and the after dinner cigar that Momma always gave him.

He kicked off his boots, lit the cigar, and said, "Hey kids, you want to hear a story?"

He laid his scarred hands, palms up, on the kitchen table for us to touch. I still remember their texture, like cool braised metal.

When Sissy and I were small and baby brother hadn't yet started to eat his fingers Daddy picked us up and held us above his head so we could fly. He had an indomitable body that seemed to be the only support that kept our rickety, dark-creak house from falling into the swamp. He filled every room he entered to full capacity. I can still see the mark above the kitchen door where he once hit his head.

Daddy let the sun into the house. He pulled back the curtains, opened the windows, and turned on the lights. He said there were too many dark corners in that house to hide in. There were too many dark corners in the universe. He made Momma pretty by throwing the sunlight in her hair like seeds. I never saw Daddy kiss her, but he danced with her across the living room floor. He chased Momma out onto the porch so that the sunlight jumped off her skin. That was the only time I ever heard her laugh, when Daddy brought her the sun.

When Daddy was here Sissy still wore her Sunday dresses and called me Bubba instead of Charles. She still let me hide inside her coat when the black moon cast its shadow across the house and the plague machines beat against the air with their chuk-chuk-chuk noises. I curled up against her ribcage and tried to guess how many birds could hide inside her bones, and she whispered, "Shhh," and told me morning would come soon.

"I'll tell you everything you need to know for a glass of lemonade," he told Sissy when she wanted to learn how to plant a garden.

He instructed her how to plant the basil, hyacinths, and tomatoes as he read the newspaper on the front porch. The hyacinths never grew, but the tomatoes flourished. He promised the hyacinths would come in next year, as if he owned the weather.

And when I sat outside with my sketchbook and charcoals trying to draw landscapes, chewing my nails until they bled because none of my sketches came out right, he was the one who sat down beside me and put his arm around my shoulder.

"Stop looking at the paper. Before you can become an artist, you have to be a scientist," he said. "Look out into the swamp and draw what you see. Not what you think you see."

One day Daddy came home from work early. He slammed the front door open with a crack and stood there for a moment, heaving. Then he lurched forward so fast I thought his head might roll off his shoulders and across the carpet. He sat down on the couch and took off his steel-toed work like he was sinking underwater. Momma handed my baby brother to Sissy. She got one of Daddy's cigars, but he declined to take it.

Finally, he got his boots off, set them down, and spoke to the wall.

"The factory shut down," he told Momma.

"What are we going to do?"

"Nothing to do," he said.

He took the cigar from Momma, handling it like a live animal. He lit it and breathed deep and his face turned slack like a snapped belt. It seemed as if the house around us shifted, grew darker, as if Daddy's protection against the shadows finally broke, so now they could insinuate themselves through the crevices in the floor. My baby brother cried out. Sissy rocked him with mechanical motions. Momma stared at the wall behind Daddy's head.

After dinner, Daddy put back on his boots with the same underwater heaviness that he'd taken them off. It was nighttime, brighter than

I'd ever remembered before. The stars cracked open and the trees in the woodland swamp festered with colors.

"You shouldn't go out there tonight," Momma said as he laced his boots. "The hell shuttles are out again. Not to mention the monsters."

Daddy went to my brother's crib, where he lay asleep. He lingered for a moment with his scarred hands on the railing, and then kissed him on the forehead.

"Don't you worry about a thing," Daddy said, to no one in particular.

Then he left.

I woke up in the middle of the night to Momma and Daddy screaming at each other in the kitchen downstairs. Momma's voice was a runaway train, halting, crashing, and squealing. Daddy's voice was congealed like syrup and glass. My baby brother wailed, but they weren't paying attention to him.

I went to the stairs. I found Sissy already there, sitting on the first step in the last stretch of shadow beyond the kitchen light. Sissy craned her neck as she listened.

"Don't go down there," she said to me. "That'll get you in trouble."

Momma argued like all wives everywhere. You don't love me anymore. Think of the children. You could've been killed. The shuttles are out and if the monsters find you then you'll never walk right again. Daddy yelled as if he understood what Momma was talking about, but he talked about the anatomy of plague machines and the monster he heard singing out in the swamp. He talked of fire he saw growing out of God's head and the memories of dead friends and cancelled television shows that followed him for years.

"I'll leave you if you go out there again," Momma said.

Daddy laughed. Not an ordinary laugh. It was a sudden pop, a wet bone crunch of a laugh.

"Where would you go?" he asked. "You've never been outside Edgewater. You'll be so lost you'll fall off the edge of the world."

After that, Daddy went out every night for the next week. Drinking with his ex-coworkers at the Legion, Sissy told me one day when Momma wasn't around. There was nothing left for any of us since the factory closed down, except this house and this town that would probably soon collapse underneath us.

One night Daddy came home with a bad back and a broken wrist. He took off his shirt in the living room and I saw from my hiding place at the top of the stairs the bite marks lacerating his back. Claw scratches welded onto his ribcage. Momma and Sissy were asleep, dreaming bad dreams that made them cry and shake. I was the only one who saw Daddy sit down on the couch in front of the television and bend over with his pearly bone exposed in his back, his back muscles masticating like a jaw. He closed his eyes heavy and when he moved on the couch his wounds made a wet sound, a tearing sound, the sound of the earth disintegrating out from underneath me.

He stopped bringing us the sun. He no longer chased Momma out onto the porch or gave us his cool hands to touch and tell us stories of metal. He stopped teaching me how to draw, stopped explaining the anatomy of plants to Sissy, and stopped tossing my baby brother up to the ceiling or kissing him while he slept. His silence ballooned upwards in our house like a column of smoke.

He stopped going out drinking. Instead he went out in the morning to scrape dead animals off the side of the road. He took up taxidermy and gutted road kill on the coffee table in the living room while watching God on the television and smoking his cigars. The living room existed in a perpetual haze. Stuffed raccoons, badgers, and possums lined the shelves in every room.

"This smoke is bad for the baby," Momma said.

She stayed upstairs and drew all the curtains down and rocked my baby brother while he cried and cried. Daddy just tapped his teeth with the tip of his gutting knife and lit another cigar. He pulled down the windows and turned off all the lights in the house except his white work lap. While he worked his bad back cast a nightmare shape against the wall. His broken wrist swelled.

One afternoon Sissy and I sat in the kitchen working on our homework. I leaned back in my chair and looked into the living room. I saw Daddy hunched over a dead deer he'd thrown, legs up, on the coffee table.

Momma came down the stairs and walked past Daddy. In the kitchen she fixed herself a hot cup of lavender tea. She leaned against the counter holding the tea, waiting for it to cool.

"Those blood stains are never going to come out of the coffee table," she said, and shook her head.

I couldn't sleep that night because my brother kept crying. I went downstairs to get a glass of milk from the refrigerator and found Daddy still working on his dead deer. The television was on, and God in his black horned mask peered out at my Daddy as he worked. His skin glowed yellow and sick underneath the work light. All of his cigars were lined up on the table by his right hand, so that whenever he smoked one down he could grab another.

I glanced over at the clock. It was about 3:30 in the morning.

"Hey Daddy," I said.

"Hey Charlie," Daddy said. "Want to hand me that jar of pickle juice over there?"

I picked up the jar of formaldehyde and

handed it to him.

"Thanks, Charlie." he said.

I went into the kitchen and poured myself a glass of milk. When I came back I stood a few feet away from Daddy, watching him work.

"What are you doing?" I asked.

Daddy stopped for a moment, his knives dripping, and tilted his head to one side.

"I'm sorry, I didn't hear you. What was that?"

"Why are you cutting up those animals?"

Silence.

I walked past him toward the stairs before he spoke.

"Hey Charlie?"

I stopped. "Yeah?"

"Before God made us the universe was a lifeless place. When we're gone the universe will go on as if we'd never even been here," Daddy said. "Life is a rather strange and dangerous thing."

He returned to working on his dead deer.

The next time Momma cooked dinner Daddy sat down at the kitchen table and insisted Momma save a spot for his stuffed deer. While we ate, the deer watched us from one corner of the table with its plastic red eyes.

"Why did you have to give it red eyes?" Momma asked, the first thing she said to Daddy in weeks. "Why not a nice amber?"

"What the hell do you care what color its eyes are?" Daddy asked.

"I just think amber would have been nicer."

She picked at her food with her fork. Upstairs, my brother wailed. Nobody moved.

"I like its eyes," Sissy said.

"There you go." Daddy said. "See? Your daughter thinks its eyes are just fine."

Silence.

"I have an announcement to make," Daddy said.

He set down his knife and fork and pushed his plate away. His voice made my stomach greasy and cold. I stopped eating. For a moment he looked at all of us, without speaking, his scarred black hands laying palm up on top of the table.

"I'm leaving you all," he said.

Then Daddy stood up, threw on his leather jacket, and grabbed the stuffed deer.

"Why?" was all Momma could say.

"Because God told me to."

Daddy stuck a fried chicken leg between his teeth like a cigar. Momma and Sissy both looked bloodshot, their mouths and eyes heavy and white, their skin cracked stiff. Daddy looked at them and laughed.

"I'm only joking about the God thing," he said. "I'm just sick of you all."

He left the house with the stuffed deer under one arm. I jumped up and knocked my chair over.

"Don't you go after him," Momma said, but I

did anyways.

Daddy left the front door open, and the wind that blew through the door scraped against the walls and whistled past my body. I ran out onto the porch and the night crept in on me. The night screamed through me. I called out for Daddy. I called out and monsters answered in response. A chill must've snuck into my lungs, making it hard to breathe. I couldn't see Daddy anywhere. The night must've swallowed him whole. The world grew impossibly large, spun off its axis, sent me down into a sickening vertigo.

Sissy and Momma found me in the woods crying and dragged me back to the house. They told me Daddy wasn't coming back. I couldn't stop crying. They told me the hell shuttles would pick him up, that God would punish him, and I couldn't stop crying.

Two

AFTER DADDY LEFT my baby brother started chewing on his fingers and face. No matter what Momma did, rock him, pacify him, feed him at all hours of the night; she couldn't keep him from eating his knuckles. His toes. He bit off his thumb in the middle of the night and spit it out against the wall. Momma and Sissy wouldn't let me see the severed thumb, but I saw where it hit the dusty wallpaper, like a flower licking a spot of blood above his crib. Momma slapped me when she saw me standing in front of the crib with my sketchpad and piece of charcoal drawing that blood-drinking flower.

There was too much jump jumping of nerves in his brain. My baby brother couldn't control the impulse to spit out his thumb and gnaw off his tongue. He died upstairs with his face torn apart and his eyes squeezed between his fists.

Lesch-Nyhan syndrome, the doctor said. A rare genetic disorder, it couldn't be helped. His genetic code missed a vital enzyme with a name too long to pronounce. One little enzyme was all that separated us from the impulse to gnaw off our faces and tongues.

Instead of burying him in the cemetery, Momma placed his body in a sweltering trash bag. I watched from my bedroom window as Sissy and Momma carried the trash bag between them, out the door to the edge of the lawn next to the swamp. They lowered the trash bag down onto the grass and walked back to the house.

I stood at the window for a long time after Momma and Sissy went inside. The sun seeped onto the bag. I imagined my brother's fingerless, toe-less limbs curled with heat. I got my sketchpad and my charcoal to capture that last image of my brother, but my hands shook too badly to draw.

Later the woman that lived in the swamp crept out from behind the tree line. She dragged her body behind her like a chained shadow. Her red hair was a nest of moss and thorns and bone. She bent down over my baby brother, grasped the trash bag, and dragged him away.

"Her name's Jolene," Sissy told me later when I asked. "She's lived in that swamp as long as anyone can remember."

"Why did she take our brother?"

"He was a gift," Sissy said, and that was all she would tell me.

After Jolene took him away she decided she wanted me too. As I tried to sleep she called to me from the dark to come join her down in the green waters. She scratched at my bedroom window as I hid trembling underneath my bed covers.

"Your mother's a cunt," Jolene whispered with her mouth pressed against the windowpane, "and your sister's a whore."

I called out for Daddy, but Daddy

disappeared long ago.

"If only this window was your throat," Jolene told me, and she scratched and scratched.

I jumped out of bed and ran down the hallway into Momma's room. I found Momma asleep wearing her sleep mask with the painted bug eyes that looked like they were popping right out of her head. Everything in her gray room rose up to attack me; the nightstand, the bed rails, the dead buttons of flowers on the wallpaper, Momma's ghost hair. Her svelte, sticky ribcage rose up like a wasteland against my knees and rolled past my body.

In the corner of the room sat my dead baby brother's crib and inside the crib his old blood bloomed into a snake. I called Momma's name but she wouldn't wake. I shook her shoulders but she wouldn't wake. I sat on top of her like in a bad dream, leaned down into her face, and screamed.

"Bubba, what are you screaming for?"

Sissy stood in Momma's doorway in her white nightgown, her hair upbraided in a snake coil, rubbing her eyes.

"Jolene's trying to kill me," I said, "and Momma's dead."

Everything in the room returned to normal. The looming furniture shrank. Momma's ribcage turned from sand back into bone. The snake of blood had been nothing but a tired spot on an unused mattress. Sissy went to the bed stand

and picked up a nearly empty pill bottle. She shook it.

"Momma's not dead. She just took too many sleeping pills."

Jolene screamed and shook the entire house. She spit my name out like a curse word and the hallway light broke. The house tumbled into darkness.

Again, I cried out for Daddy.

"Charles," Sissy said. You know he's not here."

Sissy pressed her mouth to my forehead and whispered a "Shh" that hummed against my skin.

Jolene rattled my bedroom window.

"I'm going to fuck your sister with the branches of this tree," she called to me.

Her voice shattered through the room like broken glass.

Sissy lifted me off Momma's bed. We went down the hallway past my open bedroom door. Jolene's silhouette plastered itself onto my window. Her nails were color of a sick dog, translucent and green.

We hid in the hallway closet and sat on top of boxes full of Daddy's leather jackets. I wanted to tell Sissy to make Daddy come back and save us all, but I didn't dare to make a sound. Sissy touched the back of my neck with the tips of her fingers and stroked my hair. I rattled with Jolene's screams.

When morning came Jolene left and Sissy and I were still alive. We left the closet and went downstairs to find Momma raised from her sleeping dead stupor and making coffee. Sissy and I sat down at the kitchen table with red eyes and animal seizure nerves. Sissy scratched the table with her nails. I chewed my thumbs into the shapes of meat hooks.

"Oh, you're awake," Momma said.

She poured substitute sugar into her coffee and looked out the window where Sissy's garden lay abandoned in the gloom outside.

"I thought the wisteria would've come in by now," she said.

She sighed, and her body heaved with soporific weight. Momma took her coffee upstairs and left us alone.

"Do you want some breakfast?" Sissy asked.

Her face was a lead weight, and for a moment, I saw Momma creeping into her.

"What is that monster?" I asked. "If she gets me will she come after you next?"

"You know what she is," Sissy said.

When Sissy and Momma went to sleep I put on one of Daddy's leather jackets, took a kitchen knife out of the silverware drawer, and went into the swamp. Daddy was gone, I realized that now, and I knew I was the only one to protect Momma and Sissy from everything bad. As I walked through dense fog and cold I held the kitchen knife out in front of me.

Jolene called my name and her voice shivered through the metal of my kitchen knife. I looked behind me and my house bottomed out and disappeared. I kept walking. The air thickened. The swamp closed over my head.

Jolene rose out of the green water, her limbs shining like insect wings. Her spine arched against her skin like fish fangs. She reached out toward me and clasped my knife between her palms. The knife scratched her but she did not bleed.

She smiled and her wet, dirty hair fell in a halo against my forehead. Her crown of tree branch teeth pressed into my cheeks. The tip of my kitchen knife gleamed sharp in the reflection of her eyes, those dripping, fist-sized eyes that could probably cut into bone. I shivered and shrunk in her grip. When she spoke her voice abraded my head.

"Give me the knife," she said, and she pressed her forehead to my mouth and whispered, "Shhh," just like Sissy did.

She shoved my nose into the folds of her rotting dress.

"Give it to me," she said again.

I let go of the knife. It slipped through her palms and dropped into the water. She grabbed my hair and shoved my head down.

"Look," she said. "Down into the water."

She forced me to my knees, down into the swamp and silt. My mouth and nose touched the surface of the water. Her nails dug into my scalp.

"Look or you drown," Jolene hissed.

I looked down, straight to the bottom.

There were bones in the water. The skull, finger, and hipbones of children. The bones of all the children lost to bullet wounds and SIDS and cracked heads. The bones of all the children put into black trash bags and left on porch steps so that the monster with her hands now tugging at my hair could drag them into the swamp to build her sleeping nest.

The bones were cracked open, gnawed, and left to corrode in the mud. The bones were cool blue and misery heated red, bones that never learned adult fear. Bones of girls with mouths frozen into rictus and bones of boys with empty skulls and skinny legs chewed apart. Bones of my dead baby brother. Bones that held out their hands to touch me. Bones that went down into the darkness forever.

Jolene released my hair and I stumbled backwards and fell. She laughed.

"Run home now," she said. "You'll be with me soon enough."

I left my dead baby brother and the kitchen knife and my bones behind in those dark waters.

Three

GOD APPEARED ON THE TELEVISION in a black horned mask and warned that Judgment Day was approaching. He'd been doing this for as long as I could remember. After my brother died and Daddy left, Momma threw all of Daddy's stuffed animals into our closets and cupboards. Then she sat down in front of the television and she turned the volume up a little more each day until God's voice broke through the walls and busted down the ceiling and rattled my bed so I couldn't sleep.

Momma put on her angry face every time God came onto the television. Her angry face made her look about a century older, made her mouth small and hard and her eyes big and buggy. Her body knotted against the couch like a dead tree. She grew twisted claws in the perfect shape for gripping curtains and the edges of chairs.

Yet no matter how long God screamed and cursed, no matter how much Momma's body knotted and strained and her angry face threatened to eat out her head, no matter how many times the television boomed so loud I thought the furniture would blow across the room and Momma would have to hold tight onto the seat curtains to keep from flying out the window, she never turned off that television.

"I can't sleep," I told Momma.

"Fix yourself a glass of warm milk," Momma said without looking away from the television.

I walked through a tunnel of noise to get to the kitchen. I poured myself a glass of milk and heated it in the microwave. First Daddy, then Momma, had been sucked under by that living room, bent under the pressure of its gravity. No light entered the room from outside, and all the light bulbs in the house either burnt out or broke long ago.

I took the glass of milk out of the microwave and walked back into the living room.

"Hey Momma?" I asked.

"You're blocking the television," she said.

I didn't move out of the way at first. Momma buried her claws into the couch upholstery. I wanted to ask her if she was still alive. I wanted to ask her if she still loved me.

Her angry mask slipped on, that rubbery, tight parody of a face with its shrinking lips and hollow ball forehead, and I couldn't speak.

I went upstairs and crawled into bed. I drank my milk and pulled the covers over my head, but I couldn't sleep with God's voice tearing down the house.

"Repent or you will die," God in his black mask said. "Follow me or you will die."

God never slept.

In the morning when I crawled out of bed with stiff limbs Momma was still in front of the television and God was still speaking about the death of all humanity and the flood that would sweep us away, our imminent death knoll and dirge sung by his terrible monsters. I hung onto the edge of the couch to keep from flying away and God's voice shuddered through my teeth.

"Why aren't you at school?" Momma asked.

"It's Saturday," I said. "I don't have any school."

"Go outside and play with your friends, then," she said.

She pried my fingers off the couch and pushed me toward the door, then locked it behind me.

I didn't want to tell her that most of my friends were dead.

I still thought about them even though they were gone. I remembered Wiley, who had angry purple fingers and a red butterfly birthmark that covered half his face and a death wish. He used to sleepwalk into his kitchen in the middle of the night and smash dinner plates. He picked them up one at a time and hurled them onto the floor. When his parents locked the cabinets so he couldn't smash the dinner plates anymore, he sleepwalked into the living room and smashed his mother's collection of porcelain angels. After that his parents locked him in the basement at night. In his sleep he ricocheted off the walls of the, his arms and legs whining like helicopter blades. He came to school with his face and limbs black with bruises.

Then there was Smarts, who had a body flat as a plaster fresco and punch holes for eyes. He wrapped duct tape and plastic wrap around his bald head so girls couldn't read his mind, so he said. He raised chickens to torture and slaughter because his daddy said every good boy had a little sociopath in him. Smarts talked with a lisp and walked with a limp, though Ezekiel told me had it on good authority Smarts was faking both. For what reason, though, Ezekiel couldn't say.

The twins Darling and Violetta used to wear tiny tulle wedding dresses. They buried their teeth in their ghost red hair when they wanted to read our minds. Darling pressed the tips of her fingers to my temples and told me what to think. She always said things like, "You are thinking of a warm and empty place. You are thinking of your mother's womb." Violetta, born with the umbilical cord wrapped around her throat, crouched in corners and trembled and scratched at her face.

The six of us explored of abandoned houses, houses of people murdered by monsters or dragged away to the hell shuttles. We never stole or disturbed anything, but walked through the rooms as if in a museum.

The basements and closets were as they'd been left, often with beds unmade and clothes scattered across the floor. Once I found a child's teddy bear with its head ripped off, lying on top of a chest drawer as if it was a coffin. Though the residents were gone, the houses seemed to come to life with us inside them. The attics and hallways scraped and shuddered underneath us. The ovens, sinks, refrigerators, and showers seemed to spit hot iron as we walked past.

After we finished exploring, we usually went downtown. We sat down on the street opposite the reverend that passed out abortion pamphlets. Ezekiel usually took this time to preach about the impermanence of human flesh.

"Happens fast when the shuttles take you," Ezekiel said, who'd just come back from his prophet apprenticeship at The First City with a shiny black sphere implanted in his head.

"Where do the hell shuttles take you?" I asked Ezekiel, who, I thought, knew everything.

He didn't go to school anymore like the rest of us, but instead learned with a private mentor.

"Ain't no heaven shuttles," Ezekiel said. "Does that give you a clue?

***

We went to the woods outside of town. We were drunk on the summer night, mad with mosquito bites and blood filling our ears. Summer heat drove the monsters out of their holes and we heard them scratching and hissing all around us, yet nobody seemed concerned. Darling and Violetta sewed daisy chains into each other's hair. Wiley kicked trees. Smarts and

Ezekiel walked in front of the rest of us, hands in their pockets, staring at the ground.

We came to a building half hidden by overgrown cedar and dogwood trees. The building was made of concrete and crushed rocks, like nothing I'd ever seen inside the town of Edgewater. It squatted down in the dirt like it was being crushed by its own weight.

"What is that?" I asked.

"A temple," Ezekiel said.

"God's temple?" I said. "It doesn't look like the ones in town."

The shiny sphere on the back of his head Ezekiel's head focused and squinted. I saw myself in that eye, my limbs distended and head scraping sideways.

"Let's go look," Wiley said.

We went through the doublewide entrance. Inside the temple, it was cool and quiet. The walls, low and crumbling, slouched inward and the stones dripped with monster musk.

I rounded a corner of the temple. On the walls in the hallway I saw pictograms of monsters. I recognized them as monsters that I'd been forced to recite the names of in school. Kali. Aphrodite. Jolene.

At the end of the hallway, we came to an inner sanctuary with a stone altar rising out of the floor. Broken mirrors perforated the ceiling.

On the opposite wall hung a picture of the black moon, gleaming with a silver halo, hovering over our black planet.

In the picture metallic figures hovered around the moon. Those figures were familiar and yet uncanny, both machine and animal.

Before I could get a closer look, a monster slithered out from behind the altar. It was Aphrodite, with a bird face and snake limbs. I gagged on the wet smell of her feathers. When she saw me, she hissed and nearly stopped my heart. She writhed across the sanctuary floor toward me.

Someone grabbed my shoulder. Ezekiel. We ran back down the hallway, into the empty entrance, out into the woods. Smarts and the rest already fled the temple. We didn't stop until we ran to the safety of my room and slammed the door shut. I sat for a long time on the bed clutching at my chest, those silver machines and that black moon stamped on the back of my skull.

"Be a little more careful, would you?" Ezekiel said. "I've already been to seven funerals this week."

Ezekiel and I never spoke about what we'd seen in that inner sanctuary again. But on nights when I couldn't sleep, I got up from bed and tried to recreate in sketches those metallic figures I'd seen on the temple wall.

***

Wiley stopped going to school. We found him months later in an abandoned monster nest with his head crushed into the dirt, and his hair matted into moss. We dragged him out of the nest. His arms fell out of their sockets and his head tumbled off his shoulders and rolled away into the grass. We sat by his in silence. I held his head in my lap and picked the flowers from his skull while Darling and Violetta sewed daisy chains, Smarts dug through the monster nest, pulling out bones and scraps of clothing, and Ezekiel picked at his nails and sighed loudly. After about an hour we left his body. We didn't speak of Wiley again.

Smarts disappeared shortly afterwards. One day a traveling salesman came to my door.

"Can I talk to your Momma?" he asked.

I'd never heard anyone with such a cheerful voice, so I let him inside and he sat down at the kitchen table and I fixed him a pot of coffee. Momma sat on the couch watching God on the television.

"Momma," I called. "Someone's here to see you."

"I'm not talking to that son of a bitch," she said.

The salesman folded his hands on the table and smiled sideways.

He said, "Son, you want to see something?"

He made a big spectacle of picking up his heavy black leather briefcase and placing it on the table. He waited for a few moments for dramatic tension, smiling that sideways smile, before unclasping the big golden buckles of the briefcase and letting it swing open on the table.

Photographs filled the briefcase. The salesman picked up one of them and slid it across the table toward me.

It was a photograph of Smarts. I knew it was he because he still had tape and plastic wrap around his bald head. He stood in the corner of a grainy dark room with a dirty light bulb on a chain hanging down over his head. Someone gouged out his punch-hole eyes, leaving his face a wet ruin. They'd placed a ball gag in his mouth and chained his ankles together.

"Let me see the other pictures," I said, but the traveling salesman whipped the photograph away and placed it back into the briefcase, then snapped the briefcase shut.

"Oh, those are nothing special," the traveling salesman said, and then added in his cheery voice, "just your friend performing various acts of sodomy."

"What's sodomy?" I asked.

"Five thousand dollars and he'll be returned to you."

"I don't have five thousand dollars."

"Well, I'm sure one of his friends will," he said, and he thanked me for my time, snatched up the briefcase, and left.

Later Ezekiel mentioned the salesman.

"Did anyone else have a weird guy trying to sell Smarts come and visit you?"

"Yeah," I said.

"Yeah," said Darling, her voice barely audible.

Violetta disappeared recently, and without her twin, Darling withered.

"Well I sure as hell wasn't going to pay five thousand dollars for that asshole," Ezekiel said, and then turned to Darling. "Hey, you ever figured out what happened to Violetta?"

"The shuttles took her," Darling said.

***

I was walking home from school and I ran into a hell shuttle pick-up a few blocks away from my house. I found Darling on the sidewalk in a line of prisoners surrounded by guards. She ate an apple while the rest of the prisoners clamored at passing neighbors, asking for cigarettes and last kisses.

"You too?" I asked Darling, careful not to get too close to the guards wearing their pig-nosed masks and holding stun guns.

"I'm going home," she said.

"Home?"

"Get away from her!" One of the guards shouted at me, and his pig mask nose quivered.

"You better go," she said, and smiled. "I'll see

you soon."

I ran away and didn't stop until the end of the block. I looked back in time to see a hell shuttle pull around the corner and stop in front of the waiting line.

Darling tossed the apple onto the ground. When the shuttle doors opened, she boarded first. The guards herded the rest of the people after her. Their skin turned gray with anxiety, but Darling remained white.

The next time Ezekiel and I explored abandoned houses, I said to him maybe we weren't really exploring, but fleeing. We were fleeing as fast as we could but it wasn't fast enough. Ezekiel laughed and he grabbed a teddy bear from the child's room and kicked it around the room.

"I'm not going to die like Wiley or Smarts or the twins," he said. "I'm not going to die like you."

He tapped the back of his head and the shiny black sphere smiled down at me.

Four

JEANINE WAS THE NAME for all pretty girls, the name for all girls with parents who still thought their children were virgins. She knew the flight patterns of every bird still alive in Edgewater. She memorized textbooks upside down and then took bets that she could recite the words back verbatim, and won every time. She bit her lips to turn them red because she couldn't afford lipstick, and when she got bored she scratched at her wrists until they were striped blue.

Do you know Jeanine?" I asked Ezekiel one day after school.

"She's a whore." Ezekiel said.

"Really?"

"Nah," Ezekiel said. "She's one of the crazy ones. Won't take money for it."

After that, every time I looked at Jeanine in class, her skin Technicolor underneath the projectors as we watched yet another serial killer documentary, I thought of her unzipped. I imagined blood rushing to her lips as she told me the swallows would be coming in late this year. I saw myself breathing on her bare suicide skin as she told me a scissortail warbled every morning from six to six thirty four on her balcony. I imagined I saw her naked spine bent down and a thousand cranes creep out of her back and fly away.

Jeanine and I sat next to each other in class every day without speaking to each other. I drew women with black lioness hair and eyes like spider eggs, and labeled every part of their brains. Medulla oblongata. Temporal lobe. Basal ganglia. Jeanine. Jeanine. Jeanine.

It seemed like the only thing we ever did in high school was watch documentaries about murderers. I first talked to Jeanine during the documentary of the goatherd killer.

The goatherd killer murdered sixteen girls and buried their bodies on a rocky hillock behind the grazing pastures.

While the attendants led the goatherd killer to the electric chair down a long white hallway, the walls fell away and revealed a hidden morgue. Sixteen freezer drawers flew open and sixteen half-decomposed girls in plastic wrap and hospital gowns proceeded to have a song and dance number about the vengeance they'd inflict on him in hell.

Jeanine tapped her fingers on the back of my hand and pointed to the screen.

"That's me," she whispered.

"What?" I said.

"You see that girl in the blue corpse paint, who has all her ribs showing because there's no skin on her chest?" Jeanine said. "That's me."

I looked back at her in the dark classroom.

"I wasn't really murdered," she said. "They just put that scene in there because this movie is so boring. Nobody cares about serial killers anymore.

Jeanine and the other dead girls on the projector encircled the goatherd murderer. They produced red-tipped knives from the folds of their hospital gowns and brandished them over their heads.

“But I'm not in show business anymore."

“Oh?” I said. “Why not?”

"I'm going to be an archaeologist," she said. “I’ll find artifacts we all thought were lost. What are you going to be?"

“I don’t know,” I said.

I had never thought about it.

Jeanine leaned close toward me and touched my sketchpad. Her nails left little impressions on the paper.

“An artist,” she said “or maybe a doctor. Look at the lines on her. You pay attention to details.”

The algebra teacher stepped in front of the projector. Onscreen the dead Jeanine sang, “Murder and woe, murder and woe.” The colors of the projector glowed on the teacher’s chest. The Technicolor morgue burst on top of his head.

"I told you kids to be quiet!" he shouted.

He grabbed Jeanine's arm and hauled her out of the room. The sixteen dead girls on the screen folded themselves back into the freezer drawers, the walls came back down, and the goatherd murderer resumed his walk to the execution room.

He said, "I murdered them because I wanted to be the mother they never had. I shoved my fingers down into their throats to touch the inside of their rib-cages, “he said, "Can I go home now?"

Technicians strapped his arms and feet to the electric chair. His relatives set fire to the pages of his unpublished manifesto on the responsibilities of mankind and God in an apocalyptic world. I kept hoping the girl's corpses would come back for a final song and dance number so I could see Jeanine again, but when the executioner flipped the switch and the credits rolled.

Jeanine caught up with me after school on the steps outside the auditorium. I sat on the steps, hunched over my sketchpad.

"Miss me?" she asked.

"They let you out so early?" I asked.

"My brother's a prophet down at The First City," she said, "and my daddy’s a serial killer. Once the principal figured out who I was he couldn't get me out of his office fast enough."

"Your brother's a prophet? How did that happen?"

"Strange, huh?"

She took my sketchpad and flipped through the pages.

“This is me,” she said.

“No it’s not,” was my instinctual response.

She laughed.

"Yes it is," Jeanine said. "I'd recognize myself anywhere. I'm a narcissist. My mother told me so."

She handed the sketchpad back to me.

"You're a good artist. Where'd you learn to draw like that?"

"I taught myself," I said.

I tucked the sketchpad under my arm. Ezekiel rode around the corner on a bicycle, his black coat flying behind him. He saw Jeanine standing beside me, winked, and rode past us.

Will you take me home?" Jeanine asked as I watched Ezekiel disappear down the street.

Without waiting for a response, she slipped her hand into mine and pulled me to my feet.

"Don't worry. It's not far," she said.

She took me into the back of a closed down butcher shop. The windows were boarded up and blacked out, and it seemed the shop hadn't been open in months.

"What are we doing here?" I asked.

"My father was a butcher before he became a serial killer," she said, ignoring my question. "I always got cast in those serial killer documentaries because he made the best meat costumes in the business."

She opened the freezer doors and the crystallized air inside decompressed at our feet with a hiss. Meat costumes hung from the ceiling and lay in neat stacks on the shelves. They bent forward underneath their weight, rib cages split, porcelain teeth, hair protruding from the headless throats and cracked spines.

"This was his freezer before he got taken away," Jeanine said. "Now it's mine. Would you like to see more?"

Jeanine ducked between two frozen hog heads and disappeared into the bowels of the freezer. I followed.

A forest of meat surrounded us, those trussed of bodies of cattle and costumes made from choice cuts of skin. The air cloyed with their bristled smell. I found myself looking at the way Jeanine's long lion hair fell across her shoulders, at the small of her back.

"You can touch if you want," she said. "The costumes."

I held my breath. I reached out and grasped slender girl shaped fingers of meat. Jeanine showed me her butterfly wings made out of meat, scarred with freezer-burn, and pressed between two sheets of butcher paper

"I was going to fly with these," she said, "in that documentary about the serial killer who used to tie people to red helium balloons. Remember hearing about him? He'd drive to the coast and release them there. Watch them float out over the ocean."

She told me more stories about the meat costumes as we delved further into the freezer. Here was the horned girl, with antlers made out of femur bones and hooves of black medulla, running through the forest after the Poison Ivy Widow. She touched the exposed calf skull of the Angry Baby Asphyxiator's last victim and then stuck her fingers down into the stomach of the Split Pea Gangrene Girl. She pulled them out covered in crystalline black pieces of gore.

She spoke of her meat costumes with the nostalgia of someone who'd had all the glitter squeezed out of her and now there was nothing left but the talcum powder, the mothballs, and the antiseptic. A seventeen-year-old widow of glamour.

"Of course, this was before my dad got caught," she said. "Now I'm done with all this, but I still keep the costumes. I don't know how to throw things away."

"Why are you done?" I asked.

"Done with what?"

"With the documentaries. The show business and the costumes and the dancing."

"Because it's silly," she said. "Nobody dances in real life."

She did a pirouette and stumbled on the slick freezer floor. She caught a chunk of meat to steady herself, rattling the hooks above her head.

"See what I mean?" she said.

"Try again," I said.

"That's just it," she said. "There's only one chance."

She released the chunk of meat and stepped

backwards on the balls of her feet.

"You were a friend of Wiley's, weren't you?" she asked me, "You were there when they found his body?"

She pulled her shirt over her head and let it drop to the floor. She undid the button of her pants and let them slide off her hips.

"Yeah," I said.

I spit the word out like a broken tooth.

"Yeah," Jeanine echoed, taking off her panties. "I took him into the freezer too."

I inhaled when her cold, gore covered hands slipped underneath my shirt and her nails scraped against my bare chest.

"Do you still think about him?" she asked me.

"Yes," I said.

She kissed me on the mouth and she was cold.

"Don't."

She took off my pants and when she laid me down the freezer floor stuck to my bare skin. She pressed my hand to the soft, concave pool of her stomach. I grasped her lion's hair with hands that no longer belonged to me. My hands were like chunks of meat slipping off my wrists.

She pulled out a small package tucked inside of her bra.

"What is that?" I asked.

"Condom," she said. "Don't ask me where I got it."

I thought you were supposed to say something witty before you condemned yourself to hell. Something nihilistic and darkly sarcastic, maybe. Premarital sex was the worst sort of sin after all, and if you were going to pick that way to get sent to hell, you should do it in style. But as she rolled the condom onto my penis, I could think of nothing to say. I only thought of the swaying bodies of headless cattle, the trembling lines of fat glistening like bloated, sappy stars above our heads.

Five

ANOTHER PROGRAM CAME on to late night television. It featured a man wearing a snappy suit who nursed a woman in a white room. The woman lay on a gray bed like she was drowning. She smiled a crooked dog smile. The man sat beside her with his spine straight as an oilrig, combed back his slick black hair with his fingers, and spoke to the camera.

"Dear friends," the man said. "Your weekends are wastelands of dissociative depression and existentialist boredom. You nurse the brink of destruction searching for rest. Let me help you. Let me give you the dreamless and dark headspace you've always wanted."

The man called himself Teddy and the woman, who never spoke for herself, he called Delilah. Teddy bent down and kissed Delilah on the cheek. He called Delilah his sleeping angel. He drew a black X on her forehead and promised he would put an implant in her brain so she would never wake up again.

"I bet he fucks her in the ass when the camera's turned off," said Sissy, who became a real bitch after her garden died.

"Oh, Theresa, he does not," Momma called out from the depths of the couch.

Whether Teddy fucked Delilah in the ass or not wasn't important. What was important was that Teddy sold sleep in a world where everyone was always screaming.

The back-story went that Delilah had bipolar disorder. Little high little low, it couldn't be helped. Every little high had her coming undone, flying across the galaxy with rabies spittle hanging from her mouth, spending all of Teddy's money. Every little low had her creeping through the house in search of shiny sharp objects so she could kill herself, Teddy peeling her moony eyes up off the carpet.

Delilah ended up slitting her wrists in a bathtub full of ice. When Teddy came home from work he found Delilah drawing lobster portraits with her blood on the bathroom tiles.

So Teddy dragged her to the slip implant clinic and shoved sleep inside her head. The images of the surgery repeated themselves over and over again on the television screen. The doctors cracked open her skull where Teddy marked his black X. Her brain pulsed gelatinous. Teddy took a hot wire spider and fastened its sticky hot legs to her nerves. The doctors sewed her up and she floated back to the white room, back to the gray bed.

Teddy planted his palms on Delilah's cheeks and turned her face toward the camera.

"My head is blissfully unaware of the movements of my body," Delilah said. "I no longer feel grief, or anger, or pain."

Teddy kissed the pink scars on her wrists and she laughed. Her skin flushed like she could feel his mouth, but the slip implant in her head, that hot wire spider, severed the nerves from her skin. It cut the sight from her eyes and the sound from her ears.

Teddy assured his viewers that Delilah, living dead inside the empty core of her skull, never even dreamed.

"Five years. Ten. Twenty-five years," Teddy said. "While you give your head a much needed rest your body will make you a success. Become a doctor. Write your novel. Fall in love. When you wake up, you'll have everything you've always wanted."

Teddy smiled. His teeth were the kind of teeth for eating spiders.

"Sleep clinics are opening up all over the world," he said, "Find the clinic in your area and get your sleep today."

"Ridiculous," Sissy said, blowing smoke on the television screen. "Who's miserable enough to go out and do something like that?"

But when the slip clinic opened in downtown Edgewater there were a hundred sleepy and sick townsfolk waiting for the doors to open. Jeanine and I sometimes walked past the clinic on our way home after school. We saw former neighbors, teachers, clergymen and parents going into the clinic and coming out with slack mouths like the backs of caves and bloody bandages wrapped around their foreheads. Once, our geometry teacher stumbled down the steps with Technicolor vomit running down his lips. A slip doctor in his signature gray coat, carrying a gray valise, led the teacher down the street. Wiley's mother went down the steps next. The blood on her face was thin enough to be black tea.

Jeanine and I often hung out with Ezekiel at the abandoned rock quarry where Jeanine watched over her family of swans. It was shortly after the slip clinic opened up when Ezekiel told us about deadhead tossing.

"So you got this family of four, and Mom goes out to get a sleep implant, right?" Ezekiel said. "Well, who the hell is going to want to take care of a deadhead anyhow? So Dad and the kids lead her outside and toss her into a sinkhole. Deadhead tossing. It's a party. People bring drinks and lose their virginity."

Jeanine closed her journal. "She's still in there somewhere underneath the slip, isn't she?"

"Who the hell knows?" Ezekiel said. "The wire spider could be turning their heads into hamburger, for all we know."

"One day we're going to wake up and be the only people left alive," Jeanine said.

She sounded almost cheerful when she said it. She drew me toward her and kissed me.

I went home that afternoon and found Sissy sitting alone on the couch. She spent a lot of time on the couch after she graduated high school. She had nothing left to do but smoke and watch

God on the television.

"Where's Momma?" I asked.

Sissy shrugged.

A dead deer hurtled down the stairs and smashed headfirst into the opposite wall.

"Momma!" Sissy screamed.

Momma appeared at the top of the stairs with her face like overused lightning. She gripped the banister and started dragging herself down the stairs.

"You kids are nothing but a burden to me," she said.

Sissy took a languid drag from her cigarette and tapped ash onto the carpet.

"If you're going to insult us, at least be original about it," Sissy said.

"If your father hadn't left then maybe you would've made something of yourself," Momma said. "Maybe you would go out and get a job. Maybe Charles wouldn't be up in his room always drawing those damn pictures."

"Leave Charles out of this," Sissy said. "In fact, while you're at it, leave me out of this."

Momma stopped halfway down the stairs. Her tight hands turned the color of bleached sand.

"Ever since your father left–"

"Enough about Daddy," Sissy said. "It's been over eight years, and I'm sick of hearing about it."

"We're all going to die inside this house

without him. You know that as well as I do." Momma said.

Momma left the house and started down the road.

"Momma!" I called.

She didn't look back.

"Should we go after her?" I asked Sissy.

Sissy turned back toward the television and lit another cigarette. I went back inside the house and closed the front door behind me.

***

Later that day, someone knocked on the front door.

I found Momma and a slip doctor waiting outside. The slip doctor looked like all dead men everywhere, hands bent into the shape of cabinet files, a forehead that quivered like a raw egg. Momma stared upwards so that all I could see were the whites of her eyes. She wore a bloodied bandage wrapped around her head, and a paper hospital gown with all the laces untied, her back exposed to the air. She shivered and opened her mouth, but didn't speak.

"What's this?" I asked.

"I'll tell you what this is!" Sissy called. "It's a goddamn travesty, it's a goddamn shame! But most of all it's so goddamn typical!"

"Here's my business card if there's an emergency," the slip doctor said. "And here's a pamphlet with some helpful information on it,"

The doctor handed me the pamphlet and walked away before I could ask him anything else.

"Your new and glorious life," the pamphlet read. "How to take care of friends and family with slip implants."

Momma stumbled a bit as she walked past me through the doorway, trailing her paper hospital ties behind her and smelling of antiseptic and blood. She sat down on the couch in her usual place and told Sissy to turn the television up a little louder.

Six

THE PLAGUE MACHINES SENT another horde of locusts to Edgewater. The schools and businesses shut down and we had to stay inside and drank blood-tinged water from the taps for two weeks. The machines sat outside in the streets. Their mouths opened wide and the locusts spewed forth.

The locusts wore crowns of gold and had human faces the color of angry bruises. They covered the town, dripping wings and black ichor, tormenting us until we were covered in purple wounds, and leaking blood from all orifices.

For the first two hours of the plague, Sissy and I knelt in the living room and prayed to God for deliverance.

Then Sissy said, "I'm bored," and went to watch television.

She lit a cigarette but the smoke couldn't mask the copper syrup smell of blood trickling down the windows.

"What did we do this time?" I asked Sissy.

The noise of the machines swelled in my throat.

"I sure didn't do a damn thing. I bet it was that little bitch Melissa Yeats, who brought this plague on us. She used to steal my lipstick," Sissy said.

"I want a cigarette," deadhead Momma told

Sissy.

"Get your own," Sissy said.

She stubbed her cigarette out and kicked her feet up on the coffee table.

Momma sat motionless on the couch, her mouth drooping. Her legs pooled into the carpet.

I removed Momma's bandage a few days after she came home from the slip clinic. The place where the doctors sliced into her head and inserted the implant faded to a sick gray green color. When the light from the television hit her just right, I saw the tiny black legs of the spider undulating underneath her skin.

For the two weeks of the plague she kept getting up to rifle through the kitchen cabinets.

"What are you doing, Momma?" I'd ask

"You know what your father always said," she replied. "The only way to ride out the plague was with a good stockpile of smokes and whiskey."

"Daddy's gone," I told Momma.

She kept searching.

At night, she stood at the foot of my bed and advertised for the slip implants in the hours she used to sleep.

"It doesn't hurt," she said. "You don't feel anything at all. Ever since your father left, you haven't had a good night's sleep. What pain. What pressure. What stress. Come and join me. Give your head a much needed rest."

I rolled over turned my face away, but Momma still hunched over my bed. Locusts kept hitting the window, covering the screen until it was completely black, their bodies teeming with bristled hair and over-sized human teeth. Their hoofed feet splattered tiny blood patterns against the glass.

Machine noise shattered picture frames and threw my bed against the wall. Momma held tight to the bed railings. Her hair was so alive and full in those moments it appeared to catch fire and fly up to the ceiling.

"Come join me," she whispered again. "You don't feel anything at all."

Sissy didn't tolerate any of Momma's deadhead antics. If Momma got too close to Sissy, Sissy kicked her away like a dog. I found Momma several times flat on her back with her legs flailing in the air and her dress hiked over her panties.

"Why do you have to treat her like that?" I asked.

"I don't want her touching me," Sissy said.

She turned on the kitchen faucet and blood spewed into the sink.

"You shouldn't leave her like that," I said as I peeled Momma up off the ground.

After Momma got to her feet, she rocked back on her heels and stumbled into the living room to watch television.

"Hey Charles," Sissy said, turning toward me

with a glass of blood in her hand, flecks of blood on her upper lip, "you ever heard of deadhead tossing?"

Sissy tossed the rest of the blood down the drain. She went into the living room and continued rearranging the furniture to make murder art.

Sissy pulled Daddy's stuffed animals out of the closets and cupboards. She hung owl heads over our beds. She hung kitchen knives from the ceiling hanging by threads. She stacked chairs in precarious positions on top of tables and laid dead and diseased stuffed squirrels wherever we were most likely to stick our hands without looking first.

She exposed the gut wires of refrigerators, blenders, and radios across wet floors. She placed a hundred year old scarecrow in my dead baby brother's crib. When I woke in the middle of the night and shuffled down the stairs to get a glass of milk, I found a sea of old lady upholstery had sprung up from the carpet. I crawled over a rising and rolling and tumbling armada of cat piss cushions and cross-stitched home sweet home pillows and gutted, stiff-legged chairs.

My hand slipped underneath a couch cover. I touched another dead squirrel. Ever since Sissy began placing the furniture throughout the room in particular ways to kill us all, I knew she would never leave the house again. Just like the house sucked Momma in, it had imprisoned Sissy. The only way she could express her anger anymore was through the hostile composition of the rooms around her.

As our nights trapped in the house progressed, Momma's slip implant advertising became more violent. I locked the door to my room to keep Momma from coming in and telling me to kill myself. She busted the door down at four AM and flung her body across the room, her heels making scorch marks on the wood. She planted her hands onto the bedrail and her hair reached out to suffocate me.

"What are you afraid of, Charles?" the hot wire spider asked me through Momma's mouth. "Are you afraid to let go of this useless head because you believe you're special? Are you following some self-righteous moral creed? Lay back and blow your head out of the water, Charles. The world doesn't need your head, only your body. It never wanted your head."

Downstairs on the television Teddy spilled spiders out of his hands and Delilah's laughter cracked against the ceiling. The hot wire spider in Momma's head trembled and clicked in her hollowed brain. It blew me a kiss.

"Go talk to Sissy," I told Momma's ghost. "You never bother Sissy."

But Momma just clamped her teeth down on her bottom lip, snapped her hands against the bed rails, and started her angry commercial all over again.

The buzzing locusts wore my skull down.

"Get away!" I told her once more. "Go into Sissy's room!"

I curled into bed. Momma craned her neck down until it seemed to detach from her head and she whispered in my ear once more:

"You don't feel a thing."

I thought the plague would never end and that I would be on the receiving end of Momma's abusive slip implant advertisements until God came to destroy us all. Yet one morning the locusts died. They fell out of the sky and fell off the windows and lay on the grass in carcass heaps. Water replaced the blood in the taps. The machines closed their mouths and lumbered back into the fields.

Momma and Sissy didn't seem to notice the plague was over. I ran through the house opening all the curtains now that the plague was over, touching the empty, blood-splattered windows, shaking, and laughing.

“What's gotten into you?” Sissy asked, “Stop laughing like that. You're making me nervous.”

Sissy closed all the curtains behind me, but at that moment, it didn't matter. I kept running through the house. I passed Momma in the kitchen as she crouched underneath the sink searching for Daddy's cigars and whiskey.

“Boy, what's gotten into you?” she asked, repeating Sissy's words like a spitting engine.

I ran past her. I ran through the back door and held my hands out to the sun, and the sun was bleating like a lamb and the piles of dead locusts kicked up in a flurry fell to the bottom of my ribcage as I ran. I ran to Jeanine, the only girl I knew would still be alive.

I found Jeanine in the front lawn of her house. She wore padded leather gloves and carried a large wicker basket on her hip. She scooped up dead locusts and placed them in the basket. I ran to her, grabbed her head, and kissed her on the mouth.

"Watch out for the stingers," she said when I let her go and her black hair strung out between my fingers. "I got stung by one of them and it hurts like a bitch."

She set the basket full of dead locusts down and pulled off one of her leather gloves. She held her fingers out to me and I kissed the sting wound on her ring finger. She pulled the other glove off and I kissed those fingers too.

"I've missed you," I said.

"Let's go," she said, and took me to the abandoned rock quarry.

The family of swans was still alive. They floated through the water at the bottom of the quarry, through trails of dead locusts. Their white necks dipped down to touch the lips of their reflections.

"I don't know how it happens. How they're still alive after all those plagues."

We cleared a space on the rocks and Jeanine and I lay down in the heat. Her skirts billowed over her knees. I trailed my fingers through her black lion's hair and we watched the swans swimming below.

"I'm leaving this town first chance I get," she told me. "I'm going to go to The First City or to the sea, somewhere with lots of light and warmth. One day God is going to wipe Edgewater off the face of the planet, and I'm not going to be around when it happens."

“What about the swans?" I asked, though what I really wanted to say was. “What about me?”

“They'll live," she said, "they always do. But I'll die if I stay here."

I clung to her neck. Our skin was pale and our eyes red from staying inside in the dark for so long. My fingers slid to Jeanine's cold collarbone.

"I'm going to be an archaeologist when I get out of here," Jeanine said. “I'll uncover what we've lost. Unearth our history. What are you going to be?"

I thought of Sissy and Momma back in the house bordering the swamp, crashing through the rooms in angry insect patterns. The two of them were trapped in the rictus of a spell woven by God in his black mask, by Daddy's ancient taxidermy, by the space my dead baby brother left behind.

Jeanine touched my cheek.

"What is it, Charles?" she asked. "What's wrong?"

I wanted to say, "I want to be the murderer of the monster who took away my baby brother's spine. I want to be the one who finds a new home so I can keep us safe. I want to find the crystal breathing mask that will resuscitate the dead and bring them back to me."

But dear God, I am only so much dirt, so I said nothing at all.

Seven

THE SHINY SPHERE on the back of Ezekiel's head resembled a warm bottomless pool, an empty eye with a rapacious gleam. God whispered through it to Ezekiel in the long nights. His tiny, insistent voice slithered from the back of Ezekiel's brain down the wires to his cerebral cortex, through his basal ganglia with its jump hiss bundle of nerves, all the way to his temporal lobe.

"What's God like underneath his mask?" I asked Ezekiel once.

"God is a wide black line," Ezekiel said. "This line that springs out from sky and won't stop until it's covered the entire planet in black."

"I don't understand," I said.

"Don't worry about it, I'm tired of talking about God anyways," Ezekiel said, and then he picked up a stack of resurrection pamphlets by the door, "I've got The Resurrection in a few hours. Let's go hunting."

'Let's go hunting' used to mean that Ezekiel took me into the woods with a bow and arrow to shoot stray dogs. But as we grew older it meant walking the downtown streets in search of sinners to condemn.

Ezekiel passed out resurrection pamphlets to the people left on the street that night. He walked with a snap, spine like a pressed leaf. I tread a few steps behind him, dragging my feet in his shadow.

"Resurrection at midnight, watch a legitimate miracle of God and have your faith renewed," Ezekiel repeated several times to no one in particular, in a flat, rehearsed tone.

Ezekiel held a pamphlet out to a man standing underneath a light pole. The man wouldn't reach out to take it. Ezekiel rolled his eyes, tossed the pamphlet onto the ground, and continued on his way.

"Sorry," I said to the man as I passed by.

The man's hands clenched and unclenched. Dried vomit encrusted his fingers.

"Just my luck, to get stuck with the grunt work," Ezekiel said to me, then, waving the pamphlets above his head, he shouted out. "Get your salvation here! Make God happy! Come to The resurrection!"

He continued on like this for several blocks, throwing pamphlets at the people that crouched on porch steps, the groups of ivy-skinned boys drinking mash underneath lights, girls like needles hiding behind steel grates. Ezekiel handed a few of the pamphlets to me. The cover featured block print that spelled out "RESURRECTION," right underneath a skeleton dancing beneath a heated shiny sphere. I stuffed the pamphlets in my jacket pocket.

At the end of the street Ezekiel spotted a group of girls talking outside the liquor store, dripping over passersby and asking them for smokes. He tossed the rest of the pamphlets into a trashcan and motioned for me to follow him. He walked up to a silver haired girl with punching bag eyes, her skin the color of chitin.

"Ezekiel," she said. "Where have you been?"

"You're a sinner," Ezekiel said. He smiled and held out his arm for her to take, "come with me, baby."

He took her head in his hands and kissed her hard on the mouth.

I followed Ezekiel and the girl into the woods behind the liquor store. Ezekiel and the girl ducked behind a tree. I listened to them undress each other with clumsy and frantic motions. I sat down on the other side of the tree and curled my legs tight against my chest. I waited for a long time as they whispered and laughed. I cooked in the heat of their sex. I ruptured in their climax, the moment when their smell struck me like lightning.

"Do you want a turn?" Ezekiel asked.

"No. Aren't you supposed to be somewhere?"

"We've got time," Ezekiel said. "And why not? What are you afraid of?"

A moment's pause. "Oh, right. It's because of her. That girl with the butterfly wings made out of meat."

He laughed.

"One day you're going to wake up in a bathtub full of ice and watch her escape with all your organs underneath her arms. She'll make pets out of them. Give them new names."

The girl laughed with him and even her laugh was silver.

"Her dad was a serial killer, you know," Ezekiel said.

"Isn't her brother a prophet?" the girl asked. "Jonah, or something?"

"Hey, Charles, you know I'm only kidding you," Ezekiel said. "Jeanine's a good girl. She's good for you. Come on over here to our side of the tree. Come have a smoke with us."

I sighed.

"Charles, don't feel bad. I'm sorry. Come on over here."

Ezekiel and the girl were still naked. The girl pulled her silvery hair behind her shoulders while Ezekiel fished in his pants strung on the branches for a pack of cigarettes.

"What's your name?" I asked the girl, trying to distract myself from the raw space between her legs.

"Chicory," she said.

"She's twelve years old," Ezekiel said. "Her parents just died."

"Light my cigarette for me," Chicory said.

He lit a cigarette and slipped it between her lips. She sucked on the end but didn't inhale. She crossed and uncrossed her legs. The monsters in the woods nearby screech hollered and shook the trees.

"What was that?" she said.

"Don't worry, baby, those monsters aren't going to come after us. I'm the chosen of God."

He tilted her chin back, took a kiss, and promised another miracle.

"Get dressed," he told Chicory. "I'll show you something special. Charles. You come too."

Ezekiel led us back to Edgewater. He and Chicory walked arm in arm, almost skipping as they walked, laughing, and telling jokes. I walked a few paces behind them with my hands thrust into the pockets of my jacket.

When Chicory figured out where we were going she stopped laughing. She tugged sharp on Ezekiel's elbow and dug her heels into the grass.

"Let's go back," She said.

"What did I tell you before?" he said. "Don't worry about a thing."

We stopped at the edge of town, at the sloping, knuckled hills that looked out beyond the machine fields.

I couldn't see the machines in the dark, yet I smelled the clean plated metal of their inner workings. I heard the thud of their insides shredding.

"What are we doing here?" Chicory asked.

"Watch this," Ezekiel said, and then he fell down into the grass in an epileptic fit.

Chicory dropped to her knees beside his writhing body.

"Don't touch him," I said. "He does this all

the time."

She shook his shoulders.

"Chicory," I said. "Stop."

"I don't want him to choke on his tongue," she said.

Ezekiel entangled her arms in his fit of epilepsy and they rolled together on the ground. He crushed her body beneath him. She grasped clumps of grass between her fists and pulled until the ground turned bald.

"Stop, please," Chicory kept repeating, her voice muffled underneath him. "Let's go back."

Ezekiel couldn't speak. Strained, burbling noises hit the back of his throat. The shiny sphere in the back of his head glowed bright and hot.

Down in the field the machines spewed a flash of fire into the darkness. The soil squirmed and a mass of dirty white material shot up out of the ground. It writhed until the ground itself seemed to be alive. They were bones of our dead.

As they pulled themselves up out of the soil the bones spit out their teeth and straightened their spines. They uncurled their clutching fingers. Their arms and legs rolled out from their sides and smacked the dirt. Silent, they marched out of the machine fields toward Edgewater, filing past us.

Ezekiel stopped convulsing and Chicory uncoiled herself from his limbs. He gripped her wrist but she kicked away.

"Get off of me!" Chicory cried, but Ezekiel already let go of her wrist and wasn't paying attention to her anymore.

"Isn't that something?" he said. "Look at what God did. Look at what I did."

The dead kept coming out of the fields in stark white rows as Ezekiel lay in the grass and laughed and laughed. As they approached us, the fog peeled from their faces and revealed in detail all the empty spaces between their bones, the sockets of their elbows and knees pulled apart in an invisible suspension. As they got close, Chicory was the first to recognize them.

"I know that girl. That's Reverend Elli's sister." Chicory said, as a creature wearing a black funeral dress dragged herself past us. "And look over there, that's Jenny Sikes. You know, the crazy English teacher that had sex with all those underage girls. God, she walked like she was dead even while she was still alive."

Chicory was right. These were people who all died in Edgewater. I found myself searching for the face of my father.

"I think I saw my parents up there," Chicory said. "Didn't you see them?"

She ran ahead of us and disappeared into the folds of the marching dead.

"Where is she going?" I asked.

"I have no idea," he said. "Come on, let's follow them out. God tells me they're going to

The First City."

"For what?"

"Why, to join God's army and go kill heathens and heretics of course," Ezekiel said, and he smiled a big, bloody, dinner steak smile.

We followed the path the dead made through Edgewater. I called for Chicory. No answer.

"Stop worrying about that girl," Ezekiel said.

We walked past the derelict houses and chiaroscuro streets of the night, past the closed shops, the monster holes, and preaching zones and blood spattered execution platforms. The dead always stayed a step ahead of us.

We passed Jeanine's house. She sat outside on the porch in a pink nightie, her black lion's hair pinned to the back of her neck. She smoked a cigarette with insomnia cracking her eyes. When the dead passed her house in their silent formation, she raised the cigarette to her lips without a moment's hesitation, or surprise. Then she saw Ezekiel and me. Ezekiel waved at her. She stubbed her cigarette out on the porch balustrade.

"What's going on?" she asked.

"Ezekiel raised the dead," I said.

"Again?" she asked.

We continued walking. Jeanine followed us. We found Chicory up the street, calling for Mommy, tugging on the desiccated arm of a dead woman.

"She's my mom," Chicory said. "Look at her

face. Mommy. Mommy, it's me. It's Chicory."

"Let her go, Chicory," Ezekiel said. "Mommy's dead."

The skeleton tried to drag itself forward with Chicory clinging to its hips. After a few moments it raised its fist, hit Chicory against the face, and knocked her on the ground. Chicory lay on the ground where she fell, curling her body into a cloister, covering her face and crying. The skeleton kept moving and disappeared up the street.

"Get up, silly girl," Ezekiel said to Chicory. "You're making me miss out on all the fun."

As if in response to Chicory's cries, lights flickered on all up and down the street. People came out of their houses and searched for their dead relatives. They called out the names of people we used to know. They started running through Edgewater in a heated riot, screaming and setting fires and breaking windows and clinging to once familiar bones.

All the while, the dead remained silent.

Chicory continued to cry. Ezekiel shrugged and walked off, leaving the three of us behind.

"See anyone you know?" Jeanine asked.

"No," I said. "Not anyone important."

Chicory looked like a chunk of bone, a hard white shell.

"Hey, are you all right?" Jeanine asked her.

Chicory ran off into the night.

Jeanine and I went after Ezekiel. Ahead of us

people screamed and cried, calling out the names of the people we used to know. We came across decayed faces dropped onto the asphalt, peeled, clawed, and distended from the bone. We found bits of finger bones and leg bones and the clawed away shreds of funeral clothes.

Ezekiel stood in the town square on top of a guillotine platform with one of the senior prophets of the Edgewater Prophet Headquarters. Ezekiel pulled speech notes out of his pocket and looked toward the senior prophet, who leaned against the guillotine scratching the rusted guillotine blade with his fingernails. He nodded to Ezekiel.

"Ladies and gentlemen," Ezekiel said, holding his speech notes up, "welcome to the Edgewater Resurrection. We are gathered here today to witness a rare miracle, the pinnacle of our human condition. To join the indestructible army of God is to be made immortal, the greatest honor that any human can ever hope to have bestowed upon them..."

He paused. He lowered the notes.

"Where did everyone go?" he asked.

"Wrap this up for me, will you?" the senior prophet said.

"But I still have six more pages to read," Ezekiel said.

"I'm going home," the prophet said.

After the senior prophet left Ezekiel stuffed the rest of his speech into his jacket pocket.

"They're still chasing those things," Jeanine said, in way of explanation. "Pretty pathetic."

He jumped down from the guillotine platform.

"I'm bored of this," he said.

Ezekiel left us alone once more in the stark, empty street.

Jeanine turned to me. Her hair had come undone and lay across her face in uneven streaks. She picked up a dead man's face from the pavement. When she looked at me, her eyes were white and wide enough to walk through.

"This is exactly why I'm getting out of this damned town," she said, holding the face out toward me, her thumbs hooked through the empty places where its eyes used to be.

Eight

I WOKE ONE NIGHT to Sissy hanging a kitchen knife above my head.

Sissy's knees pressed into my shoulders and her body stretched over my headboard as she knotted the thread on the ceiling.

"How come we never see that girl you're dating?" she asked.

"You mean Jeanine?" I asked

"I want to meet her."

"I'm not sure that's a good idea," I said.

"Why?" Sissy asked as she finished tying the knot.

The knife floated in suspension above our heads.

"You're digging into my shoulders," I said.

Sissy sat on top of me for a long moment without speaking. Her eyes fixed to the space above my head where the knife hung suspended. Her nails scraped into the headboard of my bed. She'd grown thin in the last months, skin like a noose, and bones like cream.

"Okay, fine," I said. "I'll bring her over."

"Great," Sissy said, and leaped off the bed, suddenly animated. "I'll make dinner."

I took the knife down from the ceiling and invited Jeanine over for dinner. Jeanine arrived at our house on the edge of the swamp the next Sunday evening dressed in spring colors. She'd painted her face with dark blue eye shadow and meat colored lipstick she stole from her mother.

I met her out on the porch.

"Watch where you step," I said. "Theresa likes to set traps everywhere. And bake needles into the rations. Oh, and don't sit down on the couch or stick your hand into anything. She likes to hide stuffed squirrels everywhere. And avoid Momma's eyes if she ever smiles at you like she's got a secret."

"You worry too much," Jeanine said.

She laughed and kissed me on the cheek. I hesitated to touch her in return. I didn't recognize her in those colors. She even smelled differently, like freesia and fake rain instead of meat and grit and hair dye.

"Look at you. You're more nervous than I am," she said.

We went inside. Sissy waited for us at the kitchen doorway across the great divide of the living room. She too, was dressed foreign, in one of Momma's lace corsets from her teenage days, and a ruffle skirt that swallowed up her legs. She hid her face behind a mask of clay.

Even though nobody was on the couch, the television continued to play loud enough to bust the ceiling. I guided Jeanine toward the kitchen. Sissy lit a cigarette and leaned against the doorframe.

"Your girlfriend looks like a whore," Sissy said.

"Please don't hate me for this," I whispered to

Jeanine.

We followed Sissy into the kitchen where she'd arranged on the kitchen table our government rations for the month onto the special occasion silverware. In the dark green light, I could almost imagine our monthly bread and meat paste was a real Sunday dinner. One from our childhood, before the factory shut down and Daddy left.

Momma sat in the corner of the kitchen next to a dead stuffed deer, her chair propped up against the wall.

"Sit down Jeanine," Sissy said, stabbing her cigarette against the edge of her plate. "Sit next to Momma."

"I want to watch the Teddy and Delilah show," Momma said.

"We're having dinner. Don't embarrass me."

Jeanine and I sat down and Sissy played host, cutting the meat paste and bread into delicate, bite-sized portions. She served them to Jeanine and me one square at a time on the tip of her silver fork. Her bones shook with the strain. Jeanine and I waited in silence for Sissy to finish, and when she did, we picked up our silverware in tandem and ate. Momma didn't eat at all.

"Well then, do you like my deer?" Sissy said, indicating the stuffed deer with hollow green eyes propped up in the corner. "My father made it. His best one he took with him. But he left this one with us."

Jeanine and I exchanged glances. I felt cut off from her, as if a pane of glacier glass separated us.

After a moment, Jeanine turned back to Sissy. The fork in Jeanine's hand quivered.

"I like it," Jeanine said.

"No you don't," Sissy said. "But that's okay. Nobody does."

"You know," Jeanine said. "You remind me of this friend I used to have. She used to collect butterflies. Preserve them and pin them up, put them in these little shadow boxes all over her room. Only the black butterflies though. She's dead now."

"I'm thinking of becoming a taxidermist myself," Sissy said. "I've always wanted to strangle and stuff a bear. I'd jump on its back and throw my arms around its neck and squeeze until it stops kicking. "

"I don't think there are many bears around here," Jeanine said.

"That doesn't matter," Sissy said. "It's just a silly idea. Why don't you tell me more about yourself? What are you going to be?"

"An archaeologist," Jeanine said.

"Oh, nobody's doing that anymore," Sissy said.

"I am," Jeanine said.

Sissy laughed. Raw flakes of makeup cracked and peeled off her face and fell into her food. The skin underneath her makeup was terracotta colored, quivering. At the sight of it, Jeanine set down her fork and felt her own face.

"What's wrong?" Sissy asked. "Aren't you hungry?"

"Ravenous," Jeanine said.

She swallowed and started examining her hands.

Sissy touched my arm. Sniffed.

"Charles. You smell like him. Are you wearing Daddy's jacket?"

"What does it matter?" I said.

"That's funny," Sissy said, "you wearing his jacket. You're nothing like Daddy. Would anyone like some whiskey?"

Sissy retrieved Daddy's handle of whiskey from the cabinet. She poured herself a shot and threw it back in one gulp.

"Anyone else?" she asked. "No? Well I'm sure Momma could use a shot."

Sissy poured another shot and slid it over the table toward Momma. Momma's slip implant scuttled inside her skull. Her arms shot across the table. She knocked the shot glass over and it shattered on the floor.

"Momma! That's good whiskey!" Sissy said. "You know that's the last we'll ever have."

She rubbed her forehead, leaving a smudge of pink on the back of her hand. She knelt down to pick up the pieces of glass. When she went underneath the table, she bumped her chair with her shoulder, knocking it to the floor.

"I'm so sorry," I said to Jeanine.

Jolene started to scratch on the windows outside. A fourteen-year-old fear crawled into my spine. I tried to set down my knife and fork but instead of reaching the table, they clattered onto the floor. I couldn't bend down to pick them up. Jolene continued to scratch and scratch.

"What's that?" Jeanine asked.

Sissy emerged from underneath the table, her hands bloodied with glass.

"That's just Jolene," Sissy said.

"Cunt!" Jolene screamed shaking the foundation of the house.

"Cocksucker!" Sissy yelled back.

Sissy dumped the glass into the sink and washed her hands.

"Don't worry, Jolene only eats children. She just likes Charles for some reason."

Momma sat upright in her chair and touched the hot wire spider in her head, making it jump and clutch at her fingers underneath her skin.

"When are you two kids going to get married?" Momma asked.

"I know why Jolene wants to eat Charles. It's because of that baby face, don't you think?" Sissy said, and pinched my cheeks. "Look at this cute face. Delicious monster food."

"I don't know, Momma," I said, pushing Sissy's fingers away.

"No son of mine is going to be a bachelor for the rest of his life."

"Okay, Momma," I said.

"Bitch!" Jolene said.

"Crazy motherfucker!" Sissy called back.

Momma stumbled up out of her chair, knocked over the dead deer, and then went into the living room to watch television.

"Momma!" Sissy screamed.

Sissy followed Momma into the living room. From the living room, I heard a crash. Momma howled. I jumped up from the table and chased after Sissy, to find the coffee table knocked over and Sissy dragging Momma across the floor by the hair. Momma squirmed, twisted, and dug her fingernails into the carpet. Teddy's pressed his face against the television screen, trying to break the glass from the inside with a hot wire spider.

I could barely swallow or think or breathe. Not with Momma's rabbit howls, with Teddy singing an aria over Delilah's gray bed, with Jolene from the swamp screaming and screaming.

"Let her go, Theresa," I said. "She hasn't done anything to you."

"You're not here!" Sissy said, gathering another fistful of Momma's hair and pulling hard so that her head snapped back. "You're not here all the time taking care of her! You don't have to keep her from burning herself on old cigarettes and force food down her throat because she won't eat!"

"Let her go," I repeated.

I laid my hand on Sissy's wrist. She jerked it away.

"No! I won't! You don't know! You don't have to tell her every half hour that Daddy's not coming back. That the baby isn't crying because he died fourteen years ago. You're always out with that girl. You've left us all behind."

"Theresa, don't make me get your father," Momma said.

Sissy backhanded Momma across the face. Blood spurted from Momma's nose, dark blood tinged with gray. Her blood spattered the walls and the television; more blood than I ever thought was inside of a person's veins.

I pushed Sissy off Momma and slammed her into the wall. A moose head crashed at our feet. Sissy's eyes went wide and her hands uncurled. She dropped fistfuls of Momma's ripped hair onto the ground. Jolene stopped screaming. The house stopped rattling. Even the television with its constant babble, slowed to a low hum.

"Charles?" Jeanine called from behind me.

"Bubba," Sissy whispered as I pressed her into the wall, my shoulders and arms shaking.

"Don't touch Momma like that ever again," I said.

I released Sissy. Momma still lay on the floor, trying to escape with her legs kicking. She squealed when I touched her.

"Momma," I said. "Let's go to bed."

I guided Momma to the stairs. Jeanine rushed to help me. Momma stuttered and drooled, blood in her spit.

At the top of the stairs, I looked back at Sissy. She peeled herself off the wall, brushing her hair back with her bloodstained hand, and gathered up the moose head in her arms.

"I'm sorry," Jeanine said.

"Fuck you," she said, trembling. "Fuck the both of you."

Jeanine and I took Momma down the hallway.

"Your girlfriend's a cunt!" Sissy screamed after us. "You should've died instead of your brother! I hate you! I hate you!"

We took Momma into her bedroom and guided her onto the mattress. She rolled onto her stomach and twitched.

"You don't feel a thing," she said, her voice muffled by her pillow. "Write your novel. Fall in love. Get your slip implant today."

Downstairs, Sissy continued to scream.

"If I ever see that girl here again I'm going to kill her! I'll kill both of you!"

"Come on," I said to Jeanine. "Stay close to me. I'll take you home."

As we walked past Sissy she stood tall and pressed the moose head close to her stomach. Its antlers pierced her cheeks. She'd become the house. She'd become dark creak hallways and dead things and old wallpaper. Soon, I thought,

I wouldn’t recognize her at all.

***

"She doesn't remember me," Jeanine said as we walked together down the road from my house.

"You knew her?”

"When I was a little girl, she gave me a flower from her garden, this purple hibiscus, and she showed me the place where the swans lived. Now she's so angry and sad. She's trapped in that house, like a bug that keeps hitting the glass over and over and over again."

“I never knew.”

"What happened to your mom?" Jeanine asked.

"She's always been like that," I said.

"She's lucky, in a way," Jeanine told me. “Your sister, I mean. If she stayed that little girl in her garden, the shuttles would take her. The shuttles always take people like that. The kind of people who tend gardens and give flowers to strangers. She's safe this way. She'll live in that house until the end of the world."

"Jeanine,” I said quietly.

“What is it?”

“What am I going to do when you're gone?" I asked.

“You’ll think of something,” she said.

I thought of Momma’s question, “When are you two kids going to get married?”

I thought of Jeanine and I sitting in the corner of the kitchen eating dinner together. I saw Jeanine dressed in Momma’s housewife clothes, feeding me whiskey and cutting off the tips of my cigars. Jeanine straddling the kitchen sink. Jeanine pulling her lion’s hair down over her eyes, naked, falling down with me into a bed full of raw meat.

"How do you stay alive?" I asked.

She pulled the hair from my eyes and pressed our hips together. She pressed my fingers into her stomach, that empty space where my hands never touched bottom. I kissed the curve of her jaw.

"We’re all afraid of dark spaces, you know, but every time I see a dark space, like a shadow, or an empty corner, or a black hole - I just think there's a man of smoke sitting in that dark space, filling it up. And his legs are open and his arms are open, real wide like, and ready to take me in. And he says, 'I'm here for you, Jeanine, I'm waiting for you in every space you're afraid of.' And that's how I can go into the woods at night and why I don't get stuck to the floor waiting for my prophet brother to come home. Because of the man of smoke. "

"That kind of sounds like God," I said.

"It's nothing like God," Jeanine responded.

"It's just another way to fill the empty spaces God left behind."

Jeanine told me goodnight and I headed back alone.

A monster chased me the entire way back home. It chased me through the woods felling trees as it went. I ran to my porch and yanked open the front door and slammed it shut behind me. I slid to the floor and the monster whispered my name as it insinuated its thin, brown fingers through the bottom of the door.

Sissy, sitting on the couch and watching television, said nothing. I tried to push my fists through my mouth.

The monster whispered my name one more time before slinking off in the night to wait. It never tried too hard to catch me. It had all the time in the world to wait for when I would be ready to be caught.

Nine

DURING HIGHSCHOOL GRADUATION, the principal walked onto the auditorium stage for his speech as if a merciless ghost pursued him. When he got to the podium and looked at us the soft, blue veins of his face squirmed. He spoke into the microphone in a tense whisper.

"This is a very important day for you all," he said. "You're about to go into the world and try to make something of yourselves. All I can say is don't try too hard. Be good, and don't draw attention to yourselves. The most successful kind of person is a quiet and obedient person. Before you pursue your dreams, you should ask God what he wants instead."

The principal looked behind him, quivering, and then turned back to the audience with his eyebrows wide and his mouth sloped to one side. He coughed into the microphone like there was gravel in his lungs.

"Good luck, kids," he said, after he'd regained his composure. "Without God's protection, it's a vast and cold universe out there. And before I let you go, we have a special guest speaker from The First City. One of the saints employed at the Bureau of Salvation. Give him a good welcome."

I sat between Jeanine and Ezekiel. Jeanine gripped my knuckles. Ezekiel leaned over to the girl in the next seat and whispered, "God tells me death is near." He kissed her all over her face and neck. His sphere pulsed.

The saint walked onto the stage wearing a white robe stained with blood, stigmata on his wrists and forehead.

He carried a flamethrower and a can of gasoline.

"And remember kids," the principal said. "God believes in you."

The prophet took the microphone from the principal, and smiled at us with red stained teeth. The principal skittered off the stage, coughing. The prophet raised the flamethrower up over his head, and blood dripped onto the stage.

"Get this straight, kids," the prophet said. "If you think you're anything but dirt, then you're in for a surprise. Ignore everything your principal said. It doesn't matter what you do. You're still going to die. You're all sinners and scum of the earth. You've spent the last eighteen years of your life fucking, cussing, and spiting at the Lord. Well, kids, when the end comes, you're going to be wishing your mother aborted you with a coat hanger and ended your miserable existence before it ever began."

He splashed gasoline across the first row of students. Before they could move, he whipped the flamethrower toward them and squeezed the trigger. The row of students went up in flames.

Ezekiel and Jeanine ran down the aisle toward the doors. I went to follow after them, but the saint splashed gasoline in the aisle and fire rolled past, blocking my exit. Students caught in the rows in front burned fast, and were soon nothing but char smeared against the seats. I turned around with the heat bubbling on my skin, my eyebrows and mouth seared, and ran the opposite way.

"Don't worry, kids," the saint called out. "It might hurt right now, but soon you'll realize this is the best thing for you!"

He pointed the flamethrower up to the ceiling. A burst of flame hit one of the support beams above. It cracked and fell, crushing a row of students below.

"Jeanine!" I called out, my voice weak from the lack of oxygen.

"The best life lived is the one not lived at all, you good for nothing animals!" the saint said.

I ran toward the exit door, tripping over my classmates writhing on the ground. When I touched the door it was so hot it seared my hand. I cried out and stumbled backwards. Another lick of flame shot above my head, catching my hair on fire. I smothered it with my burned hands.

I ran across another aisle toward the window as I gasped, unable to get enough air. I climbed up onto the windowsill and kicked the glass with my knee. The glass shattered. I rolled out the window and landed hard on my back outside in the courtyard. The auditorium groaned and shifted on its steel frame.

I ran to the street and the auditorium collapsed with a demon crack. The heat of the fire struck my back and dust and ash bloomed over my head. My classmates trapped inside screamed, and then never screamed again.

I discarded my burnt cap and gown in a trashcan by the street and I wandered looking for anyone else. I found the arsonist saint torching all the trees.

"Did God tell you to do this?" I asked, pressing my palms against my eyes to keep them from melting in the heat.

"Fuck you, kid," the saint said.

He disappeared behind the burning auditorium, brandishing his flamethrower over his head.

I continued searching for survivors outside. Smoke cloyed in my throat. The heat and lack of oxygen made me dizzy. I called out for Jeanine but my voice sounded like a broken legged horse. I circled the ruins of the school and found Ezekiel smoking a cigarette underneath a burning tree.

"Congratulations," he said. "You're still alive. Thank God for that, because you won't be alive for much longer."

"Have you seen Jeanine?" I asked.

"Who?"

He tossed his cigarette into the burning tree behind him, spraying ash downwards.

"Nice graduation, right?" he said, and walked off.

I circled the building again, but I couldn't fine Jeanine or any of Ezekiel's girls. As I walked, calling out for Jeanine in my horse voice, the heat of the auditorium made my vision white and my feet stick to the sidewalk. I started to think that the smoke that roiled off the building were the angry feet of God.

I went home.

I stumbled into the living room with my clothes smoking. Momma and Sissy were sitting on the couch watching television. I dragged myself toward them, my heels sunk low into the carpet.

"The school auditorium burned down." I said.

"You're blocking the television," Sissy said.

I crawled up the stairs and got into bed. I pulled the bed covers over my head with the smoke emanating off me in waves.

***

That night Jeanine climbed through my bedroom window and crept into my bed. She smelled of smoke and burnt meat. She rubbed at her blackened face.

"I thought you died," I said.

"Yeah?" she asked, and pulled her dress over

her head.

"Are you okay?" I asked.

"Sure," she whispered.

She pressed her dress against my mouth and slipped her hand into my pants. Her eyes were lazy, cloudy spots. Her knees stuck to my sheets. She pulled off my pants. Wherever she touched me, I burned.

"Why can't you get it up?" she asked me.

"I thought you died," I repeated.

"I'm not dead," she said. "Get it up."

"Are you all right, Jeanine?"

She slumped down into the bed, her hair falling over her face in one smooth, black sheet. She kept touching my penis with her scorched fingers. She slipped the fingers of her other hand inside my mouth and her fingers tasted of meat.

"What's wrong?" I asked, spitting out her fingers.

I pressed her close to me, touching our chins and noses together. I remained limp in her grasp.

"I thought some things were untouchable, unable to be harmed, even after all this time. But nothing is. Not in this world."

She found her discarded dress and pulled it over her head. She smoothed out her lion's hair, trailing streaks of meat through the strands, and looked out toward the window. The black moon hovered over the trees in the blacker sky.

"Do you love me, Charles?" she asked.

"I love you."

"Then why couldn't you get it up?"

I rose from the bed. I wanted her to look at me, look straight through me, like she when she took me into her meat freezer - when she scratched the hollow of my throat and suffocated me between her butterfly wings.

When she whispered, "If there were stars here they would be your eyes."

Instead, the stars outside the window caught her face in their claws and the sky threatened to pull her under. She shivered as she walked toward the window. I noticed for the first time she was barefooted, and the soles of her feet were blackened and scorched raw.

"Jeanine?"

"The swans are dead," she said, "and I'm leaving."

She crawled through the window and leaped into the darkness below. She sprinted off into the woods, and then was gone.

I chased after her. I ran down the stairs past Momma and Sissy sitting on the couch, and out the door.

"Jeanine!" I called out.

For the rest of my like I'd be chasing after people who once loved me.

I ran to her meat freezer and found the door unlocked. The butterfly wings and the suits of skin were gone. Nothing remained except the industrial whir of the freezer fans and the congealing puddles of blood stuck to the floor below where the meat costumes used to hang.

I ran to Jeanine's home and knocked on the door. I heard Jeanine's mother drag herself in her wheelchair toward the door.

"Who is it?" she asked behind the door.

"I'm Jeanine's boyfriend. Do you remember me?"

"Which one are you again?" she asked.

"It doesn't matter," I said. "Is Jeanine there?"

"She won't be coming back. Just like her brother. He's a prophet, you know. At The First City."

"Yes," I said. "I know."

"If you find her ask her if she knows how her brother's doing."

"And Jeanine?" I asked.

"That girl can go to hell."

I went to the rock quarry where Jeanine used to watch over her swans and record their names and births in her scratched black book. I found the quarry empty, and I heard no movement below.

I climbed down the sandstone face of the quarry.

The swans were dead.

They floated on the surface of the stained mirror waters with broken necks and open white wings bubbling over with black blood. Their soft heads were peeled back, split open, skulls exposed. Their reflections stared at me with sad and star filled eyes. I searched for the man of smoke that Jeanine told me she found in the dark places, but I only saw those eyes.

Ten

SISSY DIDN'T SEEM SURPRISED Jeanine left me.

"That girl was the worst kind of whore," Sissy said. "The kind with crazy dreams."

"She's not a whore," I said. "She won't take money for it."

But Sissy wasn't listening.

"I mean," she continued, "an archaeologist? Please. Nobody's an archaeologist anymore."

Sissy searched through my closet for dead animals. I sat on the bed, wearing Daddy's leather jacket. I felt Jeanine's spit in my mouth and the taste of butterfly meat on my tongue.

"I'll never find anyone like her again," I said.

"You're always so melodramatic. Nobody cares. Do you think Momma put a moose head in here?"

"Why don't you ask Momma yourself?" I asked.

Sissy laughed.

"Maybe there's an owl, if there isn't a moose. An owl would be okay. I've been looking for something to put above the kitchen table."

She pulled out boxes of Daddy's old belongings from my closet and dumped them out onto the floor. She sifted through his clothes, his glass pipes, his button beads, and jars of formaldehyde.

Momma walked up the stairs in her heavy,

shuffle stomp walk. She halted at the foot of my bed.

"Afraid to blow your head out of the water, Charles?" she asked. "You don't feel a thing."

Sissy threw a gold-edged button at Momma. It bounced off her head and rolled down into a crack in the floorboards.

"Come join me," Momma said. "You don't feel a thing at all."

"She says the same damn thing every night," Sissy said.

"You think I don't know that?" I said quietly.

"What's with you?" Sissy asked. "Are you still sobbing over that girl? Give it up."

"Give it up, Charles," Momma said in a grated, machine voice.

Sissy laughed again.

I said, "You know you're just like Momma. Even without the slip. You act just like her."

Sissy paused and her fingers shook. She stood up, turned toward me, her face stretched, and still. The heat rushed out of her body and infused the room.

"Bubba," she said, the first time in twelve years she called me that. "Bubba, you have no idea."

The next time I saw Sissy she hung on the arm of one a doctor with his gray valise. The doctor handed me Sissy's slip papers and a pamphlet about Sissy's "New and glorious life" as Sissy crawled across the floor toward the television.

Her billowing hospital dress tore on uprooted floorboards; her knuckles scraped frantic patterns against the rotted wood. As she crawled, she chewed against her bottom lip. Her eyes hid underneath her nesting hair, but her hair could not hide the hot wire spider clicking against her brain.

Sissy lay in front of the television and twitched as God in his black mask screamed.

"I know what you're thinking," the doctor said.

I turned toward him.

"In the woods. There's a sinkhole about a ten minute walk from here. Just give her a good push."

He winked at me and left me standing alone at the open door.

I knelt in front of Sissy. I stroked her hair and kissed her on the forehead like she used to kiss me.

"I'm sorry for what I said to you," I said. "I'm so sorry. I didn't know."

The spider inside her brain clicked furiously at me until Sissy cried out in pain.

That night Sissy joined Momma in her nightly advertisements at the foot of my bed.

"Come with us, Charles," Sissy said.

In the swamp Jolene screamed. The plague machines threw a hurricane that knocked over the tree outside my bedroom window, driving its sharp, roped branches through the glass. The shattered window glass flew with the storm across the room, lifting up Momma and Sissy's skirts and slicing up their faces and ankles

"You're hurt," I said as their blood pooled at their feet. "Oh God, look at you, you're hurt."

"You don't feel a thing, Bubba," Sissy said.

As the hurricane raged through my room, she smiled.

Part Two: Seven Years Later

One

CROUCHY THE FAILED ENGINEER built a hot air balloon and tried to float off the side of the. Ezekiel and I went to his house to watch when he cut the balloon tether tied to his roof. When we got there we found a small crowd already forming on the lawn, taking bets on how long before he'd crash.

Crouchy's red balloon sagged against the roof tiles. Before he climbed into his hot air balloon, he looked out over the crowd and waved with triumph.

"I'll see you on the other side!" he called out, and smiled with his jowly cat face.

"Did anyone ever tell him how gravity worked?" Ezekiel asked. "This is just fucking sad."

In the last seven years Ezekiel still maintained his sociopathically slick good looks and curly black hair and his perpetual boredom. The shiny sphere in his head grew angrier as the years passed, and Ezekiel's body warped to accommodate it, as if he was no longer so much a person but a vessel for the hard lined voice inside the pupiless black eye.

Crouchy climbed into his hot air balloon, took out a rusted silver knife from his jacket pocket, and cut the rope. We watched in an anorexic silence the red balloon rose up into the air. It started floating away with the wind, toward the east. It floated out past the temple, past the slip clinic, past the grocery store and the executioner's chair in the town square.

"I should've just stayed home," Ezekiel said.

"He might actually make it," I said.

"Hot air balloons aren't God approved technology," Ezekiel said. "He won't."

As the hot air balloon approached the woods, the trees appeared to coil upwards in response. They were like trees with branches made of daggers. I braced myself.

The balloon crashed.

The wicker basket tipped over and Crouchy fell. I couldn't hear the crash, or Crouchy's inevitable scream. Only silence. Even the crowd watching the spectacle made no noise, no cheer for bets won. They looked at the ground, covering their mouths and eyes with their hands.

"Yep. He's dead," Ezekiel said. "He should've taken the bus. Let's get out of here."

Ezekiel and I left the crowd around Crouchy's house. Ezekiel strode in front of me, each step of his like a new disease, the shiny sphere in the back of his head contracting and dilating as it received invisible signals from God. He headed toward the Prophet Headquarters and I followed him.

We passed several members of the Apocalypse Brigade. They wore monster masks resembling sharp-tongued Kali and black faced

Abraxas and passed out pamphlets about the end of the world. In the last seven years, the Apocalypse Brigade had grown from a fringe group to the predominating political influence in Edgewater.

A woman in a bird head mask shoved a pamphlet into Ezekiel's chest.

"Fuck off. See this? It means prophet."

Ezekiel pushed her, and she fell into the street, scattering pamphlets everywhere.

"I have to check in some paperwork at the prophet headquarters," Ezekiel said. "Then I'm free. Well, relatively speaking."

We walked past the slip clinic. The windows of the slip clinic were unwashed and gray. The foundation of the building buckled like an old spine. The exit doors flew open and a doctor escorted a deadhead outside, her hands and head wrapped in gauze.

"Don't worry, darling," the slip doctor said, as if he talking to a child.

His fingers tightened on her arm until he smudged it with bruises.

We reached the Prophet Headquarters. Ezekiel went inside and I waited on the steps. Even from the center of downtown Edgewater, I could see the woods, Crouchy's upside down wicker basket, the deflated red balloon draped over the trees.

"Flowers?" someone said.

A woman stood at the bottom of the steps,

holding tissue wrapped bouquets of small yellow and pink flowers. She had cropped black hair like a man and although she had a young face, her skin was knotted with old scars.

"Excuse me?" I said.

"Flowers," the woman said. "Do you want any?"

"I don't have anything to give you."

I expected her to walk away, but instead she stood there, staring at me with her wine dark eyes. She held the flowers to her chest, squeezing her fists so hard I thought she might break. From inside the Prophet Headquarters lobby the Teddy and Delilah show blasted through the speakers, Delilah laughed and laughed.

"I've never seen you before," I said. "Where are you from?"

She said nothing.

"Your name, at least? I'm Charles."

She looked behind her, toward the woods where Crouchy's hot air balloon was ensnared in the treetops. When she looked back at me I thought those eyes might tear the skin off my face.

"Did you see him fall?" she asked me.

I nodded.

"You know, they don't always fall," she said.

Ezekiel strode down the steps of the Prophet Headquarters.

"Go away," he said to the woman.

She continued to stare at me.

"I'm not joking. Go away and stop hanging around here. Every damn day, selling flowers. Maybe it wouldn't be so annoying if you were prettier."

"She's not doing anything wrong," I said.

"She's probably a host for every disease this side of the black planet."

"Why do you have to pick on her?"

"And why are you suddenly concerned? Look at her cut hair."

Ezekiel strode past me. His shiny sphere made a noise like teeth clicking.

"I'm so sorry," I said after Ezekiel left.

I headed after him.

"Don't worry about it," the woman said as I walked past. "I deserve to be a whore."

Two

EZEKIEL TOOK ME TO AN execution the next weekend. The victim that Saturday morning was Maddy the Mad girl, the baby-faced serial killer.

The executioner strapped Maddy to the ELECTRIC BABY 4000, the latest and greatest model of electric chair.

"Maddy the Mad girl has been sentenced to death by electric chair for the murder of an untold number of Edgewater strippers,"

"She could have been more original, don't you think?" said the popcorn salesman beside us in the crowd. "Everyone kills strippers. Want some popcorn?"

"No," Ezekiel said, and then turned to me. "Want any popcorn?"

Maddy the Mad girl made no movement as men in gray suits jumped up on the platform and tightened the chair's straps on her wrists and ankles and fit electrodes onto her forehead and tongue.

"No thanks. Not hungry," I whispered.

"Those jokers are back," Ezekiel said.

At the edge of the town square the Apocalypse Brigade stood on the fringe of the crowd holding signs that said, "She won't be the last," and "You're going to hell, baby girl."

"People like that shouldn't breed," Ezekiel said. "Every damn day they're crawling around in the streets. Repent. It's the end of the world.

Repent. Like we don't know already."

Ezekiel turned back toward Maddy on the executioner's platform.

"Look at her face. It's like a lake at the bottom of the world. Nothing can touch her. Fucking tragic," he said.

But I couldn't look at her face. Not after I'd seen her feet. Her bare feet, twisted back and broken. They were like vulture's feet, demon feet that could have once been dragged across the gritty floor of hell.

"God invented the electric chair so we could murder in his good name," the executioner said, "so that he wouldn't have to waste his divine punishment on scum like this."

The executioner tore away Maddy's smock, revealing her bare, bruised breasts and her belly crumbling underneath her ribs. Tattooed on her breasts were the words, "God is not real."

"Popcorn! Get your popcorn!"

Behind us, a young couple kissed frantically.

"I've taken so many girls' virginity at executions," Ezekiel said. "The heat always gets to them."

I wanted to run before Maddy started kicking and jolting in the chair, but I couldn't move in the packed crowd.

The executioner flipped the switch on the ELECTRIC BABY 4000.

Maddy's limbs hit the straps hard. Her breasts turned black, a crisscross of braised exo-veins.

Even after she burst into flames "God is not real" blazed on her skin.

The crowd started dispersing before the final shocks were administered.

"Charles, where are you going?" Ezekiel asked.

But I'd already pushed myself past the crowd and away from the square. Apocalypse Brigadiers blocked my way. I headed the opposite direction to escape them. Ezekiel disappeared.

Maddy lolled dead in the ELECTRIC BABY 4000. Even when I looked away, the image of her tattooed breasts wouldn't leave me. God is not real. Those words filled my mouth with their sharpened angles.

"Hey, are you all right?" someone asked me.

She touched my shoulder. It was the flower woman. Except for not carrying any bouquets, she was as I remembered her, all knots and scars. She wore gauze wrapped around her hands and a cloche hat pulled down over her face.

"No," I said. "I mean, yes. I'm fine."

"What's wrong?" she asked me.

She tugged on my shoulder.

"I remember what you said to me the other day, that's what's wrong," I said.

"Let's get away from all this," the woman said to me.

She slipped her hand into mine. I seized up.

"I don't know you," I said.

"It's okay," she said. "I don't know you either."

Maddy's executioner unstrapped her body from the electric chair. Maddy's skin cooled a light black, like wet tar. When the executioner dragged Maddy off the chair, I expected her to snap her head back, grow sharpened legs like a spider, and crawl away. She remained limp. The executioner tore her burnt hair off her head.

"Let's get away from here," the woman said once more.

"I don't know you," I repeated.

"Leda," she said. "I'm Leda."

I expected her to have the eyes of every lonely woman I'd ever known. I knew what lonely looked like from my mother and sister, with their nicotine-ringed, hazy, father left me faces. But Leda's wine dark eyes were fierce as teeth, and when she tightened her grasp on my hand I thought those eyes might snap and swallow me whole.

"Where?" I asked her.

"Away," she said.

I looked around for Ezekiel, but he was gone. Most of the crowd was gone as well, and the empty electric chair sat in the middle of the town square like a sad mother. Men in gray suits approached the execution platform and hauled away Maddy's corpse.

Leda beckoned me to follow, tugging on my

head.

She led me out of the town square and into an alleyway behind the courthouse. We approached the back of a shop with a steel door. Leda pulled a small key out of a storm drain, and unlocked the door. We entered the back of a flower shop. In one corner stood a humming refrigerating unit full of tissue paper. Other than that, the room was bare.

"Do you need to sit down?" Leda asked me. "I can get a chair from the front room."

"I'm fine," I said.

She tugged on the brim of her cloche hat, as if trying to pull the shadows down to hide her face. She stood in the center of the room much like she'd stood in the street several days ago selling flowers. She was like a bent tree with frozen sap. The memory of her hand in mine burned.

"I can't stay here," I said.

"Step away from the window," she said.

She grabbed me and pressed my face into her shoulder. The ground shook with an explosion. The windows burst, spraying us with glass. Shouts came from outside.

"Give us the dead whore!"

I pried myself from Leda and stumbled backwards, over the new carpet of glass, my ears ringing. She continued to stand in the center of the room. Blood dripped from the glass embedded in her forehead.

"Leda," I said, and I couldn't hear myself speak. "We can't stay here."

Leda and I went into the front room of the flower store. So strange, for flowers to still exist. The irises, chrysanthemums, and lilies appeared one dimensional and dull as dog dreams.

We moved toward the front door. Leda reached up and slid the bolt lock open, and we left. Outside a bear-masked woman with an electric cattle prod, electrocuting a prone, gray-suited man. She zapped him over and over again. Other Apocalypse Brigadiers stood on the courtroom steps on the other side of the street, watching the thin slits in their monster masks.

"Where is she?" the woman in the bear mask said. "What have you done with that whore? Give her to us!"

The others took up the chant.

"Give her to us! Give her to us!"

The man in the gray suit cried out, and as if it was a cue, other Apocalypse Brigadiers surrounded him beat him. They pulled his body apart.

"We have to go," I said.

Leda didn't respond at first. Only when I grabbed her shoulders and wheeled her around did she look at me, snapping out of her paralysis. Several of the Apocalypse Brigadiers glanced in our direction, entrails strewn between their teeth.

"Leda," I said. "We have to go."

I pulled her down the street. We walked fast. The rule was to always walk fast, never look back, even when the screaming grew louder. Because if you looked they'd come for you.

"Give her to us! Give her to us!"

We rounded a corner out of sight.

"We can't stop," she said, breathing hard. "They might change their minds and come after us."

I didn't know what else to do, so I took her home with me.

Leda and I walked up the porch steps. Only when I reached for the doorknob did I feel the heat of the explosion lacerating my back. I opened the door and blood dripped out of my sleeves.

Momma and Sissy sat in the living room. Their rickety bodies bent inside a network of blankets and breathing tubes and IV stands. God's masked face from the television turned their pale skin reptilian. Even their eyes, flickering with the movement of the screen, resembled the eyes of snakes.

"What are those things?" Leda asked.

"My family," I said. "Come inside."

We went into the kitchen and I turned on the light and the kitchen faucet. I tried to peel off my shirt and it fell apart in my hands. I placed what was left of it on the counter, smearing blood against the granite. I braced myself against a kitchen chair and started to pick the glass out of my back, piece by piece.

"Iodine?" Leda asked.

I didn't answer at first. I looked back at her with pink-tinged glass in the palms of my hands and my tongue ruched to my mouth. Everywhere she stood, she turned into some surrealist painting. Not because she was beautiful, though I found her to be so, but because she knew how to be still at all the right angles.

"Where do you keep the iodine?" she asked again.

"Down the hall. Bathroom cabinet, behind the mirror," I finally said.

She disappeared down the hallway. I wetted a rag underneath the warm water in the skin and pressed it against my shoulder.

"So when are you two going to get married?"

Normally I heard Sissy trying to sneak up on me, but the water pouring out of the faucet concealed the clicking of her slip implant and the rusted wheels of her IV stand.

"It's been so long since you've brought Jeanine over here," Sissy said. "I've missed her."

I shut the water off. Sissy ran her fingers down her dirty IV stand and the needle taped to her hand strained against its tubing. All of Sissy's features quivered. Her eyes and nose and mouth sunk into her emaciated face.

"Jeanine's not here," I said.

"We should have dinner again," Sissy said.

"Wasn't that fun?"

I tried to walk past her. She grabbed my wrist. Her fingers were leathery and thin, ready to slough off the bone.

"You know we never had a chance," she said.

"Let go of me, Sissy," I said. "Please. You'll hurt yourself."

"Not until I tell you a story."

I sighed.

"Okay, fine, I said.

She spit in my face.

She squealed, laughing, and stumbled backwards. Her IV stand crashed with a rusted squeal, ripping the needle out of her hand.

Leda reappeared. She dropped the iodine on the floor, spilling it. She grabbed fistfuls of Sissy's hair and hauled her off me. She grabbed Sissy before she fell. Sissy whined, a strained, cat sort of whine. She thrashed, throwing her head back from side to side, pressing her palms to her throat.

The hot wire spider jumped inside of Sissy's head, swollen as a tick.

Leda pushed Sissy's hair away from her ear and whispered to her.

Sissy's hands, quivering, fell from her throat. Her eyes rolled up in her head, her spit like glycerin dripping down her chin. Leda petted Sissy's sweat soaked forehead.

"Let's get you back to the couch."

"What did you say to her?"

"I'll tell you later."

Sissy let Leda lead her back into the living room and position her on the couch beside Momma.

Momma had continued to watch television, oblivious throughout the whole ordeal. She shifted inside her cocoon of tubing and gunmetal wires.

"Jeanine," she said to Leda. "Where have you been?"

"It doesn't matter," Leda said. "I'm here now."

"Jeanine," Momma said.

"Yes?"

Momma's neck creaked when she turned her head.

"You're blocking the television, Jeanine."

Leda straightened up, as if unrolling out all her bones. I hadn't taken notice of a woman in seven years, but I couldn't stop looking at her. She stood tall, taller than me. I thought she might somehow manage to break through the boundaries of my house and carry the roof away on her shoulders.

"How long have they been here?" Leda asked me.

"Too long," I said.

Later as we sat in my bedroom picking the rest of the glass from our skin, I wanted to ask her what she said to Sissy to calm her.

Yet I asked, "Can I draw you?" instead.

I sat at my desk chair. Leda sat on my bed, barefoot, her dress hiked up to her thighs. She ran her fingers through her chopped, short hair. Glass she pulled from her skin littered the floor.

"I'm not pretty enough to draw," she said.

"It's not about being pretty," I said.

"What is it about then?" she asked.

"You draw something that catches your eye," I said. "Something unusual. It's all in the way the lines around us are drawn, you know. We think we're in control of our eyes, but it's really the lines that are."

Outside, the insects ticked.

"How come I've never seen you before?" I asked.

Someone knocked on the front door.

"Charles!" Ezekiel yelled. "You son of a bitch, are you still alive?"

I went to the open window. Ezekiel stood in front of my porch with a deadhead woman on one arm. She was freshly implanted, from the looks of her turpentine skin and eyes still colored human. She couldn't keep still. She shuddered, pressing her knees into Ezekiel's ribs, her jaw into his chest.

"Where the fuck did you go earlier?" Ezekiel asked. "I wanted you to meet Boxy."

"I couldn't find you anywhere."

"Say hello, Boxy. Charles, did you know Boxy's an exotic dancer?"

"No, I didn't."

I glanced back at Leda. She stared at her hands with pain, as if she slipped them into gloves of broken glass.

"Those Apocalypse Brigadiers got all riled up after we electrocuted that girl in town square," Ezekiel said. "Rioting, blowing up the street, demanding her corpse so they can desecrate it. It's great. Come down here."

He tipped the deadhead's neck back so far I thought her spine might brush her ankles. When he kissed her she screamed in the back of her throat like night thrush and swamp music.

"I'm sort of busy," I said.

He released the deadhead with a flourish, and she splayed out onto the gravel in front of him, breathless, a choked doll.

"Sort of busy? Long as I've known you, you do nothing but draw little pictures and meander around considering the lilies. And why, dare I ask, have you yet to find a job?"

"Theresa's sick."

"She's a deadhead," Ezekiel said. "There isn't any other kind but sick."

Ezekiel sighed loud enough to make sure I heard.

"I forgot. You've got one of those savior complexes," he said. "Well, good luck with that."

He threw the deadhead over his shoulder and left.

"You should stay here if the Apocalypse

Brigade is out," I said to Leda once Ezekiel was gone. "You can sleep on my bed. I'll sleep in Theresa's room. She never sleeps."

"Sleep with me," Leda said.

I paused.

"What did you say?" I asked.

Leda leaned back on the bed and sunk down. The frame groaned with her unfamiliar weight.

"Sleep with me," she whispered.

Her frail body shook

"Charles," she whispered. "It's been so long."

I crawled into bed beside her. My head did not belong to me. My limbs did not belong to me. I didn't seem to be on my bed, but floating above it. I watched myself as if from on top of a cloud as I wrapped my arms around her and pulled her close. Her breath melted into my breath.

I lay awake with my eyes open, my mouth buried in her short hair. My back throbbed with pain, but pain wasn't what kept me from sleeping.

When her breathing slowed I crept into the hallway. My blood followed me like a second skin. It seeped through the bandages. It dripped down my back into the shape of a face and dried there, crusty and beaded, empty eyes, hole of a mouth. It trickled down my legs and pressed red imprints of my feet into the floor.

I went into Momma's empty room. I couldn't remember opening the window, and it'd been years since Momma could walk up the stairs, but there it was, blowing leaves and dust across the floor. Everything was arranged as I remembered from childhood. I knelt beside the crib and pressed my forehead to the cool plastic railing.

The floorboards in the hallway creaked.

"You're bleeding," Leda said.

But I wasn't concerned about that, because I could still see the dried spot of blood on the wall where years ago my baby brother spit out his thumb.

"What was his name?" she asked.

She touched my shoulder.

"You're shaking," she said.

I didn't notice until she mentioned it. I thought my shaking had been the room tilting sideways, the bed and the baby crib and the dresser clenching their teeth.

"You're making me remember things I don't want to," I said.

Her arms encircled me. I couldn't remember the last time someone held me.

My nerves bit down on my throat and I thought I might be crushed from the inside I wanted to cry out and scream, to jump up and down, put my fists through a window elbow up. I would've done anything to make the tension in my body go away.

"Charles," Leda said.

My name hung in the air.

"I think we're just two very lonely people,"

she said.

My nerves relinquished their grip on my throat. I tilted my head back, reached up, and slipped my fingers into her hair. I kissed her.

When we got back to the room and curled up against each other, I fell asleep almost instantly. Leda grabbed my shoulder when the screaming in the swamp started.

"What's that?" she asked. "Is someone in trouble?"

"That's just Jolene."

I went back to sleep.

I wanted to dream of Leda, warm on my lips. I wanted to dream of slipping off her dress and pressing my mouth between her legs.

Instead, I dreamed of Mad Maddy's gritty, black feet dragging across my bedroom floor.

Three

LEDA AND I STARTED meeting each other in the woods. Those were the only quiet times I remembered. We lay together on a blanket for hours, even on the nights when nearby monsters slavered awake with the heat and the Apocalypse Brigade marched the streets rallying for God. I sketched everything except her, she wouldn't let me sketch her, and while I did so she taught me her name for every flower and tree. She spoke their names like the names of abusive husbands.

We kissed like children, with all our clothes on, backs craned and legs spaced apart. Despite those vicious eyes, Leda went shy when I tugged on the hem of her dress, or when I tried to slip my hands underneath to touch her skin. She touched her face, hugged her chest, and rolled away from me. I withdrew my hands.

"I've never kissed anyone without having sex first," I told her.

She laughed with her face pressed into the grass. I didn't want to tell her I wasn't joking.

At first we saw each other every fortnight. Then each week. Then a few times each week. Soon we met every night, sloughing through poison ivy and breaking abandoned monster holes with our shoes to get to each other. When we saw each other across the clearing, our meeting spot, we walked toward each other with hesitant, lamb steps. We felt each other's heads for the heat of the wire spider.

"You're still here," I whispered, when I felt nothing but her cool scalp.

"Still here," she said.

Leda taught me to dance. She pressed my hands against her waist and showed me how to lead as we stepped over animal skulls and crumbling moss. She hummed the same song over and over. We lost music a long time ago when Sissy broke our last record player. Except for the timpani music that used to blare out of the speakers of the courthouse and the skinned drums of the Apocalypse Brigade, Leda sang the only song I could remember.

I swept her against a tree. I tried to hoist her up into the branches and rest her legs against my shoulders, but over the years, I'd become too weak. My muscles ached with the weight of her. She slipped down and I leaned into her, my face cooked with sweat. I touched the back of her neck, panting.

"You're getting better at this," she said.

She hummed a few more seconds of the song.

"Where did you learn that?"

"The ocean gave it to me," Leda said, and she smiled.

She leaned her head back. The trees quivered with sleeping birds. An owl with the face of a bear opened its fierce, gleaming. They were Leda's eyes.

"Let me draw you," I said.

"Later," she said.

We lay down on our blanket and I waited for later. The months unraveled themselves. We danced until it became muscle memory, until I thought I could take a wolf or a lizard by the waist and charm them by waltzing across the clearing. Leda's cropped hair grew long and thick until it covered her eyes.

We continued like that for a while, humming snippets of song, kissing as if we were chaste, eating weeds in the woods when the government forgot to deliver rations. Each day I hooked Momma to her IV, filled her bag with saline nutrients, and peeled Sissy off the locked knife drawer or the medicine cabinet or the upstairs closet full of Daddy's stuffed animals. I fixed myself breakfast, if there was any left in the refrigerator, and drank weak coffee while God recited the list of plagues for the month, and the various transgressions for which we would be punished for. Sometimes the noise became too much and I walked the perimeter of the house and inspect the vines growing to the second story windows, wondering where I put those clippers seven years ago.

Most of the time I sat upstairs at my desk and drew. And wait. No motion had any color to it. Everything I did had already been done for an eternity. Every monster that emerged out of the murky swamp was a monster I saw before.

But when night arrived I ran into the woods shedding the numb parts of me. In the moments before I saw Leda, I transformed into trembling mucus and raw muscle. My brain slipped wet down my nose, all of my limbs threaded with gold. A new skin seemed to sew itself over my body, the worn left to skin amongst the furniture of our house.

I lay in the nest of her hair, and I shone.

One night I opened the front door, ready to run off into the woods, only to find two members of the Apocalypse Brigade on my porch.

I took a step backwards. I groped behind me with one hand, searching for the old skin I ripped off before opening the door.

One of the Apocalypse Brigadiers was a short, chubby girl wearing a cape and a snarling wolf mask. The other was a lean man holding a knobby cane and carrying his rickets worn skeleton body behind his head like a traveling case. He leaned against my porch banister and closed his eyes, slowly, pus leaking out of their corners.

"Your name is Charles, isn't it?" the girl asked.

"What's going on?"

"We're taking a survey."

The girl tilted her head to one side every time she spoke. Sideways, the snarling wolf seemed to smile. Even with the wolf mask on, the girl seemed familiar.

"Missy Freeling?" I asked. "From sixth grade science class?"

The girl clenched her fists as if she was going to throw a punch at me. The lean man lifted his atrophied hand and placed it on the girl's shoulders.

"Her name is not important," he said. "Only the questions."

The girl relaxed her fists, but the muscles in her neck bulged.

"Continue, darling. It's all right."

"Over the course of the last three years," the girl said, a small quaver in her voice, "how many Apocalypse Brigade meetings have you attended?"

I hesitated.

"Answer the question, sir," the man said.

He coughed.

"None," I said.

"How many times have you attended a public execution?" she asked.

"Maybe one every month or so."

"Interesting," the girl said.

"Did you want to write any of this down?" I asked. "You did say it was a survey."

"No, that won't be necessary," the man said. "Missy, continue."

"Over the course of the last three years, how many times have you blasphemed against God, the creator of the universe and your immortal, all powerful savior?"

"None," I said.

The man coughed again.

"That's impossible," the girl said. "Everyone blasphemes against God. We are dirty sinners, after all."

"Are you sure that's quantifiable then?" I asked.

"This is not a joke, sir," the man said.

For a moment I couldn't speak. They'd caught me in the middle of my ecdysis, in the in between place between daylight and night. I felt as if I stood before them naked, busted at the seams. I only wanted to run toward Leda.

"Of course it's not a joke," I said.

"Who is that?" Momma called from inside the house. "Tell him to come inside for tea."

"Give me a minute, Momma!" I called back.

"Who is that?" the girl asked.

"We were told nobody else lived in this house."

"My mother and sister," I said. "They're deadheads."

"But other than that, it's just you?" the girl asked.

Her voice changed again. She spoke like a block of ice.

"There's only me."

"Are you sure?"

"Why wouldn't I be?" I asked.

They'd trapped me, and they knew it. It was

as if I could already feel the straps of the electric on my wrists. Daddy once told me it was better to kill yourself than let a monster get you. They ate you while you were still alive, they pinned your head into the ground with one paw and pulled your organs out while you were still conscience.

"If you're telling the truth, then you wouldn't mind if we searched your house," she said.

"You're not allowed in."

"You may be making a very dangerous mistake."

"Missy," I said. "Go away."

"I think we're finished here," the man.

Missy dug her heels into the porch, but a sharp look from the old man made her relent and follow him down the steps.

"Don't worry, we'll be back," the girl said over her shoulder. "Oh, and here's a warning. Don't go outside tonight."

The plague machines in the distance groaned.

That night I sat at my desk underneath a broken halogen bulb, holed up in the house while torrents of ice battered the shutters and the walls. My room rocked from side to side. The paper in front of me remained blank. Even through the storm I heard Apocalypse Brigadiers shouting on the television. The only words I heard were "End of the world" and "God" and "Repent."

I almost didn't hear the knock on the door.

I found Leda shivering on the porch, ice stuck to her skin and her eyes pink with blood.

She opened her mouth to speak but the cold laced her tongue down.

I pulled her inside and shut the door. I embraced her, rubbed her shoulders, and touched the back of her frost-covered head.

"Charles," she whispered.

"What is it?" I asked

"Did you know there's a storm outside?" she said.

I pulled away so that I could look at her face. She smiled with blue lips. I laughed and pulled her close again.

"Come here," I said. "Come upstairs."

I guided her up the stairs with the storm pummeling our ears. When we got to my room I guided her toward the bed and laid a blanket across her shoulders. Some of the color returned to her face, but she couldn't stop shivering.

"Hold on," I said. "I'll be right back."

I tiptoed past Momma and Sissy into the kitchen. The lights were out because of the storm, but I groped my way around in the dark until I found Daddy's liquor cabinet. I retrieved his bottle of whiskey and took it back upstairs.

"Whiskey?" Leda asked.

"It'll make you warm," I said, and handed her the bottle.

She unscrewed the bottle and tipped it to her mouth. She swallowed and grimaced. She placed the bottle between her knees and scratched away at its gold label.

"Something's after me," she said.

"You too?" I said.

Leda took another drink.

"Two members of the Apocalypse Brigade came over tonight," I said. "I think they're onto me."

"Why? What did you do?" Leda asked.

"I'm sure I've done something."

Leda drew the blanket tighter around her shoulders.

"What about you?" I said. "What's after you?"

She kept scratching at the gold label with her cold swollen hands. I sat down at my desk. My head felt like a dense cloud.

"Leda," I said. "How come I don't know anything about you?"

Leda took another sip of whiskey.

"I don't know where you came from, or how you got here. I don't know who you are."

"You don't want to know," she said.

I crossed the room toward her. She flinched at my sudden movement, spilling whiskey on her dress. I knelt in front of her, my palms against her knees.

"I think I could love you, but not like this," I said. "What do we do? We lay together. We dance. Sometimes we kiss, as long as I'm careful to not touch you too much. None of that means a damn thing if I don't know you. We're just biding our time. So, yes, I want to know."

Leda raised the whiskey bottle to her lips, and let it hover there for a few moments. The glass shone in her eyes like a soft film.

I rose and headed for the door.

"The ocean," Leda said.

I stopped.

"I grew up by the ocean."

I turned to face her. Suddenly, I felt very tired. The cold seemed to seep through the walls and straight to my head.

"Go on," I said.

"What do you want from me? A list of my tragedies?" Leda asked.

"That'd be a start," I said.

"My mother was a florist, my father worked for the mayor."

She paused.

"Why does this matter to you?"

"Because I want to know you," I said.

"You've never known anyone in your life."

"I want to try," I said.

I leaned against the wall, dizzy, cold. Leda sighed.

"I spent my childhood learning how to make flower arrangements and dress the way a girl should dress if her father works for the government."

"Your father worked for the government?"

"He was a small time official, not like a prophet or anything," she said. "They put the fear of God in me and I learned all the right words. I learned the proper way to dance and talk to boys."

She started talking faster, like the words had bubbled underneath her skin for years, and at this moment, she'd rupture if she didn't let them escape.

"My mother got taken by the hell shuttles when I was about fourteen. After that, well, I had this best friend named Cat. Her father worked for the government too. We'd go to dances together. I was so jealous of her. The boys always wanted her. She was gorgeous. Even as a teenager, she had this slim waist, hips that hit you like bullets. Pale blue eyes, blond curly hair. Pouty mouth, that sort of thing. She had an allure I know I could never have."

I sat down beside Leda on the bed, though I was almost afraid that any sudden movement would frighten her into silence.

"We were both sixteen when a friend raped her. The boy was named Wilco, someone we knew at school. Her father tried to cover up the scandal, but she became pregnant. The hell shuttles took her and her father away. I never understood why. Everyday I saw Wilco in school, untouched and unpunished. I watched him in class with his perpetual smirk and I kept thinking, any day now. Any day they'll take him. But they never did.

"I started talking to him during school. I

knew I shouldn't have, but I was sick with it."

"Sick with what?" I asked.

"Sick with wanting to know why he raped Cat. What was it about her that caused him to do such a terrible thing? Of course, we talked about everything except Cat, everything except what I wanted to ask him. We talked about the weather, our homework, when he thought the next plague would hit."

Leda turned her face from me.

"I got impatient. One night after a party, I followed him out into the back while he was taking a smoke break. I still remember what I was wearing, one of those silver dresses that look like they're liquid, you know, and flared out at the bottom. I had on cherry lipstick and smoky eyes because my mother said it would seduce boys into doing what you wanted. While he was taking out his lighter, I asked him how he felt about Cat.

"His cigarette drooped in the corner of his mouth. I asked him again. How did he feel about Cat? He regained his composure. He lit his cigarette and put his lighter back in his pocket. He told me that she used to be a good friend. Then he smirked. That stupid, fucking smirk."

Leda nearly drained the bottle of whiskey and her skin shone with it.

"I asked him if I thought she was pretty. He said she was "Hot as fuck," and his words torched me. I'd been getting to him closer all the while, and before I knew it I was pulling on his arm and asking him if he would do to me what he did to her. There were cat scratches on the inside of my chest. He dropped his cigarette and grabbed me by the shoulders. He shook me until I let go.

"'Baby,' he said. 'Oh baby, you're not pretty enough for me to waste my time.' Then he left me there, alone. I can still feel the static of his jacket clinging to my hair, my makeup smeared on the back of my hand. That's when I realized it didn't really matter if we were sinners or not, good or bad. We were all cursed in the same way."

I took the bottle from between her knees and placed it on the nearby bed stand. She folded in my lap.

"Leda," I said. "You shouldn't think of what he did anymore. You're beautiful."

"It's still there," she said, "No matter how many times someone calls me beautiful, it never goes away."

"Leda," I said, "I'm sorry. I wish I could've been there. I wish I could've done something."

"It doesn't matter," she said.

She grasped my hand and breathed into my palm. Kissed it.

"Do you want to know why it doesn't matter?"

And just like she did to my sister, she buried her fingers in my hair and rested her mouth in the crook of my ear.

"Because I once stood in the surf as a child and a voice from the ocean told me to not be afraid. It told me that help was coming, and we would all be saved. So we shouldn't be afraid."

She went to the window.

"They're out there waiting for me," she said. "One day they're going to find me."

"What's waiting for you?" I asked.

"Can't you see it out there?"

"I can't see anything," I said.

She pressed her face against the window. Blue cold spread through Leda's skin and turned her veins into webbed crystals. Then she climbed back into bed and kneeling, she kissed me with the storm lingering on her mouth.

"Draw me," she said. "I'm giving you permission"

Downstairs the front door slammed open and the windows burst. Leda jerked her head back, her eyes rattling. The storm barreled into the living room, knocking over furniture and portraits on the wall, beating the stairs, shaking the television.

"Not again," I said, and I sighed. "Stay here."

I stood at the top of the stairs, shivering, all the blood drained out of my head, as I tried to find Momma and Sissy somewhere in the snow. Momma howled like a rabbit, her voice trapped in ice. I ran back down the hallway, grabbed my father's jacket from the closet, and descended the stairs.

Momma and Sissy lay on the floor in front of the television, clutching at the screen with hands like bird scapula. The storm overturned their IV stands and half buried them in ice. I pressed my hands to my ears as the cold pelted me, and shouted out their names. They didn't respond. Their eyes followed the Apocalypse Brigadiers marching on the television screen. Their stoic faces sunk further into the snow.

I hauled Sissy and Momma out of the ice and dragged them upstairs into Momma's bedroom. They lay down on the bed without protest. I waded downstairs and slammed the front door shut. I nailed the windows shut with wooden boards we kept underneath the sink. When I returned to my room, I found Leda asleep.

I sat at my desk and watched her. I tried to breathe with the cold enmeshed against my lungs. I got out my sketchpad and my charcoals, but my fingers were so stiff I couldn't control them. I threw the sketchpad back against the desk. I dropped the charcoal onto the floor and it rolled underneath the. I crawled into bed with Leda, pretending I couldn't hear Momma's screams.

We intertwined ourselves around each other. Leda slept as if falling from a great height. Her hair wrapped around the iron bed rails. Her fingers and toes braced against the sheets. I listened to the television static swelling outside our door. I wanted to wake her up and ask her when this help would come, because I saw God pulling down stars to end the world.

Instead, I traced the scarred skin on Leda's shoulders as she slept and I waited to die.

The bedroom door swung open and Momma and Sissy entered the room. As the volume of the television rose, I thought I saw Teddy standing at the foot of the bed with his slicked black hair and grey suit. Delilah stood in the corner and rose up on the balls of her feet to keep the black moon from slicing off her heels. She bashed her head into the wall until blood dashed her pretty curls.

Teddy clicked his shoes together and said. "Are you afraid of what's coming for you, sir? Are you afraid of death, sir?"

He opened up his closed hands and showed me the wire spider he saved for me. It clicked and trembled in his palm. All the while, the television hummed and the floorboards rattled to the rhythm of Delilah's beating head. Momma dragged herself to the foot of my bed and her drool left a thick trail behind her.

I realized my fingers were ticking like bombs and would soon obliterate me. I cried out and turned my face away.

Leda awoke and saw me about to burst. She pulled me close and pressed my fingers into her ribs.

"Don't. You'll kill us both," I said.

"Breathe," Leda said.

"See Delilah in the corner? And there's Teddy, waiting for me."

"Just breathe, Charles. Learn how to breathe."

She held me close. My fingers stopped being bombs and Teddy and Delilah disappeared from the room. Momma and Sissy finished their slip implant advertisements and left to go watch television amidst the melting snow. I lay down in bed with the sweat peeling off my forehead, sick to my stomach.

"You don't have to pay attention to them. They don't mean anything anymore," she said. "Just learn how to breathe."

She wouldn't let me go.

Four

THE GIRL IN THE WOLF MASK and the old man visited me again. They brought a lie detector and my high school algebra teacher. While the old man hooked me up to the lie detector on the porch his hands shook so badly he could barely tighten the straps around my fingers.

My algebra teacher took out my school records from his briefcase and read off my grades for every test and notes from my conduct for every semester.

"Quiet, and unusually restrained," he read. "Completes all of his homework on time. Good grades, but not overly ambitious. His only deviant behavior seems to be associating with Jeanine Hart, the delinquent sister of one of our graduating prophets."

"Is this really necessary?" I asked while the girl took out her interrogation notes.

"I feel we didn't get to know each other under the best of circumstances," she said. "Holland, will you tighten those straps? They look a little loose."

"Have I done something wrong?" I asked.

"Of course you have," the girl said. "We just don't know what it is yet. Comfortable?"

From where I sat, I couldn't see the lie detector. I heard the thin scribble of its the mechanical arm moving against the paper as it read my nerves. My heartbeat sat on my tongue.

"Now, we're going to start out with a few test questions," the girl said. "What is your name?"

"Charles," I said.

"How old are you, Charles?"

"Twenty-five."

"What town do you live in?"

"Edgewater," I said.

It seemed as if I spoke not from my mouth, but from the mouth of a gravelly, stone-edged creature living inside of me. It pressed against my lunges and the inside of my eyes. Sounds and textures blurred. The swamp trees receded into the background, and my ancient algebra teacher melted into a shadow. I couldn't feel the straps of the lie detector on my arm, or the wooden boards underneath my feet. All I felt was the creature straining, my heartbeat.

"I really have to be going," I said.

"Negative," she said. "We went to the town hall and checked your records. We know you don't have a job. And, well, if you could see the graph, you would know you were lying."

She continued her list of questions.

"What is the nature of your association with the prophet Ezekiel?"

"Under what authority are you doing this?" I asked.

"God's," the girl said abruptly.

"Didn't God appoint a government for this sort of thing?"

The old man spit yellow phlegm into his hand and wiped it off onto his pants.

"Listen, we're not the ones on trial here," he said.

"I'm on trial?" I asked.

"Stop it! This is nonsense!" the girl said.

She stamped her feet, rattling the porch. Her wolf mask slipped past her eyes. She grabbed the mask in both hands and pushed it back into place.

I laughed. My heartbeat receded from my mouth and absorbed itself back into my ribcage. Everything came back into focus, and the three people standing in front of me lost their hard edges. They appeared silly, tattered, and sad.

"Okay," I said. "I'll stop. I'll answer your questions."

"You're not taking this seriously, young man," my high school algebra teacher said.

"I'll hear what Missy has to say."

The girl flinched when I spoke her name.

I thought of Leda whispering what the ocean said to her.

"Don't be afraid."

I laughed again. I couldn't hold it back. The lie detector scribbled faster.

"What's so funny?"

"What was the question again?" I asked.

The girl looked at the paper once more. For a whole minute her eyes searched the text.

"What is the nature of your association with the prophet Ezekiel?" she finally said.

"He's a friend," I said. "We met in grade school."

"Have you ever had sexual relations with Ezekiel?"

I burst out laughing.

"This isn't funny!" The girl said.

The old man's head snapped up. He moved with spastic, almost convulsive motions.

"Control yourself, Missy," the old man said.

"No, I've never had sexual relations with Ezekiel," I said.

"What would you consider your sexual orientation?"

"I suppose I've never thought about it," I said.

"What do you mean you've never thought about it?" the girl said.

"Well, have you?" I asked. "I just never thought we had a choice one way or the other."

"Move onto the next question," the old man told Missy.

"Yeah, okay. Fine," the girl said, and she cleared her throat loud enough to swallow the noise of the scribbling lie detector.

"What's the question?" I asked when she didn't speak.

"I'm getting to it," she said.

"Tormenting a poor child," my high school

algebra teacher. "This won't look good at your final judgment, you know."

"It seems like you've already decided that I'm guilty," I said.

"I think that's enough questioning for now," he said. "It's clear that we won't get very far with this today. Come along, you two."

The old man ripped the straps off me and tucked the huge machine underneath his arm. Missy into tears, and my algebra teacher put his arm around her shoulders.

"There now, dear. I'm sure the hell shuttles will take him away soon. He was always a fucked up kid. Nobody liked him."

He touched her on the cheek, her breast, and led her away as she cried inside of her wolf mask. The old man followed, lugging the lie detector.

***

Leda came over to my house with a suitcase just before nightfall. It'd been the first time I saw her since the night of the ice storm. She looked wild, with eyes ready to eat me alive and her hair in static knots.

"I thought I'd stay a while," she said. "If that's all right with you."

"Yes," I said, unsure if she was serious or not.

"That's fine. You can put your suitcase in my room."

When we got to my room, she placed the suitcase up against the wall and lay down on my bed, her arms over her head, her dress riding up her legs.

"I think they're going to get me soon," I told her.

"Who?" she asked, her voice muffled in the sheets.

"The Apocalypse Brigade," I said. "Or the monsters outside. Or God."

I lay beside her.

"I think I might've scared them off, isn't that strange? Because I remembered what you said to me the night before, and suddenly I wasn't afraid anymore."

"It wasn't true what I said," Leda said. "It just sounded good at the time."

"You're scared too," I said. "Otherwise you wouldn't say that."

"Charles," she whispered.

"What is it?" I asked.

I touched her stomach, her hair.

"I think I could learn to trust you."

She kissed each of my fingers, one after the other.

"All that I can think about is you," she said. "You're a good person. Do you know how rare that is?"

She withdrew her hand.

"Let's not talk anymore," she said. "When I get nervous I say things that have been said too many times."

"I shouldn't have said those things to you that night. I don't want you to go away," I said.

Leda knelt on the bed in front of me.

She grasped the bottom of her dress in two fists, so tightly that her knuckles protruded from her fingers with the strain. She pulled her dress up, slowly. In the light of my room, the cotton looked like cast-iron.

She threw her head back. She pulled her dress up over her legs, her thighs.

Her name lingered on my tongue, though I didn't remember speaking it. I wanted to tell her that she didn't have to do this for me, she didn't have to lay out her past quivering and raw. She didn't have to show me the skin of her inner thighs, crisscrossed with scars like little birds, or the edge of her cotton panties, out of place and vibrant on her heated skin. But I couldn't move, couldn't speak.

She tried to pull her dress over her head.

"Help me," she said. "Don't you know I'm in love with you?"

I unraveled her out of her dress and tossed it onto the floor.

I reached for her and touched something dry and crumbling. She'd tied a chain of daisies, browning, almost dead, around her waist.

"I have three more flowers to lose," she said.

"I want a nine flower waist."

I paused. My hands hovered in the air next to her waist.

"I know, it's silly, but I can't stop," she said. "Nine would be the perfect number."

I opened my mouth to speak but she grabbed the back of my head and pulled my mouth into hers. The motion was clumsy, almost violent.

"I just wanted to be beautiful, but look at me now," she said. "I'm hardly human anymore."

She took my hand and guided me to touch her cheek, her nose, her neck.

I pulled her into me.

"If only I could show you what I saw," I said.

She was softer than I imagined. She spilled into me. I'd never been able to touch her like this, grasp her, and take whole chunks of her in my fingers. I kissed her neck, her stomach. I knelt down and kissed her in-between her legs. She tasted like I always imagined her to.

She tried to take my clothes off, but I had to help her because she was clumsy, uncertain. She wiped the sweat off her forehead. I wanted to tell her we could do this another time, but then she pushed my penis inside of her in one fluid motion.

She gasped. I thought of the voice in the waves. I pinned myself to the waves. I rocked inside her slow, as if I we might shipwreck ourselves if we moved too fast.

She turned her head from side to side. She

held onto me like she might fall if she let go. I closed my eyes. A small, low noise escaped from my throat.

Leda pushed me. I pulled away and she propped herself up on her elbows, flung her hair back.

"What's wrong?" I asked.

"From behind," she said. " I want to watch the window. I want to see what's coming for me."

I turned her over. I buried my fingers in her hair and drove into her. She cried out. I tasted her sweat. It seeped through my skin. For one moment, the shadows fled and I couldn't feel the bed sheets underneath me. I only felt her, touched her.

"I love you, Leda," I said.

"Fuck me," she said. "Please."

She squeezed my penis inside of her, pinned my body to her. I wanted to peel away the layers of her, pink by pink, unfold each one until her womb busted down. I slipped my fingers inside of her and licked the juice away. I pulled her hair, fistfuls, until she was forced to throw her head back. She groaned. The walls peeled away. I thought my head might peel away as well, leaving nothing but a smear on the wall.

I dug my nails into the back of her neck and there I found the hint of a blue tattoo, poorly inked.

I slowed my pace, even while she squirmed

underneath me, pushed against me. The tattoo was well hidden at the base of her skull. It was a number.

"What is this tattoo for?" I asked.

"Stop," Leda said.

"What's wrong?"

"Stop. I said stop."

She stood up and I slipped out of her. I touched her shoulder. She grabbed my hand and pushed it away as if it was a foreign creature. She knelt with the headboard at her back, quivering, hands in front of her breasts

"What did you see?" she asked.

I couldn't speak.

"Tell me. What did you see?"

She gathered up her dress and hugged it to her chest. The wildness came back into her face.

"Tell me," she said again. "What did you see?"

"A six," I whispered.

She jumped off the bed and ran across the room. I chased after her. By the time I caught her around the waist, snapping her flower chain, she'd already grabbed the handle of her suitcase and hauled it toward the door.

"No, let me go," she said, gasping.

Her dress tore in my fingers. She dropped her suitcase and the back of her head hit the wall. Dead daisies scattered across the floor.

"You're going to turn me in," she said. "Have you known all along? Did you draw me?"

She pushed me away with such force that I fell. She rushed to my desk and rummaged through my drawings. She tossed several sketches onto the floor as she searched.

"What does it mean? The six?" I asked, pulling myself off the floor. "I don't have any idea."

She paused and turned to look at me with my drawings crumpled in her hands, red veins bulging in her eyes. For a moment, I thought of Daddy's stuffed deer, hunched in the corner of the kitchen.

"Are you going to turn me in?" she asked.

"Of course not."

I embraced her. She was smaller than I'd ever remembered her, all tree knots and skinless bone. She dropped my drawings and they scattered onto the floor. The dress drifted to the floor. At first she stiffened, as if she was going to pull away again.

"It's waiting out there for me," she said.

"For all of us," I said.

"Promise you won't turn me in," she said.

"I promise. Never."

Her body relaxed. I led her back to bed. The smell of crushed flowers overwhelmed me.

"What does the number mean?" I asked.

"Don't tell anyone," she whispered.

"I won't."

When she went to sleep I rose from the bed, gathered my crumpled drawings, and tossed them away.

Five

"YOU'RE BORING NOW," EZEKIEL told me. "How come we never have fun anymore? Let's go have fun."

So after Ezekiel finished damning souls for the day we went to The Legion.

A heretic bombed the slip clinic that night, so all the wannabe deadheads with their ghost lips and burnt out limbs were at The Legion instead of the clinic waiting room. They stood at the edge of the hazy, blue-lit stage clamoring for the three strippers. The strippers danced like insects jump, nervous and frenzied. One turned on a pole, revealing her backside. Someone wrote SLUT on her ass in red lipstick.

"I think I know that girl," I told Ezekiel.

"Sorry," he said.

I edged closer to the stage while Ezekiel went to order a drink. The stripper colored her hair like the stage lights, orange at the roots, blue at the tips. Her PVC boots sparked against the stage when she walked. She slung her dirty hair behind her shoulder and unclasped her brassiere, then let it drop to her feet. She knelt down to collect money from the wannabe deadheads. A line of spit ran down her chin.

That's when I noticed the furious red sore on her forehead, the faint lines of the hot wire spider's legs clicking underneath her skin.

"She's a deadhead," I said.

“They all are. Cheap labor,” a man on my left said. “And of course they don't complain.”

Ezekiel approached me with his arm around the bartender, a man with nicotine stained fingers and blacked out eyes like holes. His silver nametag read “Eugene”.

“Hey Eugene, this is my friend Charles,” Ezekiel said. “He doesn't come here much. He’s sort of a loner type.”

“I think I know that stripper up there,” I said.

“Doubt she'd remember you now,” Eugene said. “Want a Bloody Mary? House specialty.”

“No thanks,” I said.

The stripper heaved as if she had trouble breathing. Her fingers curled over her anorexic breasts and her hair rained down on the wannabe deadheads below. They grasped at her crackling PVC boots and her raw white calves and smeared the red lipstick SLUT into an indecipherable mess.

“If you want to fuck her you're going to have to talk to her doctor,” Eugene said. “This one's been having bolts lately. Her implant is going all screwy.”

“No thanks,” I said.

"The strippers have been a real life-saver after business slowed down. End of the world and all, you know. Plenty of drunks in this town, but drinking just isn’t enough for these sad fucks anymore.”

"I can’t imagine it would be.”

"Though it sure is a busy night tonight, with that slip clinic getting attacked by that heretic and all. You'd think they'd just kill themselves, instead of trying to grab tits and drink all night."

Lucky for you they don't," Ezekiel said.

"Right, man, right," Eugene said. "It's been so busy I had to get Millie to make drinks. You know she can't make drinks worth shit, but nobody here cares."

Someone crawled on top of the bar and turned on the mounted television. Delilah smiled her crooked dog smile while Teddy addressed the camera.

"Well Edgewater folks," Teddy said. "We just got news of the firebombing at the slip clinic. Sorry to say, four doctors, three nurses, and six patients have died, and the heretic responsible is still on the run. We didn't want you to have to wait to get your slip, so we've set up a makeshift clinic just down 5th street, in what used to be the Babel Tech building. And just like your regular clinic, this one will be open twenty-four hours a day."

Delilah bounced on the bed and clapped her hands. Everyone turned away from the stage and faced the television behind the bar. The strippers continued to dance in her stop jerk motions.

"Oh my God," I said. "I remember. That's Jeanine. That girl up there. Don't you remember Jeanine?"

"Can't say that I do," Ezekiel said.

"What is she doing back in Edgewater?"

"Shut up," Eugene said. "Pay attention to the television."

I left Ezekiel and Eugene and edged closer toward the stage.

"Come on down to the slip clinic tonight," Teddy said. "Get your hot wire spider and turn your life around. I've been saying it for years, but you have to get it to believe it. You don't feel a thing."

Several wannabe deadheads pushed past me and ran out of the bar, leaving behind empty glasses, singed hair, and bloodied scraps of clothing. Soon The Legion emptied out, except for a few regulars, Eugene and his staff, Ezekiel, me, and the strippers on stage.

"Rest assured that God will bring this heretic to justice," Teddy said. "Even if he has to destroy this entire damned town to do so."

Teddy leaned down and kissed Delilah on the cheek.

"Fuck me," Eugene said. "Look at the mess those bugfucks left behind. Millie, get out from behind the bar and clean this shit up. Fucking damn."

As I approached the girl on stage, she ceased to dance. She ran down like a toy and her hips stopped grinding a pulse against the air. She stood at the edge of the stage, shivering and naked.

"Hey sweetie," I said to her. "Hey, you remember me?"

She twitched and her head tilted toward me. Her wide white eyes shrunk down into her head.

"Jeanine. Come off the stage," I said. "How did you get here? Take my hand and come down."

"The show isn't over, baby," she said.

"It's over," I said. "Now come here."

After a moment's hesitation, she reached out to take my hand. Her fingers were clammy and wet.

"Yes sir," Teddy said. "God always gets his revenge."

"Watch it!" Eugene said as I took Jeanine into my arms. "I told you, if you want to fuck her you're going to have to talk to the doctor. And looks like he's out on another smoke break."

Jeanine continued to shiver as if stuck on an electrical circuit, her bones shuddering like strung out nerve wire.

"Are you cold?" I asked her.

I took my jacket off and draped it over Jeanine's shoulders, but she wouldn't stop shivering.

"She's a damn deadhead," Eugene said. "She doesn't give a fuck one way or the other. Millie, get your scrawny ass out from behind that bar and clean this shit up like I told you to."

"Charles," Ezekiel said. "We have to go."

Ezekiel stood by the bar holding his half-empty glass of Bloody Mary. Heat came off the sphere in the back of his head in sharp, glass-cut red waves.

"God's going to wipe out this entire district. He's bringing in the machines right now. Don't you hear them? Eugene, turn off that television. Turn it off so Charles can hear the machines."

When Eugene turned off the television, cutting off the Teddy and Delilah show, I heard the grating noises of the machines wheeling themselves through the streets outside, the clicking of their inner organs preparing another doomsday.

"We have to go now," Ezekiel said, setting his Bloody Mary down on the bar and striding over toward me. He grabbed my arm and pushed me toward the exit. "Let's go."

I pulled Jeanine away from the stage and strip lights.

"Hey kids, wait for me," Eugene said as we left the Legion and went out the back alleyway.

The door swung shut behind us. Overhead the stark black moon swung low in the blacker sky, and the steely, silent heads of the machines loomed over the bar.

Ezekiel ran and I followed his shiny sphere through the dark as I dragged Jeanine behind.

Fire came down from the sky. It destroyed the bar and the surrounding buildings in a single flash. The heat tore at our backs. We kept running.

Six

TEDDY'S VOICE SPILLED into the streets from every home in Edgewater. Soon his voice became indistinguishable from that of God's, hard-edged, and crackling at the corners.

"You know what happens to the sinful," Teddy said. "Don't you know by now that you never escape?"

As I ran after Ezekiel, I saw the Teddy and Delilah show on the television in every living room we passed. First I saw Teddy leaning over Delilah on the bed. Then Teddy wearing a black, pig-snouted mask, his hands extended over Delilah's face like panic claws. He was transforming himself into God. Next I saw Delilah wearing the same mask. Then God again. The storm sirens blared. People closed their curtains and locked their doors. I couldn't see Teddy and Delilah anymore. Fire scraped the sky in the shape of God's terrible face.

"This heretic will be found and punished for defying me," Teddy said in God's grinding voice. "I will not rest until I hunt him down and destroy him."

I followed Ezekiel down an alley, through a neighborhood rupturing in two, across a stretch of woods, and into a hovel on the outskirts of town.

The sirens continued blaring. People who couldn't take the noise anymore unlocked their doors and spilled out of their houses.

"You're the heretic, aren't you?" one woman screamed. "I should've known when I caught you fucking my daughter!"

"Yeah?" someone said in response. "I think you're the heretic. You don't close your eyes when you pray!"

Apocalypse Brigadiers appeared and started breaking windows and throwing rocks at the heads of passersby. One man stood on his roof with a megaphone and screamed at everyone that passed.

"Don't you look away from me! I know what you've done! Don't think you can hide!"

"Ezekiel?" I called, moving into a corner of the hovel. "Where are we? I need to get home."

"Quit your bitching," Ezekiel said. "This used to be Job's shack. We should be safe here until the storm passes."

My eyes became situated to the dark. The hovel was nothing more than a single, dirt-covered room with a television shoved into one corner.

Jeanine convulsed and kicked my shins with her PVC boots. I winced.

"Be still," I said.

"The show isn't over, baby," she said.

A bomb exploded nearby and a storm of heat swept through the hovel's open entrance. Jeanine squealed and twisted in my arms.

Ezekiel turned on the television. Teddy and

Delilah sat motionless on their bed, their faces concealed by God's black masks. They remained silent, their legs straight, their hands crossed against their laps. The emitting from the television was a loud emptiness, the sort of emptiness that spasmed and stretched and screamed.

"The machines. They're right outside."

"I'm not worried about them here," Ezekiel said.

Jeanine tried to run out the door. I grabbed her arm and pulled her back inside as a machine stuck its bristling head through the open doorway and its eyes lit the hovel red. It scanned the room and noticed Ezekiel, who rolled his eyes and tapped the sphere on the back of his head. The machine withdrew, casting the room back into darkness, and continued down the street.

Another explosion rocked and ruptured the earth. Delilah's hands twitched. I thought of Leda back home at the edge of the swamp alone with deadhead Momma and deadhead Sissy. I saw monsters rising from the green waters and crawling up the porch steps.

"I have to get home," I repeated once more.

"Shut the fuck up," Ezekiel said. "God told me we would be safe here."

The sound of the machines clattering and grinding grew and grew, chewed my ears out, broke a heavy board against the flat of my ribs.

"Oh fuck," Ezekiel said, and he ran out the door.

I grabbed Jeanine and followed him out into the street, where a full-fledged riot was taking place. A low piercing whine filled the air, and then the hovel exploded into flames behind us.

"I thought you said we would be safe," I said.

"Oh, fuck you," Ezekiel said. "Fuck you and that fucking hooker you got there."

I followed Ezekiel as he cut a swathe through the rioting crowd.

"Prophet coming through!" he shouted. "Get the fuck out of the way!"

An Apocalypse Brigadier in a crocodile mask tried to block Ezekiel's way. He shoved the Apocalypse Brigadier away and he cracked his face against the pavement.

We went into the woods. The hairy trees surrounding us exploded in firework bursts. Their spindly branches fell all around us and caught my shoes n fires.

"I think we're being chased," I said.

"Oh, no kidding," Ezekiel said as he dodged machine gun bullets.

We ran deeper into the woods but as the bullets and fire beat at our backs.

Jeanine fell down into the grass trembling and clutching at my father's jacket. I tripped over her and struck the dirt. Ezekiel stopped running. Two figures approached us with their fingers spitting sparks. I pushed Jeanine into the hollow of a tree.

She whined. I pressed my fingers to my lips in a “Shh” motion.

She curled her knees up to her chin, and hugged my father's jacket to her chest.

I stood up. The first figure that approached wore a long trench coat that couldn't hide the skinny parabola of his body. He lifted his head and the black moon struck the electrical nodes where his eyes used to be, struck the curving shine of the plastic wrap around his bald head.

"Smarts?" I whispered.

"This asshole?" Ezekiel shouted.

"I've been looking for you," he said as he approached Ezekiel.

A young woman trailed behind him, holding a machine gun and wearing a teddy bear pink slip. Both of them wore armbands with the number six.

"I should have known it was you who blew up the slip clinic," Ezekiel said. “You being such an asshole and all. You couldn't do me a favor and stay dead, could you? And you ruined my shoes."

I placed my head against Jeanine's hiding tree and its trunk trembled.

"I'm sorry," I said.

"Are you apologizing to Smarts?" Ezekiel asked me.

"I'm sorry I didn't have five thousands dollars to save you," I said.

The young woman lifted up her machine gun. Ezekiel whipped a pistol out from his coat and shot her in the chest. She stumbled backwards and fell into the dirt. Machine gun fire burst up above us, hitting the trees.

"What?" he said as he turned to look at the surprise on my face. "I'm a prophet. I'm allowed a deus ex machina every once in a while."

Smarts opened up his trench coat. Inside he taped a row of explosives.

Smarts clicked on a lighter.

"You're blind," Ezekiel said.

The shiny sphere on the back of Ezekiel's head flared up and Smarts' electrical nodes busted. The lighter snapped off. Smarts trembled and touched his broken artificial eyes. He searched for his taped explosives with shaking fingers, patting at his coat until he dropped the lighter in the dirt. He got onto his knees to search for it.

Ezekiel kicked Smarts in the ribs and knocked him on his back.

"What are you?" he asked Smarts. "You're nothing."

Ezekiel straddled him and grabbed his plastic-wrapped head. He leaned down and screamed into his empty face.

"I have God on my side, you idiot!"

Ezekiel pulled off Smarts' coat and threw it into the grass. He started beating Smarts, tearing at his clothes, biting at his unraveling head.

Smarts twisted and scratched at Ezekiel's face but his nails left no marks. I stood transfixed in the gleam of the Ezekiel's shiny sphere. My limbs slowed into calcified trash. I heard the blood in my ears flowing through me like the blood that God churned through my kitchen taps.

"You worthless asshole," Ezekiel said to Smarts. "You're dirt compared to me. You're dirt and what you did to the slip clinic was all for nothing. You're going to die like all heretics die."

He shoved Smarts' face down and stuffed his mouth with grass and dirt. Smarts head seemed to balloon if it might pop off his neck. The dirt spilled out of his mouth as fast as Ezekiel shoved it in. Bits of blood and dandelion fluff came up from Smarts' throat and Ezekiel pushed them into Smarts' empty eye sockets.

Smarts lifted his head in my direction and I thought those empty eyes looked straight through me.

I ran.

"Charles!" Ezekiel called after me.

I didn't stop running.

Monsters chased me on all sides. I couldn't see them, but I felt the heat of them as they uprooted the trees and tore wide lines into the dirt.

I ran into town and became swept back up into the street riot. Someone in a bear mask grabbed me by the lapels.

"You're the heretic!" he said.

He hit me and bruised my jaw.

"Let me go!" I said. "There aren't any heretics anymore. Can't you see that?"

"You did this to us all!" he said as he hit me again and again. "You killed my baby girl! You damned everyone!"

I wanted to tell him that he was wrong, but when I spoke, I said:

"I saw two good men die tonight. Please hit me again."

He raised his fist again, his knuckles raw.

"I left someone I loved all alone in the woods. Please hit me again," I said, nearly sobbing. "Hit me."

"You're crazy," he said, laughing until he choked.

He let me go.

The monsters grabbed people and dragging them off into the night. My eyes stung with sweat and blood, and soon I couldn't distinguish the Apocalypse Brigadiers from the monsters that swept in and out of the crowd.

"This is your punishment for your disobedience!" one of the Apocalypse Brigadiers shouted.

"Tell us something we don't know!" someone shouted back.

I struggled through the crowd with one hand over my eyes and the other held out in front of me. Someone grabbed onto my arm and screamed in my ear. The screaming stopped abruptly when a monster ripped their body away and dragged it headfirst through the crowd.

Several feet away I pried the person's severed arm off me and dropped it. I never took my hand off my eyes. I felt that if I looked, I would die.

I wanted to drop to my knees and smash my head into the concrete. I could lie there until the heartbeat of the plague machines became my heartbeat, and the dirt piled on top of me.

But then I thought of Leda, alone in my room while a lonely death slithered onto the porch, and I kept going.

The plague machines smashed their fists into the street and transformed it into a hill. I tumbled backwards into an Apocalypse Brigadier, knocking her mask off. Before she could say or do anything to me, I was crawling back up the hill, hand out in front of me.

I got to the top of the hill where the air cracked with heat. People reached out to grab me but I slipped out of their grasps. I descended the other side of the hill.

I slogged through a pool of tar. People thrashed and reached out for my ankles. I stepped on a girl's hand on accident, and when she cried out the tar bubbled out of her mouth.

I wanted to reach down and pull her up out of the tar, but instead I thought of Leda, kneeling on my bed, the scars like little birds flying away. I left the girl and kept going.

When I reached the end of the street, I let my hand drop from my face and I ran down an alleyway away from the riot. Teddy in God's black mask pointed at me with an accusing finger through every open window. The plague machines and the monsters built a chasm for me to fall into, but I climbed out of it. I peeled the gore and charred remains of the Apocalypse Brigadier off my face. I choked on the dust of buildings falling around me. I made it to the edge of the town with all of my limbs intact, and when I saw my house at the edge of the swamp, I sucked in a cry.

I crawled up the porch. I crept inside the front door.

"Leda!" I called out over the blare of the television.

No response.

I went up the stairs. Sissy and Momma sat on the couch, listless, smoking cigarettes. I ran up the stairs. I panted so hard I thought my bones might break. My bruises stuck to the wall where I reached out to keep myself from falling.

I opened my bedroom door. Leda was gone.

Seven

SHE NEVER CAME back.

I went to our meeting place in the woods and waited for her. I touched trees and tried to pull them into my hips to dance, because I thought Leda might've really turned into a tree, and she was calling for help inside their bark. I scratched at tree roots looking for her face. I crushed flowers searching for her smell.

When daybreak came, I wandered through the ruins of last night's riot, calling out her name. There was no response except for the cries of people trapped in various stages of dying, the rumble of the plague machines returning to the field.

I went to the flower shop where she worked and approached the old woman who sat behind the counter picking dandelion fluff off her wrists and painting red roses blue. She didn't look up when I went to the counter.

"Sorry to bother you," I said to her, and then rapped on the counter.

The old woman looked up startled.

She dropped her paintbrush. Her face was an ashy blank.

"Has Leda been to work recently?" I asked.

"Do you work with the government?"

"You're not going to help me, are you?"

The old woman picked up the paintbrush again and gave me this knowing, sardonic smile

– a smile full of weeds.

"You got it," she said.

I went back home when night fell.

I left the light on so she could find her way home.

I rubbed the teeth marks Leda left on the back of my neck. I picked up the flowers ground into the carpet, and emptied her suitcase and hung all her dresses in my closet. I discovered a butterfly she breathed on the bathroom mirror, and I stood there for hours tracing its shape until it wore away. In the middle of the night, I thought I heard her creeping down the stairs so I got up and ran down the hallway to greet her, only to be met by the endless face of the empty stairway.

When I returned to the bedroom alone, I threw open the window and the black moon came down from the sky to stay with me. The black moon slept in the warm spot on her side of the bed and cast her shape against the wall.

Teddy and Delilah stood at the foot of my bed. An ocean of television static swirled at their feet. My bed floated toward the ceiling. I gripped the sheets to keep from falling into the static below, and I turned my face toward the light. If I wanted Leda to return to me, I couldn't let the light go out.

I remembered something Sissy once told me back when flowers still grew in her garden. She told me the cells in our bodies were completely replaced every seven years. The cells of my body were igniting and dying and being reborn. Soon I would have fingers that had never touched Leda's hair and warm skin. Soon I would have eyes that never saw her face.

Momma told me Leda was gone for good, but I knew she didn't know one way or the other. Teddy told me the only way to fix a broken heart was to not have a heart at all. Delilah only stretched out on her gray bed and quivered as she watched an invisible monster on the ceiling.

I called the police about Leda's disappearance. They took me to the station and sat me in a colorless room underneath a leper colored light. I sat there alone for two hours, until the sheriff shuffled in, wiping at his nose and twitching.

"What seems to be the problem?"

"I wanted to report a missing person."

He snorted.

"Your wife?" he asked.

"I suppose you can say that."

"We don't investigate missing persons anymore," he said.

"You're the police. Isn't that what you're supposed to do?"

"You know what? I think I'd like some coffee," the sheriff said, leaning back in his chair. "Would you like some coffee?"

"Why aren't you taking me seriously? I need someone to help me."

The sheriff stood up from the desk.

"I'm going to go get some coffee," he said. "You wait here."

"Hey!" I called out, but he'd already left the room.

The door banged shut behind him. I waited in the room for another half hour, counting the granules on the ceiling. The sheriff came back into the room empty-handed.

"How was the coffee?" I asked him.

"What are you talking about?" he asked. "What coffee?"

The sheriff sat back down at the desk.

"What were you here for again?" he asked.

I tried to make out the sheriff's face in the dim light, but no distinguishable features rose up out of the gloom. For all I knew he could have been a swarm of insects. I tried to clear my throat before I spoke again, but my words came out hoarse and thick anyways.

"I wanted to report a missing person," I said.

"Oh, that's right," he said. You said she was your wife?"

"There has to be something you can do."

"Did she commit adultery?" the sheriff asked me.

"What?"

"You know… was she fucking someone else?"

"What does that have to do with anything?" I asked.

The sheriff sighed and looked down at the desk, which was empty, and then back up at me.

"If you like I could get the department to pray for her," he said.

"Yeah, sure," I said. "That'd be great. Thanks."

I went back home. I crawled on my hands and knees to reach the second floor. I managed to climb into bed and draw the blankets over to my head when I heard the familiar sound of an IV stand being dragged down the hallway floor.

"Maybe she just didn't love you," Sissy said, appearing in my doorway with her eyes about to run down her face.

I said nothing and Sissy slipped away.

The nights passed by and Leda's absence wore a hole in my throat, but I still couldn't believe she was gone. I kept turning over in bed, expecting to see her curled up and lying beside me, only to find the black moon warming the sheets. The trees scraped against the side of the house and the black moon kicked. I rocked on the floor and thought the space Leda left behind might close in to devour me.

Out in the dark I heard the machines. I wanted to ask them where Leda went. I wanted to ask them why she left me here alone with my dead family.

But I imagined they would only say, "God gave her to you and God took her away."

Eight

"YOU ARE THE WORST kind of idealist," Teddy told me, "lingering in the torment of your inertia."

I sat on the couch, wedged between Momma and Sissy as we watched the Teddy and Delilah show. Momma and Sissy smoked cigarettes that turned their fingers and teeth yellow. The smoke drew a noose around my neck. I couldn't see through the haze, and I knocked a glass of whiskey off the coffee table.

"No," Teddy said while I cried as the whiskey soaked into the carpet, "I take that back. You're not just the worst kind of idealist. You're the worst kind of human being."

"You're so melodramatic," Sissy said. "Hand me another cigarette."

"We have a very special guest with us today," Teddy said.

On the bed beside Delilah sat a small woman with a dog's face and red cat-eyed glasses, her knees drawn up to her chin and her sallow face slipping off her cheeks. She wore a breastplate made out of animal bones, and she kept tapping it with her purple painted nails.

"Look at the camera, darling," Teddy said. "Can you smile? There you go. Our guest with us today is Slim Sarah, a woman of extraordinary devotion. Let's run the clip again. Smile, darling!"

Slim Sarah, played in the clip by a faceless, sexless silhouette wearing a woman's mouse brown hair, lived the suburban apotheosis with her husband and twelve children. Her husband sat in front of the television every night with the twelve children. As Teddy and Delilah sang lullabies and danced with human sized spiders, the children basked in the carnal glow of the screen inside their pristine house.

One day while Slim Sarah's husband was away at work, God told her to line up her twelve children in the living room and kill the ones he disapproved of.

"Are my children bad?" Slim Sarah asked.

"It's not about whether they're good or bad," God said.

He climbed out of the television and handed Slim Sarah a meat tenderizer and a bucket of water. His body bristled and spread out through the entire room in a toxic haze.

"Is this the one, God?" Slim Sarah asked.

She approached the first child in the line. Kelly, the youngest, wore red bows in her hair and scratched smiley faces into the wall with the heels of her baby doll shoes.

"No," God said, and Slim Sarah beat the girl to death with the meat tenderizer and shoved her head into the bucket of water.

"Is this the one, God?" Slim Sarah asked of the next child.

This was Terrance, classical music aficionado,

and you can be sure everyone hated him for it. He kept making sideways glances as if he could see shapes coming out of God's fog.

"No," God said, and Slim Sarah picked up the meat tenderizer from the carpet, slick with tender young blood, and murdered Terrance.

"Is this the one, God?" She asked of the next child, while Terrance lay face down in the bucket of water.

"No," God said, and "No," and, "No," until eleven of Slim Sarah's children, beaten and burst and bloody, lay out on the carpet, their bodies wet and stiffening.

Slim Sarah approached the last child. Streaks of child's blood dripped through Slim Sarah's hair. Chunks of gore stained her cookie-making apron. The last child was shy little Meadow, with overdeveloped hips and breast and her limbs shooting out of the hull of her waist like gangly cannons. Meadow often crawled on the floor so she could know how cats lived, who hid inside closets to watch the migration of dust.

"Is this the one, God?" Slim Sarah asked.

And God said, "Yes."

Slim Sarah's husband came home and found all their children dead. He stood in the doorway and tore out chunks of his hair, big bleeding scraps, and threw them at his feet. He knocked Slim Sarah on their marriage bed and busted her lip. Meadow hunched in the corner, screaming like an elephant, while her father beat her mother and clawed at her bleating throat. God sucked himself back into the television.

A militia of prophets and saints busted down the door of Slim Sarah's house and shot her husband in the head. They escorted Slim Sarah and Meadow out of the house and to the backstage of the Teddy and Delilah show.

"And we're throwing a parade in her honor," said Teddy.

He touched Slim Sarah's cheek, and accidentally smeared off some of her powdered make-up hiding her blackened, bruised flesh beneath.

"The parade is coming!" Sissy shouted, and threw her arms up in the air.

"A parade!" Momma said, and she jerked her head up off her chest so quick I thought I heard her bones snap.

Momma and Sissy jumped up and down on the couch in a parody of excitement, their limbs short-circuiting, and hair flying. Their skirts ballooned up over their heads.

"Momma," I said. "Stop, you're going to break your hip."

They ignored me and continued to jump until exhaustion. Momma fell onto the floor onto the whiskey stain. Sissy sat down, her skin flushed, and lit a cigarette.

"Will you take me to the parade, Bubba?" Sissy asked me.

"Don't call me that."

"Bubba?" Sissy asked. "But I always call you Bubba."

"Be quiet Charles," Momma said as the whiskey stained her cheek. "Can't you see your mother is watching the television?"

"Be quiet, Bubba," Sissy said.

She dropped her cigarette and ground it into the floor with a bare foot. Her flesh hissed.

"Don't do that!"

I went down on my knees to retrieve the cigarette butt and found Sissy's feet covered in a latticework of cigarette burns and braised scars.

I called the slip doctor.

"What is it this time?" he asked.

"Theresa's been smoking cigarettes and putting them out with her bare feet," I said.

"I'm sure she'll be fine," the slip doctor said.

"Didn't you hear what I said? There are fucking burns all over her feet."

"All right, don't get so worked up," the doctor said. "I'll be over in the morning."

The doctor hung up. The phone slid out of my hands and I went back into the living room. I found Momma still resting against the whiskey stain, her fist stuck inside the broken glass. Sissy was gone. Her IV stand lay overturned on the coffee table.

"Where did Theresa go?" I asked Momma, and as if in response, the open front door banged against the wall when a gust of wind hit.

Momma remained silent.

I found Sissy standing outside in the middle of the dirt road beneath a bower of trees.

"You shouldn't be out here," I said.

The wind tossed Sissy's unwashed hair off her shoulders and cut its mouth against her skirt. I looked beyond the road into the indomitable nest of woods, and thought of Jeanine left alone in the hollow of that tree.

"Let's go," I said.

I took Sissy's arm.

"Where does the road go?" she asked.

"It doesn't go anywhere."

I took Sissy back into the house and locked the front door. She sat down on the couch. Everything glowed gray in the nightmare texture of the television. Teddy kept tapping Slim Sarah's chin and telling her to look into the camera.

"Not since Abraham dragged his son Isaac up the mountaintop to sacrifice him has there been such an act of courage, folks," Teddy said. "This truly is a remarkable woman."

I dragged Momma off the floor and the couch. I wiped the whiskey off her cheek.

"Will you take me to the parade, Bubba?" Sissy asked.

"Would you kill me if God asked you to?"

She smiled. "Yes."

I took a cigarette out of her hand and stubbed it out on a nearby ashtray.

"No more cigarettes, okay?" I said. "No more

cigarettes until the doctor gets here."

Nine

I WOKE UP IN bed with a stuffed deer. It stared at me with button eyes framed by ladylike, sweeping eyelashes. Its gelatinous hooves melted into the sheets. I wanted to push the stuffed deer off the bed, but I couldn't bring myself to touch it.

"Did you put that deer in my bed?" I asked Sissy later that morning.

She sat in front of the television with her feet propped up on the coffee table and her thumb in her mouth. She of course, said nothing.

I went into the kitchen, grabbed a kitchen knife, and went back upstairs to my bedroom.

Before I could kill myself, someone knocked on the door. At first, I thought it was the guards coming to take me to hell. But it was the slip implant doctor, visiting to check on Sissy. He came into the house carrying a gray valise and a machine hooked into his veins. He told me years ago if it wasn't for that machine his blood would turn into shit.

"You said you were going to come by a week ago." I said.

"What are you doing with that kitchen knife?" he asked.

"Nothing," I said, setting the knife on top of the television. "Come on in."

The doctor placed his gray valise on the coffee table.

"Let me see your feet, sweetheart," he said.

He knelt in front of Sissy and treated her cigarette burns with iodine and bandages.

"She's probably just repeating the past," he said. 'Nothing to get too concerned about."

" My sister would never do that to herself. Something's wrong with the implant," I said. "Use your diagnostic scanner."

"That won't be necessary. Stand up, sweetheart," the doctor said. "Lift up your dress, sweetheart."

Each of the doctor's "Sweetheart's'" crystallized in my mouth. Sissy lifted her dress and showed the doctor the hunger curve of her stomach. I looked away.

"She looks fine everywhere else," the doctor said. "Just keep an eye on her. Okay, you can put your dress back down. There you go."

"Check my mother too," I said.

We found my mother in the kitchen, rummaging through the cabinets looking for cigars.

"Your father is such a bear when he doesn't get his nicotine," she said.

"Daddy's not here, Momma," I said.

The doctor didn't call my mother sweetheart when he told her to lift dress. He didn't find any burns, only raw gray moles and the outline of her bones that resembled upset faces.

"Has she been taking her pills?" the doctor asked.

"She spits them out. Like everything else. Why do you think I have the IV?"

"You ever had a dog before?"

"...No?"

"Try giving her the pills with a little peanut butter," he said.

The doctor picked up his gray valise and shit for blood machine. I chased him out onto the porch.

"You can't go," I said. "Can't you see that they're still broken? My mother, she doesn't eat, she's searching for cigars for a man that's been gone seventeen years. And my sister, she's going to burn her feet straight off her ankles."

The doctor paused for a moment, his bottom lip drooping down as if it might fall off, his fingers shaking as he reached for the balustrade to steady himself.

I watched the doctor's blood flow through the tube in the machine.

"Your mother and sister are dead, don't you know?"

Blood like ichor, passing out of his veins, then transformed into sour pink plasma before passing back.

"Face the truth," the doctor said, "we're nothing but glorified morticians, dressing our relatives up pretty. Suicide just has a friendlier face now. When these people come out of sleep after their first ten years are up, nothing will have changed. Most of them will be back asking for another slip implant in less than a week."

The doctor's tubing undulated slowly in the wind, and the blood flowing through cast a shadow like a snake on the porch. His knuckles turned white as they gripped hard the machine.

"Your eyes look like a terrible secret," he said. “Did you know that?"

He headed down the road.

"Wait," I said, following him. “Wait. Please."

He kept walking.

"I have a question. My sister. I found her standing outside in the road one night, and she's looking down it like it goes on forever. And she asks me 'Where does the road go?' Why did she ask me that? My sister's never said anything like that."

"Misfiring synapses," the doctor said. “You should have listened to my advice about what to do with her seven years ago."

I watched him walk away. I stood in the road breathing heavy, feeling as if I might collapse, until he left my line of sight.

I went back into the house.

"Who will take care of you when I'm gone?" I asked Sissy when I came back into the living room.

"We will take care of each other," she said. She leaned forward on the couch and reached out to touch my forehead, as if to reassure me.

I went upstairs where the stuffed deer lay in my bed, hooves poised toward the ceiling.

If the deer could speak, I knew it would say, "You've failed everyone you've ever loved. You've failed Momma and Sissy, and Daddy too. You've failed your childhood friends, Smarts and Wiley, Darling and Violetta. You've failed Jeanine, the first girl you fell in love with, and the only person you ever thought might actually have a chance. You've failed Leda. You've failed yourself.

"You've even failed Ezekiel and the shiny sphere on the back of his head."

And if the deer could speak, its mouth would grow into a parabola, a long echoing chamber, and it would speak in the voice of my father.

"It's time to give up."

As I lay in bed nuzzling the deer's cheek, Jolene came to my window holding a bird in her first. She ate the bird and then smiled at me with gritty, bloodstained teeth. She slunk back into the swamp. I stared for a long time at the empty window, the feathers caught on the casement.

Ten

I WENT TO the slip clinic the next morning. I crawled over a horde of plastic chairs and scabbed would-be deadheads to get to the receptionist.

"Name?" she asked without looking up.

"Charles," I said, "I just wanted to ask–"

"Fill out these forms," she said, and shoved a clipboard full of papers into my arms. "Give them back to me when you're finished."

When I finished filling out the forms, she handed me a number, and I waded into the sea of waiting patients. Televisions lined every flat surface in the clinic. The Teddy and Delilah show droned on without pause. Slender faced girls stood by the wall, clutching their bleeding throats. Grizzled men tugging at their melting faces surrounded them. A bald headed junkie waited on top of a plastic chair, stepping from foot to foot, sticking her fingers into her stomach. We were careful to never touch each other.

I clung to the walls and watched Teddy juggle hot wire spiders on the television.

After four hours, someone over the intercom called my number. An attendant carrying my forms took me down a long, white hallway. Scorch marks from the bombing still lingered on the whitewashed floors. She led me into a white room full of crooked white beds, all of them occupied by people watching television screens on the ceiling.

"Undress," she said.

She placed my forms on the bed, handed me a white hospital gown, and left.

I shouldered the wall as I took off my clothes. A doctor walked over to the boy in the bed beside mine and knocked him unconscious with a mask that resembled an iron cage. Nurses in latex uniforms, carrying steely medical instruments, filed around the doctor. A nurse handed the doctor a six-inch saw. He sliced the boy's forehead in half. A second nurse placed a hot wire spider in the doctor's hand. The closer the spider got to the boy's head, the more it trembled. I looked away, finished undressing, and put on the white hospital gown before lying down in bed.

In the bed next to mine, a girl was having what looked like a seizure. When she saw me she tried to speak, but could only stutter. Spit ran down her chin, and on her forehead grew a boiling, black mass of tissue in the spot where the implant rested underneath. She had electric orange and blue hair.

"Jeanine?" I whispered.

Another doctor and his nurses entered the room. They surrounded her. They lifted up the sides of her bed sheets like white wings as they performed their surgery, obscuring her from my view. The silhouette of her hand pushed against the sheets. I almost believed she reached out for me.

The doctor dropped her crumpled, bloody spider into a metal tray. A nurse produced a needle and nylon thread and sewed up her head. They dropped the sheets back down. Jeanine lay unconscious.

Her arms lolled over the sides of the bed. Yellow fluid seeped through her sewn-up wound.

The doctor who just finished surgery on the boy moved toward me. He glanced at my forms while the nurses hovered behind him.

"Let's see what we have here," he said. "Reason for getting a sleep implant: Everyone I've loved and will ever love is already dead, etcetera, etcetera. Looks like we have another philosopher here, girls."

He handed the forms to one of the waiting nurses. I grabbed his hand before he placed the mask over my face.

"Why is she here?" I asked him about Jeanine. "What happened to her?"

"She's fine. See you in ten years."

He tried to fit the mask over my face. I grabbed the base of the mask and ripped out the tube. The hisssss of gas escaping from the open tube punctuated the air. A nurse grabbed my shoulder and pushed me down.

"Someone turn the gas off!" the doctor shouted.

I shoved the nurse away. I fell off the bed and knocked over a surgical tray.

The doctor grabbed my hospital gown as I dragged myself across the floor to the unconscious Jeanine. Her hands curled in sleep. I reached for her. The doctor pulled me back. I dug my heels down into the whitewashed floor. My hospital gown tore.

"Someone get me a tranquilizer!"

"There aren't any left. We used them all!"

On the television screens above our heads, hundreds of Teddy's and Delilahs opened their mouths and screamed in static. I tried to tear myself from the grip of the doctor. I buried my face into the folds of the hospital gown and gasped. I pounded my fists against the doctor's thigh.

The room erupted. The boy who had the spider inserted into his head only a few minutes before threw his hospital sheets off and ran straight into the wall. The rest of the deadheads broke out into a wave of indecipherable noises, screaming and hissing. Delilah struck the ceiling of the room. Teddy rammed his fist into her jaw.

"What did I tell you, girls?" the doctor screamed. "Never trust a philosopher!"

I reached for Jeanine, but all I could see was the newly implanted boy running into the wall over and over again until his forehead bloodied.

"What is wrong with you?" the doctor asked.

"I don't want to die anymore," I said

The doctor released me. I got off my knees and stumbled toward Jeanine. I grasped her hand.

“I’m sick of this shit. I’m going on my lunch break,” the doctor said.

"She's coming out of the slip. Her implant was faulty. Be careful with her," one of the nurses said to me, a young nurse, with blood still in her cheeks.

But already I was grabbing Jeanine's shoulder and trying to wake her. Her lips parted slightly and her spit dripped on my knuckles.

"I don't want to die," I whispered to her. “I shouldn't have to want to die."

Jeanine inhaled a sharp breath and opened her eyes

"Charles?" she said. “Where am I?”

"The slip clinic. We have to go."

The deadheads lay back in their beds. The nurses left with their anesthetic makes and surgical tools. The crackling hissing static from the television dissipated into silence. Teddy and Delilah closed their mouths and sat motionless on the bed.

I tried to carry Jeanine out of the clinic. She carried me.

Eleven

JEANINE SAT ON the edge of my bed, wrapped in dusk light. I sat on the floor rocking back and forth. For the longest time we didn't speak. I lay out some of Leda's clothes for Jeanine to change into but she didn't touch them. She squeezed the sleeves of her hospital gown. After a while, Jeanine went into the bathroom down the hall, dragging her hospital ties behind her.

"Charles?" she called out to me after a few minutes.

She stood in the bathroom with both hands against the mirror.

"What happened to my hair?" she asked.

I didn't know how to tell Jeanine that her hair was colored like the gauche lights that used to be in the Legion bar, orange at the tips, blue at the roots. Or that the first time I'd seen her in seven years she was insect dancing in front of a stripper pole, wearing PVC boots and smeared lipstick on her ass.

"I'm so tired," Jeanine said.

"You've been asleep for a long time."

"What year is it?"

I told her.

"Three years too early," she said.

Jeanine touched her sutured head wound. Her veins rose to the surface of her flesh like a broken garden.

"It was only moments ago," she said. "I was still young and the doctor put that mask over my face. Now I'm unbelievably old. Like a corpse. That's all it takes. Just a moment, and then it's all over."

She pulled off her hospital gown and let it fall. She touched the war zone of her breasts and ribcage, bent down until the bones in her back cracked.

"You know when you go to sleep and you wake up and feel like you have this really important dream that you can't remember?" Jeanine asked. "It's like that. There's this blister where a memory used to be inside my head. And it seems really important, but there's only a blister left, and no matter how hard I think I know I'll never get that memory back."

She touched diseased spots growing on her chest and gray skin flaked off her.

"They said everything would be better after I got the implant out," Jeanine said. "They told me I would find love."

"I'm sorry," I said.

She continued to look at herself in the mirror and touch her body like a stranger. Even without the implant, seven years had seemed to go by in an instant, as if the girl I used to love appeared in the mirror and shed everything good, her milk and honey, her butterfly wings of frozen meat, her anthropology dreams.

I once loved that girl, but I looked away for

only a moment and turned back to find nothing left of her but a pile of gray flakes on a dirty bathroom floor.

Jeanine went back into the bedroom and put on one of Leda's dresses.

"You had a girl?" she asked me.

"She's gone now."

"That's how it always goes," she said.

Jeanine touched the tulle sleeves of the dress. Her decaying body seemed to collapse within Leda's clothes.

"Was this hers?" she asked.

I nodded.

"I figured," Jeanine said. "Theresa would never wear a dress like this."

Jeanine looked through Leda's clothes in my closet. Jeanine touched Leda's soft-soled shoes and her collection of black leather gloves.

"What were you doing at the slip clinic?" she asked.

"I wanted to die," I said.

"So why didn't you?"

"I don't want to die anymore."

"Why not?" she asked softly.

"I found you."

She laughed.

"Charles," she said, "Charlie. You didn't find anyone."

"Maybe you're right," I said.

"What have you been doing all these years?" she asked me.

"Looking after Momma and Sissy. Trying to keep things from falling apart."

She glanced at my desk, now empty.

"Do you still draw?"

"Not anymore," I said.

"Anything else?" she asked.

I said nothing for a long time. The silence formed a hard casement around us.

"I think I'm a heretic," I finally said.

"You're a what?" Jeanine asked, and then laughed softly, nervously. "What makes you think a thing like that? The shuttles haven't come for you, have they?"

"No," I said. "But I think they will soon. Ezekiel doesn't visit me anymore. Right before he stopped coming by the house, his sphere looked straight through me, like it could read my thoughts and it didn't like what it found. And when our old friend, his name was Smarts, when he became a heretic and bombed the sleep implant clinic, I told him I was sorry. I told him I wished I could have saved him. And I remember I would have pushed Ezekiel off of him and rescued him from death if I could. And I think Ezekiel knows that."

"Wow," Jeanine said. "Why would you go and do something like that? Become a heretic?"

I expected God, who was on his nightly apocalyptic tirade, to crawl out of the television and tear the foundation of this rickety house apart. I expected monsters to rise from the swamp and the woods and the machine fields to devour me whole. But God continued to speak from within the safe four walls of the television box, and the monsters lurking outside didn't come any closer.

"I don't know why," I said. "I didn't even know what was happening until it was too late."

I swallowed hard.

"You see things that shouldn't have happened, that should have never been brought into existence, and it corrodes your brain a little more each day. And then it happens that you see something really terrible, something so profoundly awful that you think you will tear apart or go insane if you see another moment of it. You realize this isn't the way things are supposed to be. Something's gone wrong. There was this force set in motion from the beginning that was destined to go wrong. And we're all caught up in the wheels of it, unable to escape, because it's a mechanism so much more powerful than any of us."

"Wow," Jeanine said again.

"And it's controlling each of us, driving us toward this ultimate outcome which none of us can comprehend, even though we're stuck right in the middle of it. It's bigger than the black planet, it's bigger than God. It's probably even bigger than the stars and the places beyond the stars. It's this mechanism at the center of the universe, which decided our destinies a million billion years before we were even born."

From the look on Jeanine's face, it was obvious I'd gone insane.

"I first felt it when my baby brother died," I said quietly, "and I've felt it pulling me, driving me, ever since, like I could have been nothing but a heretic. Like nothing I could ever do would change that outcome."

Momma appeared in the doorway. Her hair broke between her fingers.

"Your sister's gone," she said.

Outside in the swamp, someone screamed.

I ran past Momma and down the stairs. I yanked open the front door. I ran toward the tree line. The door banged shut behind me.

The sun plunged down. I reached the swamp and it rose to grab me. It sucked the shoes off my feet.

I heard the nearby machines pulsing and grinding in preparation for another plague. I ran blindly in the dark, listening for another scream, but I heard nothing except the machines and the wind barreling through the tree.

"Sissy?" I called out. "Where are you?"

I slowed down. Twisted branches scratched tiny symbols into my skin.

"Sissy?" I said, softer this time.

I brushed back a low hanging curtain of Spanish moss. Jolene stood waist deep in chilly water. Lichen grew on the north side of her face, obscuring half her nose, one eye, a lilt-upturned corner of her mouth.

She held her hand out to me and the skin on her fingers curled away.

"It's been a long time, Charles," Jolene said.

Fireflies trembled in her teeth. I stood immobile in the bower of trees, holding the curtain of moss between my fists.

"Did you bring another knife to try to murder me?" she asked me. “Do you remember our special time together?”

I took a step backwards.

"Come here, Charles," she said, "there's no running away. You've known that for a long time."

I couldn’t run away, like I couldn’t as a child. I could only look at the buzzing fireflies trapped in her teeth.

"Charles," she said, and her voice darkened, as if grinding glass. “Come here."

I stepped forward curtain of moss fell behind me. I approached the edge of Jolene's pond, swallowing softly. My eyes became stuck to the bones lying at the bottom of the water where my dead baby brother still rested.

"I'm looking for my sister," I said.

"There's no one here but you and me," Jolene said. “Soon there won't even be that."

She buried her dripping hand into my hair. She forced my head up, exposing my throat to her sharpened teeth. Her breath smelled of rotting feathers, sorghum, blackened leaves.

It was as if time brought me back into a circle to this moment, as if I had become old and bitter and doomed, only so I could become a child again.

Jolene forced me to my knees in the wet dirt, and it seeped through my clothes.

"Look down into the water," she said.

"I can't," I said. "Please. I can't."

She pushed my head closer to the tepid water. I dug my hands down into the muck with my spine trying to tear itself from my back, my jaw trying to unhinge from my face.

"Look or you drown," she said.

"Please," I whispered.

But just like the first time, I looked.

The dust settled at the bottom of the swamp and the black moon hit the green waters, illuminating the bones underneath. The bones were as I remembered them, molested, gnawed, and broken. Bones that went down into the dark forever. The history of all humanity. Our origin and epitaph. Bones.

"I know," I whispered. "I know that I am nothing, all right? I've been learning that my whole life."

She traced the shape of my forehead with her sucking fingers and fish gut thumbs.

"I'll tell you a secret," Jolene said.

I couldn't say anything in the overwhelming folds of her rotting, tea green dress.

"That girl passed through my swamp the

night she left you. She was being chased by a big bad thing."

"Leda?" I said.

Down in the water the bones formed into the shape of long decayed bodies, Sissy and Momma, Daddy, Jeanine, Smarts. They were all down there.

"Are you saying Leda's alive?" I asked.

"Maybe," Jolene said. “Maybe not.”

She released my hair. I fell back.

"Do you remember you’ll always be mine?" Jolene asked.

"I haven't forgotten," I said, swallowing big cold rushes of air.

I crawled away from Jolene's pond toward the bower of moss.

"If you find her,” Jolene said. “Tell her I said hello."

Twelve

WHEN I ARRIVED BACK home I found Sissy hiding in the cupboard underneath the sink. She put a finger to her lips when I opened the cupboard door.

"Shh," she said.

I sent Sissy into the living room and went upstairs. Jeanine stood by my window, looking out over the trees.

"I think Leda might be alive," I said.

"That's your girl, right? What makes you think that?"

"A monster told me."

"What happened to you?" she asked when she saw me bare-footed, red in the face, covered in swamp mud and slime.

In the bathroom I turned on the shower faucet and sloughed off my clothes. While I stood naked near the shower, covered in grit and mud, Jeanine knocked on the door.

"Can I come in?" she asked.

"Hold on," I said.

I got into the shower and closed the curtain.

"Okay," I said.

The door opened and closed. Jeanine closed the toilet lid and sat down.

"Did you love her?" she asked.

"Why are you asking me that?"

"Can't you just tell me? Did you love her or not?"

"Yes," I said. "I loved her."

The bathroom door opened and closed a second time. I finished showering and went back into the bedroom. Jeanine sat in the chair beside the window with her legs splayed out in front of her. She buried her fingers in her blue and orange hair.

I turned the light on, as I had done every night since Leda's disappearance. Jeanine didn't move.

"Why did you get a slip implant?" I asked. "I thought you would be the last person to ever do anything like that."

Jeanine shifted in the chair. I sat down on the edge of the bed.

"It's okay if you don't want to tell me."

"I don't."

"I can make up Theresa's bed for you," I said.

My limbs burned with fatigue, and I ached to close my eyes.

"I'm sorry if I upset you," I whispered.

I lay down in bed and almost instantly, fell asleep.

I awoke later and found Jeanine hovering over me. She pressed her knees into my hips. The curve of her back shot off like a bow in the dark.

"Isn't it strange, the sort of things that come back to haunt you?" Jeanine asked. "The memories that we are doomed to repeat over and over again?"

I reached out to touch her exposed thigh. The cold burned my fingers.

"You were right, about what you said earlier," she said. "We were destined to be wrong from the beginning."

Jeanine leaned down and the orange colored tips of her hair brushed against my mouth.

"We should go look for her. Your Leda." Jeanine said quietly. "You know my brother? He's a prophet. We can find him at The First City. He can help."

"Why?" I asked.

"You said she might be alive, didn't you? A monster told you she might be alive. That's more of a chance than most people ever get."

She scratched her bare stomach. Flakes of gray skin drifted onto my face.

"I don't have anything left to live for," she said, "but you still might."

I heard shouting outside. Lights like swamp gas drifted through the trees.

Jeanine rose from bed and pressed her hand against the window.

"It's the Apocalypse Brigade," I said. "They always come around right before a plague hits."

"Those motherfuckers are still around?" she asked.

"Well, you know. It's always the end of the world."

The fire in in the woods drifted closer. Figures emerged from the woods. Apparitions of men, with distended limbs and vegetable shaped heads. They were chanting something about the death of all humanity.

As they came closer, I saw they were being led by the old man and the girl in the wolf mask, both bearing butane torches and knives.

"Charles!" the girl called out. "We've come back for you!"

I pulled Jeanine away from the window.

"Okay, you've convinced me," I said. "Let's go look for Leda."

I ran to the closet and grabbed two bags. I threw one at Jeanine.

"Pack," I said.

I stuffed clothes into my bag and ran downstairs. I almost ran into Sissy standing at the bottom of the stairs, smoking a cigarette and lugging her IV stand like a carcass behind her.

"Hey Bubba," she said, and smiled.

Jeanine ran down the stairs behind me, carrying her bag.

"Wait," I said. "I forgot about Momma and Sissy."

"Dead meat," Jeanine said.

"We can't just leave them here," I said.

"Yes, we can."

She pushed Sissy out of the way, then grabbed me by the shoulder and pulled me into the kitchen. She opened the window above the sink.

"They've only got three years left," I said as

Jeanine opened the refrigerator and stuffed our bags with all the rations I had.

"They have nothing left."

"Where are you going, Bubba?" Sissy asked, standing behind us in the doorway.

Jeanine crawled through the open window and jumped into the grass below.

"I wish I could've helped you," I said to Sissy.

She spit in my face once more.

Apocalypse Brigadiers shattered the windows in the living room. Missy climbed through the window with a knife. Momma screamed.

I followed Jeanine through the open window.

As we escaped through the woods the plague machines grew louder and louder.

I waited for lightning to strike us, for the blood to flow through the rivers. I waited for God to come out of his four sided box and tap, tap, tap over what was left.

Part Three

One

THE NIGHT JEANINE and I left Edgewater our former classmate Lucy Pele set herself on fire. She once chewed on the insides of her wrists and stuck dandelion heads in the open wounds. She opened her coat in the school auditorium and released half a dozen white pigeons into the rafters. Now she stood with prisoners waiting for the hell shuttles as they were pushed and jostled by pig-headed guards.

“Can I have a cigarette?” she asked a passing priest.

He pushed a quart of gasoline into Lucy’s arms. Lucy spilled the gasoline so that it pooled into her sunken eye sockets, the crumpled half of her beaten head, her stomach, her navel. The priest held out a lit match. Lucy went up in flames. Jeanine and I watched the entire thing.

We sat on the other side of the street, waiting for the first morning bus out of Edgewater.

"Burn pretty, baby," one of the guards told Lucy, as she became a column of smoke. “You know what you're good for."

"I'm having second thoughts about this," I said to Jeanine.

The shuttles arrived. One of the guards tossed Lucy’s smoking bones into the gutter before herding the remaining prisoners into the hell shuttles.

"That should have been me in there," I said as

the shuttles drove off. “Lucy never did anything I wouldn’t have done.”

“Well, it wasn’t you.” Jeanine said.

She rested her skinny bent legs on top of her duffel bag. She wore half-moon sunglasses and one of Leda's summer dresses, the one with the electric blue flowers against cream white.

"Do you think your brother can really help us?" I asked.

Jeanine touched the scar on her forehead.

"He's a prophet," she said.

"But do you think he can help us find Leda?"

"If God wills it," Jeanine said.

I said nothing.

"What was the color of her eyes?" she asked.

I tried to remember the color of Leda’s eyes, but I couldn’t. I only remembered their whiskey sheen, her head tilted back toward the ceiling with the bottle between her knees.

"You didn't know her very well, did you?"

"What does her eye color matter? That doesn't mean a damn thing."

The bus arrived. Jeanine and I gathered our bags and boarded. We were the only passengers.

"Where you folks headed?" the driver asked.

"The First City," I said.

"For the Slim Sarah parade, I bet.”

I opened my mouth to respond, but Jeanine interrupted me.

"Yeah, you guessed right," she said. “For the parade."

We paid the driver and headed to the back. Before we sat down the bus hitched forward. Jeanine and I took seats opposite of each other. I lay down and used my bag as a pillow. Jeanine sat on her knees and looked out the window until Edgewater disappeared from view.

I almost expected the world to be different outside of Edgewater, as if the town I lived in all my life was nothing but a strange little curse in a normally friendly universe. The hell shuttles, the plague machines, the swam monster who lived in her pool of bones - all of it would disappear like a bad dream once we left the county lines.

It didn't.

We drove underneath the same ash gray sky. We passed the same gray towns with flood-damaged buildings and hell shuttles taking away sinners. We drove through a plague of locusts that spattered the bus windows in blood and wings.

"Maybe you're right," I said.

"Right about what?"

"That I don't know much about Leda."

"Maybe she was like you," Jeanine said. "Maybe she just needed someone."

"It was more than that," I said.

"Was the sex better?"

"Jeanine. Don't ask me that."

"You can tell me. I'm not a child. I can handle it."

"What does that matter?" I asked. "That was

so long ago. I don't even know. It doesn't matter."

"It doesn't matter," Jeanine said, mocking me. "You keep saying that. So what does matter?"

The bus stopped. More people boarded, including a gray-haired woman carrying a baby in a sling close to her chest, a couple of feral children, and a deadhead girl in wrist chains led by a slip doctor.

"Move over," Jeanine said. "I don't want to be next to a deadhead."

She grabbed her bags and sat down beside me.

The bus lurched forward again. A glowing map above the seats tracked our destination. Jeanine and I had a few days of travel before we would reach The First City.

After a while of looking out the window at the grey landscape and the crumbling buildings, I closed my eyes and went to sleep.

***

When I awoke, it was night. Jeanine leaned against me, asleep, with her sunglasses drooping down her nose. I draped my Daddy's coat over her shoulders. The bus halted and a man with the mark of Cain boarded.

"I'm not letting that man sit near me!" someone shouted. "Look at his forehead!"

"Sit down and shut up or I'm throwing you

out!" the bus driver said over the intercom. "He can sit wherever he damn well pleases. God's orders."

The man slung his bag in an overhead compartment and sat opposite Jeanine and me. He took out his knife collection, set it on his lap, and cleaned the blades with a dirty, oiled rag. He shoved a wad of chewing tobacco in his mouth and balanced his plastic spit cup between his boots.

A baby started crying. Jeanine twitched in her sleep.

"There's nothing more I hate than crying babies on public transportation," the man said. "Some people just have no consideration for others."

The gray-haired mother made "Hush, hush," noises to her child, but the child continued crying. Several people shifted in their seats and stared.

Jeanine reached for my hand in her sleep and pressed her fingers into my palm. I closed my fingers around her hand and squeezed.

"Hello folks," the bus driver said over the intercom. "Looks like we won't be at our next stop until well after dawn, so strap in."

"She was a deadhead, huh?" the man with the mark of Cain asked me.

He cleaned an alligator-gutting knife as he spoke, one with a hooked blade and an etched silver handle.

"How did you know?" I asked.

"That cut on her forehead. My sister's a deadhead," he said. "Is she your sister?"

"A friend."

"Damn shame."

The baby let out another high-pitched wail.

"Will somebody shut that damn baby up?" he shouted, waving the knife over his head.

The mother continued to make "Hush, hush," noises. The man lowered his knife and turned back to me.

"What's your name?" he asked.

"Charles."

"And her?"

"Jeanine."

He didn't offer up his own name. He spit a wad of chewing tobacco into the spit cup balanced between his boots and kept cleaning his knives. The baby quieted down. From his control station the driver flicked on the televisions mounted above the seats. Teddy and Delilah were on. Teddy stood in front of Delilah's bed, waving his arms like a magician, and Delilah's bed spun around and around.

"Oh, turn that shit off!" Cain yelled.

The televisions shut off.

"I can't handle that bullshit," the man said. "That's all they play these days. Day in and day out."

"It's God approved!" a man in the seat ahead of mine said.

I couldn't make out his face. He wore his coat over his face and there were owl feathers glued to his shoulders.

"Yeah?" Cain said, tapping his scarred forehead, "well, so is my ass. Now shut the fuck up."

Silence. Cain turned toward me once more.

"So where you folks headed?"

"The First City," I said.

"Yeah? What's there?"

"I don't know."

He laughed.

"You're not going to find much there, Charles. That was your name, right? Charles?"

I nodded.

"Whatever you're chasing, you won't find it. That's how they get us, you know. They make us chase something when there's nothing there at all."

Cain put away his knives and his spit cup. He hunkered down into his seat with his knees pressed into the back of the seat in front of him.

Jeanine roused from sleep.

"Where are we?" she asked.

"We have a ways to go," I said. "Rest a little while longer if you can."

"Charles," she murmured, leaning down and laying her arms across my lap.

For a moment, I thought the mouth of her wound spoke to me, from some inner recesses of her irreparable brain, but then I felt her lips move against my shoulder. I rested my hand on the back of her head and she became still.

The baby started crying again. I looked over at Cain to see if he would do anything, but he'd fallen asleep.

I cupped Jeanine's chin underneath my palm.

"Let's go back, Jeanine," I said. "Let's just get off at the next bus stop and go back. We won't find her."

Cain, this strange man with an angry mouth on his forehead and a wad of chewing tobacco tucked in the pocket of his cheek, knew more than I ever could. I wouldn't find Leda at The First City, or anywhere else. She hadn't left me. God found her, or Ezekiel's shiny sphere, or any one of the monsters roaming the woods.

She was gone, and I should've expected this from the beginning.

I could go back home and become a soft skeleton, a mild-mannered suitor for a local alcoholic. I could linger for the rest of my life in the bower of the swamp waiting for Jolene to drag my bones to the bottom of those green waters.

"Jeanine?" I whispered.

She'd fallen asleep again. I shook her.

"Jeanine, did you hear me? Let's go back."

Jeanine groaned.

The windshield shattered and the bus careened off the road.

Two

THE BUS CRASHED into an abandoned farmhouse. We found the driver dead with a striped spear driven through his chest, pinning him to his seat.

Cain sent a distress transmission through the bus driver's radio.

"What do we do now?" I asked.

"Wait," he said.

The passengers on the bus talked among each other about their quests of salvation. Most were doomed from the start.

A yellow man with a body like a beaten flute told us he collected slivers of the black moon - slivers that fell from the sky and dropped down into his metallic bag.

"One day I'm going to build my own moon," he said.

Despite several wanted him to open the metallic bag so they could look inside, but he kept it fastened shut and clutched tight to his stomach.

"I'm looking for my lost son," said the woman with the crying baby.

"He's dead," said several passengers simultaneously.

"He's not dead," the woman said. "He sends me dreams through the television. He was always so bright. I knew he'd figure out a way to reach me."

An abandoned, yellow-eyed child tugged the sleeve of my jacket.

"I know what you're looking for," he said. “You're looking for love."

"Yeah," Jeanine said, "Charles is always looking for love."

"You can marry my cousin," the child said. “She's got tiny shoulders like the naked women in pictures, and a gap in her teeth, and she's always crazy at night.”

"He'll keep that in mind," Jeanine said.

The child left to go to another part of the bus.

Jeanine hunkered down in the back seat and drew her knees up to her chest.

“Are you okay?” I asked.

"It's been hours.” Jeanine said. "Help isn't coming."

"She's right, you know," said Cain.

“Then what have we been doing sitting here for hours?” someone asked

Several passengers opened up the emergency exits, clambered out, and disappeared into the night.

"I wouldn't leave just yet," he said.

The chuk-chuk-chuk of plague machines was nearby. I heard another sound underneath them, a heavy, rhythmic pounding against the dirt.

A woman wearing three-inch thick scars on her cheeks, crashing her arms like battleships came over to Jeanine.

"This is the third time I've been in a bus

crash," the woman said, "Isn't it strange?"

"Not really," Jeanine said.

"What's on your head?" the woman asked.

"This thing?" Jeanine said, touching her forehead. "It's my birthday present."

"I know what that is," the woman said. "That's where you get a hot wire spider. Everyone in my family is a deadhead except for me."

"That's nice," Jeanine said.

"I couldn't stand taking care of them anymore, so I tried to get away. But whenever you want something the universe does everything it can to stop you. Like this bus crashing. I was going to go to the university at The First City - get a degree in something. It didn't matter what. Anything so I wouldn't have to stay in the house all day wiping the spit off my brother's chin."

The woman leaned against Jeanine's seat. Her eyes were filmy with cataracts.

"What were you going to do?" the woman asked. "I mean, before we crashed."

"I wanted to go to a bar," Jeanine said. "And ride a mechanical bull. I'm the best rider there ever was."

Jeanine continued speaking.

"And if you're going to get a degree, whatever you do, don't get a degree in archaeology. Nobody's an archaeologist anymore."

"Would everyone be quiet?" The man with the mark of Cain said. " Someone's coming."

So I hadn't been the only one who heard the

heavy pounding against the dirt. And it felt closer this time. I looked out one of the bus windows and a seething mass of bodies appeared on the horizon.

"What is that?" the battleship woman asked.

"Those are people on horseback," Cain said, in a flat voice, "with spears. How anachronistic."

"Another damn cult, by the looks of it. I could be wrong about this, but I'm pretty sure they're coming to kill us all."

More passengers jumped out of the emergency exits. A few climbed through the front shattered windshield and down the hood of the bus. I grabbed Jeanine's arm and pulled her close to me. Jeanine tensed and pressed her fingertips into my ribcage. I was about to leave the bus when Cain stopped me.

"Take this," he said.

He handed me the alligator-gutting knife and took his bag out of the overhead compartment.

"Charles," Jeanine said. "Look."

I pressed my hand to the window as if I could stop the fleeing passengers from running headfirst into the approaching cult. They were tall warriors riding speckled horses. They wore chainmail and pig snouted God masks. The passengers kept running across the field away from the bus, their limbs disintegrating in the light of the black moon. The warriors impaled them on their striped spears and dragged them away.

The baby let out a wail.

"There's that fucking baby again," Cain said.

The woman with the crying baby stood in the back of the bus near the emergency exit. The exit opened and sucked the curls of her hair out into the dark.

The warriors tore down the walls of the collapsing farmhouse. Cain held his arm against my chest to keep me from running.

"Wait," he said. "Wait until most of them have caught someone. You'll have a better chance of surviving."

A pig snouted God mask appeared in the window next to Jeanine.

"Charles," she said.

"Wait," The man said again. "Fucking cults."

The warriors rocked the bus. Most of the remaining passengers ran out of the bus to try to escape, only to be impaled, gut wrenched, wrists broken, and dragged off on the heels of horses.

"Now," Cain said. "Run for those hills you see over there. Come on. Now."

Cain shouldered his bag, grabbed a machete from his knife collection, and ran toward the back emergency exit. He shouldered past the woman and her baby, jumped out of the bus, and headed for the machine fields.

Jeanine and I bolted to our feet and chased after him. A horse's flanks filled the space of the emergency exit, blocking our way. A man in a God mask, carrying a spear, jumped down into the bus and grabbed the arm of the woman holding the wailing baby.

I lunged at the man with my new knife. He knocked me back into Jeanine. She lost her balance and fell back in the aisle. The knife flew out of my hand. The man rammed his spear straight through the woman's ribcage and killed the baby with a sharp blow to the back of its head.

He slung the dead mother over his shoulder, jumped onto his horse, and rode off.

Jeanine clamored to her feet. She grabbed me to keep me from falling.

"We need to go," she said.

We jumped out the emergency exit. I touched the siding and my fingers came away slick with the woman's blood. Jeanine pushed me flat against the side of the bus as two men thundered past on black horses. They carried lit torches and dragged busted and slack jawed children behind them. I looked for Cain, possibly somewhere on the horizon, but I couldn't make anything out in the dark.

"Our bags," Jeanine said. "They're still in the bus."

"Leave them."

"I'll get them," she said.

"No."

"I'll get them. You go. Run for the hills past the field, like he said."

Jeanine climbed back into the bus before I

could argue anymore. The men on horseback threw their torches into the farmhouse and the dry wood burst into flames.

I ran toward the hills across the open field. It seemed for my entire life I ran with heat on my back. The weeds and fennel and rye grass of the field glowed and cracked and bent. Screamed. They screamed. I kept looking back to see if the bus had caught on fire, to see if I could catch sight of Jeanine. I tripped and fell several times. I got up again and again, shaking, my knees and elbows scraped hard. I rubbed the woman's blood over my mouth and I waited for hoof beats behind me. I waited for the death that sat with me every morning eating breakfast to finally reach over and drag me away.

But I reached the hills still alive. I tried to hide in a low bank but I found a young girl already hiding there. She wore a wolf mask and held tightly to her bleeding arm.

"Can I hide here with you?" I asked.

She snapped and growled at me, digging her bare feet into the dirt, her toes curled so tight I thought they might break.

I moved on, searching for another place to hide, or for Cain.

I found another girl lying on her back. She wore God's mask with its black, velvety pig nose and goat horns. She clutched a black striped spear to her chest. Her skirts billowed out on the grass, hiked over her panties, revealing the pale, wretched space of her broken legs.

"Hey," I said, but I couldn't hear myself over the throb of the machines.

I said it again. Said, "hey," as I bent to touch cheeks with her God mask. I pried the spear out of her hands and threw it into the grass. Her hands stiffened. I peeled off her God mask and met the smile of her blood-encrusted jaw, the upside down twitch of her nose sliced in half.

She whispered something to me.

" What did you say?" I asked, yelling over that unbearable, increasing noise.

The girl squeezed fistfuls of my shirt between her fingers and died.

Someone touched me on the shoulder. I whirled around and tripped over the dead girl. Jeanine stood there with her hand held out toward me, the two bags slung over her neck and shoulder. She stepped over the dead girl and helped me to my feet. She touched the dried and cracked blood on my mouth. Her fingers and face were greasy hot. She smelled of smoke and when she tipped her head ash fell from her hair.

We left the dead girl behind and walked into the field of machines.

That was the first time I saw the machines up close.

There were shiny, hard machines that sat on the graves of our dead. There were machines with dirty hearts and piston pumps and grappling arms heated red. Efficient and inhuman, hurled straight from heaven. There were machines that looked almost human, with their seraph faces, baby limbs - but they were nearly inoperable. Newer models were overtaking them, machines that looked like nothing a human could have ever created, machines spinning wheels and dripping loose skin from their jaws. Still others were like black boxes with steely mouths, bulging nests of plague locusts swinging from their arms.

Jeanine and I tried not to get too close.

Three

WE ARRIVED AT A city in the middle of the desert, a small thing, little more than taupe and silver buildings jutting out the yellow sand.

We stopped in front of a sign sticking halfway out of the sand.

It said, "Welcome to Sodom."

"This can't be Sodom," Jeanine said. "My brother used to tell me stories about God destroying Sodom. It was completely obliterated. There was nothing left."

"Well, the sign says it's Sodom." I said.

"It can't be the same one."

Just outside the city limits we came across a hell shuttle line-up a mile long. It wrapped like a streamer around the gray buildings. Old men with ring scars asked to feel Jeanine's breasts. Young girls in tulle skirts and orange lipstick asked for cigarettes and kisses.

"I'm sorry, I don't have any," I said, over and over again. "I don't have any."

Jeanine took my arm and led me away. We continued into the city.

"I can't go on anymore," I said. "I need to rest."

"I don't have time to rest," Jeanine said. "I'm going to die any moment. My heart is crashing. It wants to quit."

She had a rabies grin and the smoke in her eyes made her look wild and inhuman.

"What happened to you? Weren't we going to find your brother?"

"Didn't you hear what I just said?" she asked.

Instead of finding a place to rest, Jeanine took me to the nearest bar.

Someone smashed all the television in the bar, and "Dance you cunts" was written across the walls in blood. I lay my bag down against the bar.

"I just cleaned the blood off that thing!" the bartender yelled.

Without a pause, he turned to Jeanine.

"What can I get you?" he asked.

"I don't care," Jeanine said. "But I'm dying tonight so you better make it good."

The bartender poured her some water in a plastic cup. Jeanine downed it like a shot and slammed it down on the bar

"Feel my heart," she said to me.

"No."

"It's a dying animal."

Jeanine ordered another drink.

"What are you doing?" I asked.

"We do crazy things when we're about to die," Jeanine said. "You saw those girls outside."

I felt my face and heart slipping away. The entire bar seemed to drift down into snow. A man approached Jeanine, and he was made out of snow as well. He tapped on her shoulder. Jeanine turned around in her chair with her hand pressed to her chest. Her water spilled across her lap, and the man laughed.

"I know you," he said to Jeanine. "You used to strip at the Legion. Back in Edgewater."

"That hole in the wall?" Jeanine asked, "Where all the sad, old people hung out?"

"You had nice tits," he said. "Nice body for a deadhead."

"I'm not a deadhead. Not anymore."

He smudged the ash still on her cheeks.

"Everyone called you the gasoline girl," he said. "You were the always on fire girl."

"I've been on fire more than anyone else I've ever known," Jeanine said.

She touched the tips of her blue and orange hair.

"Was I any good?" she asked.

"You're the best deadhead stripper I've ever seen," he said.

"Maybe love is real," she said.

Jeanine touched the man's face. Her fingers lightly cupped his cheek.

"Do you want to go to my hotel room?" he asked.

Jeanine stood up and slipped her hand around the man's waist.

"Charles, I'll find you later," she said.

"What about your brother?"

"Don't be selfish. I only have one more night left to live."

She left the bar with the man, and I was left alone.

"Get your hands off the wall!" the bartender yelled at me, "Don't people know decency anymore?"

I left before the bartender could yell at me again. I wandered the streets of Sodom hugging my arms to my chest. Around me people chanted about the grapes of wrath, the wine press of wrath, the blood that would overflow until we would be forced to drink it. Other people huddled together like animals and cried for deliverance with their backs bared to the cold.

I wondered if Jeanine would have stayed with me if I told her I didn't get a slip implant that day because I wanted to save her.

In the distance, I heard a familiar, dry and violent sound, and I realized why the people were outside, repenting and wailing. The plague machines were approaching.

I could barely open my mouth it was so dry. I went into a diner. I the shut front door as people outside started screaming.

The waitress approached me.

"All the other employees are in hell, and I can't cook," she said.

"Can I get a drink?"

The waitress sniffed hard and walked back into the kitchen. She returned shortly with a glass of water, and then went into the back room. I heard her sobbing.

I sat by the window with the glass of water. I

trembled as the machines pounded closer, hugging my bag to my chest. The door swung open again and Cain sat down beside me.

"You need to get out of this city," he said, "It's about to be destroyed."

The waitress, her eyes now streaked black, came back into the front of the diner to take Cain's order.

"Water, please," Cain said.

The waitress left the table scratching at her wrists.

"You survived," I said.

"Of course I did," he said, tapping a finger against his mark of Cain. "That you survived is the truly remarkable thing

"Jeanine told me something," I said. "Sodom was destroyed before."

"She's right. And it will be destroyed many more times."

"I don't understand."

"Understanding is useless," Cain said. "Look outside."

It was snowing. The snow turned the sky a dirty white. It blew into the gutters and stuck to the windows. It obstructed the buildings from view.

"It's not even cold," I said.

"Look closer," he said.

When I looked out the window again, the snow grew edges. It turned metallic and stuck out tongues of black ink.

It wasn't snow. It was pieces of paper, with "Repent" printed on every side.

"The last bus out of the city leaves in an hour," he said, "and you look like someone who needs to get somewhere."

"I don't know," I said.

"Know soon," he said. "Where did that waitress go?"

For a moment, it seemed as if the blizzard of paper muffled all sounds, all the screaming and pleading, the gnashing of the machines, everything except the crying of that waitress.

"Forget it."

Cain got up from the table.

"Don't go," I said. "Please. There's so much I don't know. What does God want? Where did the monsters come from?"

"One hour," he said. "I hope for your sake you're on that last bus."

He left the restaurant. I followed him, but lost sight of him in the storm of paper. I went back to the bar and found the bartender standing on top of the counter with his fist stuck through a smashed television.

"You remember that woman who was in here?" I asked him, "The one with the orange and blue hair?"

"That man took her to the hotel down the street," he said, pulling his bloodied fist out of the television. "Room 65. Now get the hell out of here before you smudge something else."

I went outside back into the paper storm. The machines grew louder. I pressed my hands to my ears but the noise drilled straight through me

I reached the hotel and entered the lobby. I ignored the man sitting at the desk and ran up the stairs searching for room 65. The stairs were built like coffins, and the ceiling slipped down over my shoulders like dirt. The plague machines opened their floodgates and water spilled through the windows. I reached the top floor of the hotel drenched in black water.

I wrenched open the door and found the man sitting up in bed. His hands, engorged and snow white crab claws, fell over the side of the bed and down into the rising water. Jeanine lay across his lap with her orange and blue hair stuck to the headboard, her ribs rising out of her skin like plaster molds.

"Jeanine, we have to go," I said.

"There's nowhere she needs to be," the man said.

The slips of paper, each one with the tiny "Repent," spilled through the open window and stuck to the man's skin, to his crab claw hands.

"Can't you see I'm dying, Charles?" she asked me.

I shouldered my bag and waded through the mold-draped water, past the floating desk, the undergarments swirling in a maelstrom.

I pulled her out of the man's lap. She slipped

off the bed and down into the water below. She came up gasping. I squeezed her wrist tight, grabbed her bag off the bed, and pulled her out into the lobby.

"My heart," she said. "Can't you feel my heart is about to explode?"

She grabbed her shirt as it floated past and she pulled it over her head. Then she dredged up her panties. The windows inside the room broke and a paper storm surrounded us. Repent. Repent. Repent. The wailing of the machines and the people outside all screamed, "Repent."

Together we went out into the streets of Sodom. Pink blood tinged the papers. Faces came in and out of the storm, faces of everyman and everywoman, the face of Daddy, Momma, and Sissy, the faces of those who went into the woods and never came back out again. "Repent" peeled to my nose. To Jeanine's implant wound. I tried to keep going forward without being pulled away by those familiar faces.

We found the bus stop by following its faint headlines from down the street. We boarded the crowded bus and were pushed against the windows. Jeanine's panties pressed a wet outline into the glass. I enveloped the both of us in my Daddy's jacket as we were jostled on all sides. Pieces of paper pushed through the doors and the machines shook the earth.

"My heart's going to burst," she repeated. "My heart's going to burst."

The bus pulled out of the stop and left the city.

"What was the point of all that?" I asked her, shouting so that she could hear me over the roar of Sodom being destroyed. “Do you feel any better after going to that hotel? After having those drinks?"

"What is the point of any of this?" she asked.

She hissed steam through her teeth. She drew an angry face onto the glass.

"Was there a point to what we did?" she asked.

"What the hell are you talking about?”

"I took you into my freezer," she said. “I showed you my swans. My secret place. Was there a point to that?

“You were the one who left, Jeanine.”

"It doesn't matter," she said. “We’re all dying. In a single moment, I fell asleep and woke up old. One more second and I'll be dead. It doesn't matter if I left or not. I want to go home."

"It mattered," I said.

"Fuck you," Jeanine said.

She tried to hit me, but we were so tightly pressed against the window she couldn't move to face me.

"You told me you wanted to go back," Jeanine said, "when were on the bus. I was half-asleep, but I remember. Why don't we go back?"

I leaned my forehead against her wet hair.

"I was kidding myself," I said, “There's

nothing to go back to. If you could turn around to look you would see there was nothing there at all."

Four

AFTER WE ESCAPED Sodom the bus driver sold all of us to slave traders.

Someone placed a bag over my head. They tore me away from Jeanine and ushered me off the bus. We went down into a twisting labyrinth, and when the bag was taken off my head, I found myself in a room without windows. A lone chair stood in the center of the room. Several men and women, silent, stood in the corners of the room.

A woman approached me. At first, she seemed to be nothing but a silhouette that peeled itself out of a hazy gray fog. But then she leaned over me and the shadow lifted from her face. The veins in her forehead were cut like crabmeat.

"Sit down," she said.

“Where am I?” I asked.

She slapped me across the face. She wore gloves braised with metal rivets.

"Sit down," she repeated.

I fell back into the chair, rocking it off its back legs.

"Do you have any friends or relatives we can contact?" the woman asked. “Anyone who would pay good money to have you back?"

“Please,” I said. “I just want to know where I am.”

She slapped me again.

Everyone else in the room remained silent and frozen-faced. Still.

"Do you know anyone who would pay good money to have you back?" she asked again.

"Everyone is dead," I said quietly.

She placed the bag back over my head. Just as quickly as I was escorted into the room, I was escorted back into the tunnels.

"Where's Jeanine?" I asked. "What did you do with her?"

A door slammed shut and locked behind me, and I was left alone.

When I pulled the bag off my head I found myself in an underground abattoir. Dirt pushed its way through the wooden slat walls and dead animals lay in a pile underneath a chute. There were dead suckling pigs, spine wrenched cattle, broken-necked swans. Two concrete killing slabs were set in the center of the room, and blood ran in trenches through the floors.

I pressed my hand over my mouth and noise to keep from gagging.

The room trembled and dirt rained down on my head. More dead animals tumbled through the chute. The bottom of the pile squirmed, and a man emerged wearing a stained apron and clutching a pig by its hindquarters.

He threw the pig down on one of the killing slabs. It landed on its back against the concrete with a crack of bone and a thud of wet, congealed organs. The man picked up his butcher tools and sliced the pig in two. Its body ruptured, its skin deflated, and its blood and fluid poured down the corners of the slab.

My lungs grew tight and I breathed inside my hands, but I stilled smelled pig's blood and shit.

"You'll get used to it," the man said to me without looking up. "Everyone does. Come over here and help me with this, will you?"

With my hand still pressed over my nose and mouth, I stepped over the trenches of blood and walked over toward the killing slabs.

"What do they call you?" the man asked me.

"Bubba," I said, the word muffled by my hand.

He laughed and said, "Bubba? Strange name."

"No," I said, peeling my hand away from my mouth. "That's not what I meant. My name's Charles."

"But they call you Bubba?"

"Not anymore," I said. "Just Charles."

He told me to call him Number Seventeen.

" Number Seventeen?"

"It's how I keep track of time in this place. I count the number of people who come in here and die, or get taken away, or what have you. So I'm Number Seventeen, and when you're gone, I'll be Number Eighteen.

"Oh."

"You look a bit shaken up, Charles."

"I've never smelled anything like this before."

"You'll get used to it," Number Seventeen said

once more, "The guy who was here before me, back when I was still Number One, he told me the human body has an enormous capacity to adapt to its surroundings. He was a crazy bastard."

Number Seventeen handed me a knife.

"You ever butchered a pig before?"

He taught me. When we finished the pig lay dissected on the killing slab in several bloody, quivering chunks. Its heated blood and gore dripped down my arms, and its scent clung to my tongue. I hardly recognized what it used to be.

"This is your job now," he said, "until you disappear. We butcher the animals. Then we push them through the flap over there to be collected. You don't get to know what happens after that."

I glanced over at the flap, a small, bloodstained metal sheet cut out of the wall. It hung slightly open like a deflated mouth, dripping gore from its edges.

"What happens when we run out of animals to butcher?"

"You don't," he said. "There are so many dead things."

"But in Edgewater, we hardly ever ate meat," I said. "They told us there was a shortage."

Number Seventeen retrieved from the pile of dead animals a black swan with a bolt running through its brain. He laid it out on the killing slab just like he'd laid out the pig, with a crack of bones, a slap of skin and feathers. The black looked like a prop, some kind of joke, with its tongue unrolled out of its mouth and its feathers stuck together in congealed blood.

"The meat goes to the priests and the favored of God," Number Seventeen, "and that ain't either one of us."

"How do I get out of here?" I asked.

"You don't. You've always been here."

"Where did the others go?"

"There's no one else."

He chopped the swan's head off and it rolled off the killing slab. I expected the swan's severed neck to spurt blood, like a great fountain, but its blood only dribbled out onto the concrete in a quiet stream.

"You don't understand," I said. "I need to get to The First City. I was with a girl. Do you know if she's somewhere in here?"

Something pounded against the wall, as if someone in another room was trying to get our attention.

"What was that?" I asked

Number Seventeen ignored me and went back to butchering the swan. The pounding continued. I stepped over a trench of blood and moved toward the wall. I pressed my hand against the wall and it reverberated through my skin.

"You better work," he said. "If you don't work

they won't give you anything to eat."

"I need to talk to someone," I said. "I need to get out of here. I have somewhere I need to be."

"Didn't I tell you that you've always been here?"

"You don't understand. I can't stay here."

Number Seventeen held out a butcher's knife for me to take.

"Only when you realize you're trapped do you want to be freed, but you've been trapped all along. They took you into the dark room, they took you out of the dark room, and there's no going back to illusion. Now work, or they'll hurt you. If you don't I'll be alone again."

I hesitated for a moment as the stained surface of the butcher's knife quiver in his grip. Number Seventeen stared straight through me like a ghost would.

I took the butcher's knife from Number Seventeen's grasp, and helped him cut up the black swan.

***

I spent weeks, maybe months, in that underground abattoir, butchering the dead animals that kept piling up underneath the chute. We pushed raw meat through the chute, and food was pushed back for us to eat. At first I wouldn't eat, because I couldn't without thinking about the bloody mouth of the chute and the dead of those sick and broken dead creatures. But I got too hungry to resist for long.

Number Seventeen taught me how to use the knives. He taught me to turn my face away when I sliced the heart so the blood wouldn't spurt into my eyes. He taught me how to forget that I ever existed anywhere else but this black iron prison, this lonely underground abattoir.

We slept against the wall. Number Seventeen told me another year would soon pass us by. We no longer knew day from night. Every time we woke up and went back to work, Number Seventeen said the world above us had been destroyed and rebuilt while we dreamed.

The pounding against the wall continued. Some days Number Seventeen told me it was the pounding inside his head. Other days he told me it was the noise of his heart sliding down into the grease trap of his bowels.

"I used to wait for the day when they would come and get me," he told me, "like they came for everyone else. But that day never came."

I cracked the breastplate of a newborn foal with a blue tongue. Its fluids spilled out onto my fingers like gasoline. Despite what Number Seventeen said, I never got used to the smell.

"I started looking for myself in the guts of these dead animals," Number Seventeen said. "One day an animal will come down that chute. When I slit it open, I'll find who I used to be inside of it, curled up and small, like a red fetus.

I will know when I see it. The last part of me that ever hoped to escape this prison."

"What then?"

"I'll know there's nothing left to hope for."

The pounding in the wall continued when I slept and when I woke. The noise never stopped.

"I saw the person you used to be," Number Seventeen told me once when I awoke.

He stood at an empty killing slab, smiling.

"Did it say anything?" I asked, feeling delirious.

"I found the unborn fetus of you. It was cradled inside the stomach of a black swan."

"What did you do with it?"

"I ate it," he said.

The pounding through the wall grew in intensity. I pressed my hands against my head to keep my brain from being ground into pulp.

"I'm tired of this," I said. "We shouldn't have to live in a world where we drive ourselves crazy just to survive."

Number Seventeen buried his hands into the pile of dead animals. Blood crept up his hands. It filled the gaps between his teeth, pooled in the space between his lips. He didn't respond.

When I wasn't butchering animals or talking to Number Seventeen I drew on the walls with charcoal and blood. I drew buildings of Edgewater, the animals we butchered, Jeanine dancing with rigor mortis limbs in the grip of a hot wire spider.

“I didn’t know you were an artist,” Number Seventeen said.

“I’m not,” I said. “I mean, I stopped doing it.”

“I was an artist once,” he said. “But I started to forget what was real and what wasn’t.”

“I don’t care what’s real,” I said.

“Only someone who’s tired of life would say that.”

"I'm tired of travelling from one meat freezer to one slaughterhouse after another," I said. "I'm tired of all the dead things. I'm tired of waiting to die since I was six years old.”

Number Seventeen laughed.

"Sounds like something you'll have to take up with God," he said.

He dragged another carcass to the killing slab and I pressed my hands against my eyes as the pounding bore into me.

Then the pounding stopped. I lowered my hands.

There was now a small hole in the wall.

"Was this here before?" I asked.

"Don’t pay any attention to that."

I pressed my eye to the hole in the wall.

A woman stood in the center of a room on top of a metal plate. Bright colors illuminated her hair and skin. Orbs of light and electricity bounced off her limbs and sparked in her hair. She wore a dress of transparent gauze, and when she turned, her spine bent down like a bird’s mouth.

"Jeanine?" I whispered.

She came over to the hole in the wall.

"Who's there?" she asked.

"It's Charles."

"You're not Charles."

"Yes I am. What are you doing?"

"I'm a ghost. They're taking ghost pictures of me."

"Ghost pictures?"

"They sell them to parents with dead children."

"Get away from that wall," Number Seventeen called out to me. "Stop talking to the wall. There's nothing there."

"Jeanine, is there any way to leave this place?" I asked her.

"No," she said.

The light swelled in her hair, grew to an intense violent-green, and then diffused into red. It sparked off her mouth like dandelion wisps. They disappeared when they touched her clothing.

"Did you put this hole in the wall?" I asked her.

"Yes,"

"Why?"

"I was lonely," she said, "I have to go. They need more pictures."

She returned to the center of the room and turned around slowly so the light could gnaw her.

"Get over here," Number Seventeen said. "There's so many animals coming in we're going to drown if you don't start helping me."

I didn't get another chance to talk to Jeanine until Number Seventeen fell asleep. As he and I sat up against the wall, Jeanine whispered to me through the hole.

"Can I call you Charles?" she asked.

"I am Charles," I said.

"I was traveling to The First City with a man named Charles before they imprisoned me here. I told them my brother was a prophet, but they didn't believe me. They said everyone had a brother who was a prophet down here. Then they put me in this room. I thought I was dying until they put me in this room. Then I realized I've already dead."

"You're not dead, Jeanine," I said.

"Be quiet please," she whispered. "I want to tell someone this before I forget. If I don't tell you it'll be lost forever. Seven years ago, when I was still a girl, I got a slip implant put into my head."

"I know," I said. "I'm Charles. I know you."

"Be quiet," she said, her voice soft and insistent, "I was going to be an archaeologist. I lived in this little town called Edgewater, on the edge of nowhere. My brother was a prophet, he lived in The First City. I thought nobody existed unless they lived in The First City. So as soon as I could I left Edgewater and headed for The First

City. I enrolled in the university there and joined the archeology department. I thought I could uncover the things we thought were lost. All the things we lost from the very beginning.

"But I found out I wouldn't uncover a damn thing. I was one of the few students in the department. Everyone else were training to become slip doctors, or morticians. In the archaeology courses I was taught what was beneath the ground, and how we would teach others what was beneath the ground. We saw pictures of what was beneath the ground - these glossy, fake photographs of ruins and animal skeletons.

"When I asked one of our instructors when we would get to excavate the earth, he rebuked me.

"'It doesn't matter,' he said. 'You must learn to stop asking questions like that.

"'But what about the buildings that have been burned to the ground?' I asked, 'What about the thousands of graves, the earth piled on top of the earth? There has to be something nobody has found yet.'

"'Only children ask questions like that,' the instructor said. 'Do you want to be treated like a child?'

"'No,' I said quietly, and I stopped asking questions.

"He said to me, 'When you've finished your education in the archeology department you will become an instructor. You will take these pictures and show the world we have found everything that needs to be found.'

"He pushed a glossy photograph across the desk toward me. It was a photograph of a dead butterfly pinned inside a shadow box. I took the picture. Then I left the archeology department and never went back.

"I suppose that's when I realized that what I'd been running away from my whole life would follow me wherever I went. Or maybe that whatever I was running toward didn't actually exist. I couldn't go back to Edgewater. The swans were dead. My meat freezer was empty. I couldn't stay in The First City with the archeology department and the fake photographs, but I couldn't go back to my old life. So I went to a slip implant clinic and asked them to make me forget."

"I'm so sorry, Jeanine."

"I don't want you to be sorry. If you ever see Charles, you can tell him I'm sorry."

"Why him?"

"Because he loved me. Because he took me home from the hospital, after my body rejected the sleep implant. I never told him I saw he had become a ghost. I thought I was the one slipping away, but while I was gone he died on me. Gave up. So I went with him on this stupid journey to find someone he loved. Like it would mean both of us could stop running away if we found her."

I pressed my hands against the wall. I wanted to reach straight through and touch her fingers, sparking with light.

"We're going to get out of here."

"Oh," Jeanine said, "you know you shouldn't promise things like that."

The door banged open and several men and women rushed into the room. Number Seventeen awoke and grabbed my hand. A woman tore his hand away. A man grabbed my shoulders. I bit and kicked whoever got close to me. Then someone punched me in the throat and I couldn't breathe. A bag went over my head. They dragged me out of the abattoir and back into the tunnels.

Number Seventeen sobbed as they shut and locked the door. I struggled to get away. In response they smashed my ribs, suffocated me, ground my knees against their boots. I fell onto the floor and cracked my chin against the stone. The bag came off my head.

Someone grabbed a fistful of my hair. It was the woman with the crabmeat veins who'd interrogated me when I first came to the labyrinth. Instinctively, I reared back and head-butted her in the face.

She cried out and let go of me. My captors swarmed around me. They struck my arms and face and chest again and again. I cried and twisted my body away from their blows. They dragged me across the floor like a husked skin.

Shouts echoed from down the hallway. My captors stopped. The woman with the crabmeat veins pulled out a gun and pushed me face first down into the concrete.

A volley of gunshots rang out and everyone fell dead around me.

"Get up."

A lean man towered over me. He wore God's mask and held a rusted rifle.

He grabbed my arm and pulled me up.

"Get out of here," he said. "We're tearing this place down."

"Who are you?" I asked. "You're not a cultist?"

Only then did I notice he wore an armband embossed with a bold number six.

"Go back the way we came and you'll find your way out."

"There's someone I need to find."

"You won't find them."

Several people, also wearing black masks and carrying old guns, ran past me. The lean man followed them. They left me alone in the corridor with my dead captors, slumped around me and bleeding like animals.

I walked back the way they came. In distant parts of the underground I heard people shouting and gunfire going off. I kept walking until I found a clay door. I pulled it open and walked out into the desert.

It was nighttime, the air cool and the black

moon small. Dust blew across my clothes. I sucked in fresh air and breathed out slow. In the distance, I saw the bus from Sodom we'd arrived on. Now it was busted and broken down, its wheels missing. People newly freed from the slavers wandered off into the distance. The black moon pooled around their feet and dark halos swelled on their heads

Two figures in black masks stood nearby. One man held an assault rifle. He wore a cracked God mask that exposed his blacked out eyes and forehead. A dark skinned woman stood beside him. She wore a stained purple dress with a butterfly bow.

"I don't like running around in these 'fuck you' masks," the woman said. "It makes me uncomfortable."

"Cults are popular these days," the man with the assault rifle said. "Easy to slip under the radar."

"It's the principle behind the thing," the woman said,

"You're going to talk to me about principle?" the man said. "You just shot a woman seven times in the chest because she said she didn't like your dress."

"Who are you people?" I asked.

The two stopped arguing and turned toward me, as if seeing me for the first time. The woman reared up like a snake.

"We're friends," the man said.

"Why did you break into that place? Why did you save me?"

"We know what you've been through."

We stood at the entrance of the slave trader's tunnels for a long while. I watched paint flakes fall off the man's face. I thought of Smarts and his number six, and the unknown woman with the machine gun that followed him.

"You're heretics." I said.

"We're friends," he repeated.

The lean man came out of the slave trader's tunnels and stood beside me. He cradled his God mask in the crook of his arm. Implanted on his face was one mechanical eye, the pupil dilated to the size of a coin.

"You could go with us if you wanted," he said. "We could help you."

"Charles!"

Jeanine ran toward me. Her sheer gauze clothing was torn and her lip busted. Someone had ripped out patches of her hair.

"Charles," Jeanine said, breathing hard.

"You know who I am," I said.

"Of course I do."

She touched the collar of my shirt and it crumbled in her fingers. Only then did I realize my clothes were ragged and streaked in blood.

"I'm sorry," I told the man with the mechanical eye. "There's somewhere I have to be."

I took Jeanine's hand and we walked away.

Five

WHILE JEANINE AND I wandered in the desert, we told each other about our perfect worlds.

"No more clothes," Jeanine said. “We could fuck on the streets. While in line at the grocery store. On the porch steps while our grandmothers are making lemonade."

"No more corpses," I said. “No more dead skin and bones. When something dies I want it to disappear."

"No, we need bones. A record of what we lost."

"Okay, we can have bones. But no blood."

Jeanine and I walked in the desert for days. We followed the black cloud on the horizon that Jeanine said would lead us to The First City. In the day, we burned, and in the night, we froze. We sucked the moisture from our clothes buttons to keep our mouths producing saliva, and as we walked pieces of our clothing fell off and dissolved in the sand.

As we got closer, the black cloud grew hard edges. It rose above the landscape like an outstretched claw.

“That's God's castle, isn't it?” I asked.

Jeanine nodded.

I measured our progress across the desert by the details that formed out of the black cloud. The details of parapets and windows encased in spider-webbed iron bar took shape. Then, I saw the metallic buildings. God's castle made even the tallest of them appear diminutive in comparison.

"When we get to the city we'll find my brother," Jeanine said. "He can help us."

My eyes almost sealed shut with sweat and heat. My face cracked with sunburn. We passed the cracked bones of animals picked apart by birds. We passed bones of men and women holding hands and curled inside of each other like fused fossils.

Jeanine touched my face. Her fingers came away slick with my sweat.

"In my perfect world it would always be dawn," Jeanine said. "A thousand sunsets every moment."

We made it to the city in the early afternoon. Unlike in flood-damaged Edgewater, the buildings of The First City gleamed metallic white. The streets lay austere like the unrolled silver tongue of a machine. Televisions were everywhere, bolstered onto the surface of buildings, on the sidewalks underneath thick panes of glass, in storefront and house front windows.

Jeanine knelt in the street and drank from a puddle. I licked the glistening faux rocks of the post office building.

Then, as if they'd been waiting for a cue, the city came alive. People came out of their houses and gathered in the streets with ticker tape and colorful floats. They talked excitedly as they held banners and put on grotesque white stage make-up. They placed the banners for Slim Sarah's celebration parade, with Slim Sarah's cat glasses and dog face blown up to huge proportions, from nearly every building in the city. The Teddy and Delilah show broadcast from every television.

"I'd forgotten about the parade."

"That stupid show is still on?" Jeanine asked. "Whatever, it's not important."

I wanted to stop and rest but since we lost our bags after leaving Sodom we had no money to rent a room. As the people in the streets prepared for Slim Sarah's celebration, praying and beating their backs with whips and throwing colored confetti into the air, Jeanine and I continued on to the Prophet Headquarters. It sat underneath the shadow of God's mountain.

The silhouette of God's castle descended down upon the walls like a sharp edged tornado.

The guard post leading up to the Prophet Headquarters was empty. Jeanine and I walked into the building unnoticed. We stood for a few moments in the empty lobby just so we could feel the cool air-conditioner blowing on our skin. Every surface glittered and gleamed as if cooling under ice.

"Why wasn't there anyone at the entrance?" I asked Jeanine.

"The parade, I guess." Jeanine said. "Let's go find my brother."

We found no one else on the first floor. The receptionist desk was abandoned. All of the offices were empty behind their glass walls. We explored the vast floor. Its cool and sprawling corners expanded outwards like an echo chamber.

We approached a pair of elevator doors and they sprang open. A guard walked out with a prophet in handcuffs. The guard pushed the prophet forward. The prophet groaned. His cheeks were swollen and his face blue with bruises. His shiny sphere twitched like an acid-stained eyed.

The guard walked past without acknowledging Jeanine or me. Jeanine and I slipped into the elevator before the doors closed. The elevator descended.

"They're arresting prophets now?" I said.

"I didn't think the apocalypse was scheduled until next month," Jeanine said.

The elevator doors opened into a basement. Jeanine and I stepped out into what appeared to be a seemingly endless corridor. The walls were lined with a series of doors that went from the elevator to perpetuity. Each door had a number written on it in red paint.

"This is it," Jeanine said.

We went down the corridor and Jeanine began checking door numbers. From behind the thin walls I heard clicking teeth and subdued crying. Occasionally I heard the slam of furniture being thrown across a room, or people chattering hymns underneath their breath.

"This is where the prophets work?" I asked, my voice a whisper.

Down here there was nothing left of the pristine, austere ice world we'd seen in the lobby. The walls were gritty gray and smeared with smoke. The carpet underneath us was stained and old and embedded with dead insects.

Jeanine opened a door and we entered her brother's office.

Jeanine's brother sat in the corner of a room at an overloaded desk underneath brown, claustrophobic wallpaper. He was hunched over a large object that emanated light, typing. At first, I didn't recognize what it was.

“That's a computer, isn't it?” I said. “I haven't seen one in a long time.”

He continued to type without looking up.

I could see the family resemblance between him and Jeanine. They both had shiny wide eyes, dark hair, and sharp bodies with railroad track bones. And like Jeanine, he had aged well beyond his years. His skin appeared melanoma sick and his face ran greasy and pale. His cheekbones threatened to slide down his chin.

His typing hands bulged with throbbing, gnarled veins.

"Jonah," Jeanine said.

He glanced up, but he didn't stop typing.

"How do you know my name?" he asked.

"It's Jeanine," she said. "Your sister. Don't you recognize me?"

His fingers stopped typing for a brief moment.

"What did you do to your hair?" he asked. "It looks awful."

"I came to see you."

Jeanine walked toward Jonah's desk. He shrank into his chair. He wore a suit and tie too big for him. The space his clothes left behind only accentuated the cold, small knot that remained of his body.

"We need your help," Jeanine said.

She reached out for Jonah's hand. He twitched when she touched him.

"I'm kind of busy," he said, indicating his computer monitor. "I still have to type up these salvation reports, and then I have a meeting with some of the other prophets to discuss our recent divine revelations. And then after that I have to catch up on my conversions. I'm behind quota."

He resumed typing.

"Jonah," Jeanine said.

He didn't respond. He didn't look up.

"Jonah!"

"I told you, I'm busy. If I don't finish this I'm

going to be in trouble."

"We're looking for someone. Someone Charles knows who went missing about a month ago. We thought you could help, seeing as you're a prophet and all. Like, you could check the shuttle records to see if anyone by her name was transferred, or if any residential transcripts came in."

"That isn't my department," he said.

"But surely you can do something. You're a prophet of God."

"People go missing all the time. We don't keep records on that anymore. Too much of a hassle."

"Please. I know you can help."

"Jeanine, I'm really quite busy. You don't know what kind of trouble I'm going to be in if I don't finish these reports. The high priests have been breathing down my neck because of my drop in productivity, and they've been getting rid of a lot of prophets lately."

"I'll write her name down for you. Do you have a pen?"

"Jeanine."

She started opening his desk drawers.

"Jeanine, please."

She pulled out a pen and a legal pad and wrote Leda's name. She pushed the legal pad in front of her brother's keyboard.

She leaned into him, her stripper body just as cold and hollowed out as his.

"I missed you, you know," Jeanine whispered. "You don't know what's happened these last few years. Maybe if you were home you could have stopped all those horrible things from happening."

"What was I supposed to do?" Jonah asked. "Nobody can do anything anymore."

"Did you know at our graduation the guest speaker burnt down the school? And someone murdered my swans. And Daddy got executed after they found out he was a serial killer. Did you hear about that?"

"I don't have time for things like that," Jonah said.

He'd been chewing on his bottom lip for years. There was a red split right down the middle of his lip where he dragged his teeth.

"Why do they have you down here in the basement?" Jeanine asked. "You're a prophet. Everyone always said you were special. I thought prophets lived in high rise apartments and had harems full of beautiful women and drank vintage wine and ate crepes all day."

"Do you see any fucking crepes around here?" Jonah asked.

"Jeanine," I said. "We should go. He isn't going to help us."

"They always told us in school," Jeanine said, "that prophets get the best of everything."

"Have I not made myself clear? I'm very busy and if I don't make my quota the high priests will get rid of me. I'm not just some small town prophet who can make a few salvation and damnation reports and then spend the rest of the day lounging around and drinking in dive bars. This is The First City Prophet Headquarters, and things are different here."

In a nearby office someone screamed and swore, then threw a heavy object at the wall.

"Let's go," I said.

"I missed you," Jeanine said.

She traced a small pattern against Jonah's back. He stiffened.

"Prophets always have to make sacrifices."

"He's more scared than we are," I said. "Look at him. He's closer to God than any of us and he's terrified."

"I'm calling the guard," Jonah said.

He picked up his phone and began dialing for the guard. Jeanine grabbed the phone out of his hand and slammed the receiver against the side of his desk. Jonah jumped out of his seat. She tried to pull him by his tie, but when she tugged it unraveled from his skinny neck and fell to the ground.

"Don't you dare call the guard on us," she said. "I haven't seen you in ten whole years, and you can't even give me five minutes? Who are you?"

"Who are you?" Jonah asked.

He jabbed a finger into her oozing head wound. Jeanine cried out and jerked backward.

She hit her head against the wall. I rushed over to help her, but she pushed me away and wheeled around, panting, to face her brother. She opened her mouth as if to speak, but said nothing. Her hands clutched and dragged across her face, as if checking to see if she still had her head.

"Who are you, Jeanine?" Jonah repeated. "You want to know who I am, but you're the one with a hole going straight to your brain. You think I've changed? As far as I'm concerned you're dead and all that's standing in front of me is some stranger wearing my sister's worn out body."

"Will you be quiet?" the prophet in the adjacent room screamed. "Some of us are trying to work!"

"Shut up!" Jonah screamed back.

He grabbed his chair and hurled it at the wall. It smashed into pieces.

"Don't talk to her like that," I said to Jonah. "You know she doesn't deserve that."

"And who the hell are you again?" Jonah asked me. "Get out of my office. This isn't a public forum where you can just walk in and voice your complaints."

He picked up the phone receiver again. The shiny sphere in the back of his head turned heated red on the edges and white in the center, like a wound full of venom.

"We'll leave," I said.

My voice came out slow and calm, even though my body shook.

"Just put down the phone. We'll leave if you put it down, and we won't come back."

"You expect to make demands on me?" Jonah said, but when Jeanine and I moved toward the door, he put the phone receiver back into the cradle.

"I'm telling Mom," Jeanine called from the hallway.

Jonah slumped against his desk. I closed the door behind us and we headed back toward the elevator.

"What a bastard," Jeanine said as we went up in the elevator.

She leaned against the elevator wall. She pressed her palms against her eyes and tried to hide her tears from me.

Six

OUTSIDE WE FOUND Slim Sarah's celebration parade in full swing. Floats made to look like bloody fetuses, children's hair, and murder weapons lined the streets. Apocalypse Brigadiers and people streaked with fake homemade blood danced on top of the floats and in the middle of the road. Others banged on drums and kettles, blew trumpets, brandished meat tenderizers, or carried signs with Slim Sarah's face printed onto them. Parents smeared their children with blue and yellow powder to resemble the bruises of a corpse, and carried them on their shoulders.

"What is going on? Who is Slim Sarah?" Jeanine asked.

We held hands to avoid getting lost in the crowd and walked as close to the sides of the buildings as possible.

"She killed her children," I said, "so God threw her a parade."

"Horrible."

"I know."

"She's so ugly. Couldn't God have picked someone prettier?"

A loudspeaker boomed from atop one of the floats.

"Hello citizens of The First City City! Today we are here to celebrate the extraordinary devotion of Slim Sarah. Not since Abraham has a person shown such obedience to the glorious maker of Heaven and Earth. We should all take Slim Sarah as our role model, and learn to be more receptive to the commands of our supreme father. Let's celebrate for God!"

The crowd cheered. I pressed my hands to my ears to try and block out the noise.

"Where do we go now?" Jeanine screamed into my ear.

"I don't know," I mouthed.

"Slim Sarah! Slim Sarah!" the crowd chanted.

Jeanine pointed to the woods north of The First City, just underneath the shadow of God's castle. I nodded. We headed into the street and moved toward the trees.

A man wearing a bloody baby head mask slammed into my side and knocked me on the ground. When I scrambled to my feet, Jeanine was gone.

"Jeanine!" I called out, but I knew I'd lost her.

Costumed people assaulted me on all sides. They knocked me onto the ground again and again. Blood filled my mouth. My palms scraped raw against the pavement.

"Slim Sarah! Slim Sarah!"

I crawled away from the street on my hands and knees to avoid being crushed by a parade float. Someone kicked me in the ribs. The pain shuddered up my bones and into my stomach. I called out for Jeanine again, but I couldn't even hear my own voice.

"Slim Sarah! Slim Sarah! Slim Sarah!"

Slim Sarah passed by on a red parade float. She sat slumped on a plastic throne, her dogface even more bloated and jaundiced in real life than on the television. She wore a crown of white flowers and a purple robe. Her single remaining child, shy Meadow, crouched at the foot of the plastic throne in a dirty white gown.

The more the people cheered the further Slim Sarah sank down into her throne.

I reached the edge of the street and managed to get up. I pushed past women lifting up their skirts and revealing the wasp hives glued to their thighs. I dodged past men shoving charbroiled plastic body parts into my face, and I ran out of the city toward the trees.

The sun sank down into the western desert sands, turning the air cold. The black moon emerged from the treetops. Behind me, the parade continued to rage. I ran into the woods.

"Jeanine!"

A low groan answered in response. The trees shivered.

"Jeanine?" I whispered.

I walked further into the woods. Between the leaves metal flashed. The trees opened up into a clearing, and in the middle of the clearing I found a cage.

The cage was full of prophets and saints.

They stood together naked and stripped. Someone had cut their hair and stripped them of their magic staffs and flamethrowers. They'd ripped the whispering machines from their chests and pried the shiny spheres out of their heads, leaving them hollowed out.

"Charles, is that you?"

I approached the cage.

"Who said that?"

"In here."

Jonah spoke to me from inside the cage. He motioned for me to come closer, and then pressed a finger to his lips in a gesture of silence. I touched the bars of the cage. They were so cold my fingers stuck to the iron. Jonah pressed his forehead against the bars and left cold red marks against his face.

"Where's Jeanine?" he whispered.

"I don't know. I lost her back in the parade."

"Is she dead?"

"I don't know. Maybe."

The prophets and saints huddled together, some trying to cover their nakedness. Some were brain damaged from the removal of their implants. They scratched marks at the corners of their mouths and plucked at the tender wells of their wrists. They sat on the floor of the cage with their heads between their knees in states of delirium and bad dreams.

"What are you doing in there?" I asked.

"I've fallen from grace," Jonah said. "I told you I was behind quota. Couldn't keep up the demands of being a prophet of God. I haven't slept for months, you know, not really. Or maybe it's been years. Hard to tell."

I said nothing.

"Anyway, since you're here now, I wanted to tell you I'm sorry for kicking you out of my office. It wasn't your fault for what happened to me, or Jeanine's, for that matter. I knew I was going to be punished like this for quite a long time."

"Punished?" I asked. "You're a prophet. Prophets don't get punished."

"If you want to ignore the evidence," Jonah said.

He tilted his head and pointed to the empty space where his shiny satellite used to be.

"See this? Now Jeanine and I both have holes. We can never go back to who we used to be."

"Charles?" someone else called from inside the cage. "Charles from Edgewater? Your sister is Theresa?"

"Yeah," I said. "That's me."

Another prophet appeared beside Jonah at the bars of the cage.

"Ezekiel?"

"Nice to see you again, Charles," he said.

"What are you doing in here?"

"I fucked your mom."

"What?"

Ezekiel laughed.

"Just kidding. You should have seen the look on your face. Got any cigarettes?"

"No," I said. "Sorry."

"Too bad. Well, as you can clearly see, I've fallen from grace. Just like Jonah, Just like everyone else. Daniel and Elijah over there didn't have high enough conversion rates. Moses forgot to circumcise his baby. The women over in the corner? Saints who couldn't perform enough miracles."

"I don't understand," I repeated, my voice a whisper, "I thought you stopped seeing me back in Edgewater because you thought I was a heretic."

"They took me away the night I killed Smarts. Seems I'd been on God's shit list for a long time. We all fall from grace sooner or later. Maybe one day you forget to look both ways when you cross the street, and then it's all over for you. God casts you out of his sight forever."

"What about forgiveness?"

All the prophets and saints laughed.

"Do they still teach that to the kids in school," Ezekiel asked. "Forgiveness?"

I said nothing.

"Hey, can I ask you something?" Jonah said to me. "If you ever see Jeanine again, can you tell her something? Tell her... tell her that-"

"-That you loved her, right?" I asked.

"Don't tell her that. It's too late for that."

Another groan shook the earth and the trees. Whatever it was, it was getting closer.

"It's time for you to leave, Charles," Ezekiel

said.

"What should I tell Jeanine?"

"Oh, I don't know," Jonah said, and laughed this miserable, dry laugh. "Tell her I still don't give a damn about her."

"Didn't you hear me?" Ezekiel said. "Leave. Do you want to die? Charles. Look at me. You need to leave."

I pressed my face against the cold bars. I tightened my grip on the bars until my nails cracked.

"I need to know what God wants from us."

"If we knew that do you think we'd be in here?" Jonah asked.

"Where do monsters come from?" I asked. "Why do slip implants exist? And why did that murderer get a giant parade thrown for her?"

Ezekiel threw up his hands.

"Okay, I'll tell you what I know. Seeing as how we've got about three minutes left to live, I might as well make the best of it. And I actually liked you, Charles. You know, before you started hanging out with that crazy ass bitch and avoiding me."

"We know the end times are approaching," Jonah said, "God threw Slim Sarah a parade to set an example for others. To cow us into obedience right before the end."

"But you make it sound so foreboding when you say it like that," Ezekiel said, and rolled his eyes.

"When is the world ending?" I asked."

We know it's going to happen soon, but we don't know when," Ezekiel said. "We really don't know anything. We're given the quotas by the high priests, we're told how many sinners to damn, how many miracles to perform, etcetera, and even the high priests themselves don't know anything."

"You decide who gets sent to the shuttles?" I asked.

"Yes," Ezekiel said. "But it's completely arbitrary. A random process. We just have to fill the quotas the high priests give us, and it doesn't matter how. When you get sent to hell, just consider yourself unlucky."

"Everyone's a sinner, right?" Jonah said.

Another groan. The ground shook, and I struggled to stand upright. Several of the prophets and saints inside of the cage cried out and held onto each other.

Ezekiel reached through the bars of the cage and grasped my shirt.

"Get out of here, Charles."

"Why are you so worked up?" Jonah asked him. "He'll be dead soon enough. He's searching for his girlfriend or something like that. Couldn't even see that my sister was in love with him."

"Jeanine wasn't in love with me."

"Are you really that ignorant? Why else would she risk her life coming here to help you? You're looking for someone who's probably dead, when you had Jeanine all along. But now she's gone too, and it's all your fault."

"Maybe if you would have helped us this wouldn't have happened," I said.

"I hardly had a role to play when it came to you dragging my sister halfway across the world on a mad quest to look for a dead woman."

"Why do you even care?" I asked. "You were so concerned with yourself you wouldn't speak to her after being estranged for over ten years."

The slow and lumbering footsteps were getting closer. I thought the earth might split apart.

"You know I couldn't have helped you," Jonah said.

"I'm really glad I get to spend the last few seconds of my life listening to you two bitch at each other," Ezekiel said. "This is a great way to go out, let me tell you."

"I'm not finished asking you questions yet," I said to Ezekiel.

"I'm not going to be able to tell you what you want to know," Ezekiel said, "but I can tell you this."

Ezekiel's dark eyes were shiny and hard as glass.

"The human brain has the unique ability to doubt the reality presented to itself. To comprehend the dissonance between ideas and the truth of the surrounding world. God knows this, and it infuriates him. It terrifies him."

"There's no point in telling him that," Jonah said.

Ezekiel ignored him and continued speaking. "From the moment we are born we are forced into fear. Even the prophets and saints, even the high priests. A human in fear can be easily manipulated."

I breathed heavy, as if I couldn't force enough air through my lungs. I grasped the bars of the cage until I thought the bones in my wrists might break. The musky scent of a dirty animal, oak, rot, and hair, blew through the trees.

"Remember that," Ezekiel said. "Remember why you shouldn't be afraid."

"It won't do him any good when he goes back to Edgewater and the flood waters rise up to his neck," Jonah said.

"I'm not going back," I said. "I'm going to search for Jeanine. And if you're right about her, if she really does love me, then I'll quit and go home. I won't put her through anymore of this. But if I can't find Jeanine, then I'm going to keep searching for Leda."

"She's dead, and you know it. You've run out of options."

"Maybe. It doesn't matter," I said. "I'm still going to the ocean."

A chilled shadow loomed over the cage. Several of the prophets and saints looked up in its direction.

"One more thing," I said. "Is God real?"

"Oh, he's real all right," Ezekiel said. "And you better hope you never meet the son of a bitch."

A monster approached the cage. His body expanded between the trees as if to fill the entirety of space. His hooves scraped crescent shapes into the dirt. He had an elongated deer face, with a quivering brown nose and blue woman eyes. His velvet tipped antlers, draped in kudzu, and bloodied clothing, rose upwards like the branches of a tree, snarled and growing upwards.

"Get the fuck out of here, Charles," Ezekiel said.

The monster ripped open the door of the iron cage. He grabbed a prophet in his enormous, leathery hands and crushed him. Blood spurted from out between the monster's fingers and the prophet died with his spine piercing his tongue.

"Thank you," I whispered to Ezekiel as the monster tore off half his head.

Ezekiel's face went blank and his eyes turned pale. He slumped face down to the floor of the cage and the empty space in the back of his head filled up with incandescent blood, almost like a pool of oil. The monster then grabbed Jonah and ripped his throat out with his teeth.

As I ran, I expected the screaming to start, as it always did. But I only heard the quiet chuffing of the monster's breath and the breaking of bones.

Seven

THE PARADE ENDED by the time I got back to the city. Floats and masks lay discarded in the streets. On televisions across the city Teddy hovered on a string over Delilah's supine body.

"I declare this parade a smashing success!" he said.

Delilah laughed and convulsed.

I roamed the streets searching for Jeanine, calling her name. The police approached me.

"You need to leave," one of them said.

"I'm looking for a girl," I said.

"The parade is over."

"I think she loved me and I can't find her."

They laughed at me.

"Go home. People get lost all time. And she probably didn't love you anyways."

I tried to squeeze my hands into fists, but I had no energy left. They remained limp and sick by my sides.

"Why are you still here? We told you she didn't love you."

"It doesn't matter, whether she did or not," I said, my voice hoarse. "I still love her. At least, I think I did once."

"Get the fuck out of here."

I left The First City and collapsed outside its walls in the desert.

A girl in a vellum dress found me face down in the sand. She circled around me for a long time, making noises like a vulture. I couldn't move. The heat ensconced me like a second skin. Eventually the girl grabbed me by the ankles and dragged me down into the ruins of an abandoned temple.

Inside the temple she hauled me on top of a slab of concrete and rolled me over onto my back. I opened my eyes and the mosaic of a blank faced monster on the ceiling stared at me.

She stripped off what remained of my clothes and drew symbols on my chest with red paint.

"I'm not dead yet," I said.

"Yes you are," she said.

She stuck a finger into my mouth. I bit the tip of her nail and she jerked her hand back.

The girl pulled her hair away from her face, and I saw it had been burned away. Her eyes were caverns of empty space. Her cheeks were chasms full of powder. When she turned her head her rotting teeth were visible underneath her translucent skin.

She pulled a knife out from beneath the folds of her dress. I gripped the edges of the slab. I realized I sat on a sacrificial stone.

A sacrificial altar.

"Let's not hurt each other," I said.

She growled and lunged at me. I kicked her face and it collapsed. The knife clattered away and the girl hit the floor. I rolled off the concrete slab and dragged myself across the floor toward her. She ceased breathing, and her face no longer resembled anything human.

"I'm so sorry," I said.

I buried my face in her dirty hair.

For a long time I knelt beside her on the floor, stroking her burnt neck and shoulders and arms. I called her Leda. I called her Jeanine. She crumbled into dust.

When I finally let her go, I explored the room and found her living space in the corner, underneath the icon of a monster with seven heads and seventeen arms. She once slept on a thin pallet, and the only possessions she owned were a few bottles, syringes, candles, and some rations. I drank her water and ate what little rations she had left. I retrieved my bloodied clothes from the floor, put them back on, and stepped over the girl's dissolving body toward the exit.

I found myself lost in the ruins of the abandoned temple. It stretched out in all directions, and it was much larger than the temple Ezekiel and I once explored outside of Edgewater. The mosaics on the walls depicted the same sort of strange monsters I'd seen as a child, many legged, many armed, with lash whip tongues and scepters of light in their mouths.

Looking for the way out to the desert, I uncovered abandoned room upon abandoned room. I found one with a fountain in the likeness of a headless stone monster with wings and a hovering halo, crouching over the dry spout. I found another room another empty except for the bloodstains splashed upon the ceiling and the walls. I found a small room with a sacrificial altar drenched in dried black and red fluids, vegetable husks and beaded jewelry scattered onto the floor.

Occasionally I came to a window looking out across the desert sky. Yet even though I could see the outside world, inside the temple I felt at the center of the universe, outside of time. Inside the temple, searching for the way out, retracing my steps and passing the dead girl over and over again, I'd finally found a place swept aside by God and abandoned by the circle of eternity.

I came across sandstone pictograms in the last hallway. The first pictogram depicted the black moon threatening to swallow the earth as it hovered over the black planet. Once-glittering machine shells floated around the moon like birds. Monsters waited below the moon with open mouths, as if ready to swallow the shells.

In the next pictogram, the machine shells were hurtling to the planet below. In the next, the machines fought the monsters and tore them apart.

From childhood we were taught that nothing changed. When bones sank downwards they sank into the darkness forever. Butterflies never metamorphosed, and remained untouched and dead inside shadow boxes. Inside the pagan temple I realized the world had once been different, and I'd never realized it before.

Nobody had, yet the evidence existed all around us. I saw it for only a moment as a child in the temple out in the woods, and now it'd come back for me.

I came across a black room without windows or mosaics. It was painted so dark that it seemed like a sphere without shadows or corners. I thought if I entered the room, I would fall down into an abyss.

Yet when I touched the floor the room lit up. A storm of living fire blew from one end of the room to the other. An immense cloud heavy with lightning rose to the ceiling, swirling with white light.

I jerked back as if burned. When I stumbled out of the room back into the hallway, the light and the storm shut down, casting the room back into darkness.

The fire had passed through me without hurting me.

I stepped back into the room and the fire once more blew through the room. This time, I didn't fall back into the hallway. The cloud rose once more and lightning struck the center of the room. The glowing fire danced upon the walls, the floor. I held my hands out toward the storm and it flowed straight through me.

Shapes emerged out of the fire and the lightning. They kept shifting in and out of different forms, with no discernable identities. One minute the figures seemed to have wings and the heads of animals. The next they dissolved into abstract shapes, wheels and intersecting locks and glittering, geometric curves.

A voice emanated from the center of the room.

"Stand on your feet and I will speak to you," it said.

"Hello?" I called out.

I grasped my shirt. My face and hands broke out in sweat.

"Stand on your feet and I will speak to you."

"Hello?" I repeated. "I don't understand."

"Stand on your feet and I will speak to you."

"Who are you?"

"Stand on your feet and I will speak to you."

"What do you want?"

"Stand on your feet and I will speak to you."

The fire continued to blow through me. The cloud of lightning expanded until it filled the entire ceiling. The light in the center of the room grew so intense that I had to shield my eyes. A hiss filled the room, like gas escaping from a valve. The cloud shook.

I stepped back into the hallway. The room dropped back into blackness. Into silence.

"Are you still there?" I called to the black room.

No reply.

"Hello?"

No reply

I left the room and went back down the hallway. Soon I found my way out of the temple and back into the pale desert. I kept touching my arms, my face, as if my skin might blow away.

Eight

AN ELECTRICIAN APPROACHED ME as I lay half-dead on the steps in front of his office. I didn't remember traveling through the desert to that town. I didn't remember collapsing on the steps. I only remembered a dream in which I bent down to drink from a pool of water that transformed into Leda's hair, dreaming that wherever the sun burned me the girl I murdered in the pagan temple was touching me with her crumbling tongue.

The electrician cupped his hand under my nose to see if I was still breathing. He woke me up from my stupor with the creaking, of his arthritic bones and the smell of leather.

"Did the monsters get you, son?"

I grasped his hand. He squeezed my wrist gently in response. I tried to speak, but only gasped.

"What was that, son?" the electrician said.

His words were slow and cracked. He spoke like a fragile relic.

"Have I made it yet?" I managed to say.

"Where were you hoping to make it to?"

"The ocean," I said.

"No more than a few hours to the east."

"Thank you," I said.

I passed out in his arms.

I woke up a few moments later, sick and lightheaded, with my head against his chest. He laid his hands against my back, and he attempted to pull me up off the steps. I passed out again.

The next time I awoke, I found myself inside the electrician's shop, lying on top of his desk beside an industrial fan. The electrician held out a glass of water for me to take, and I sat up trembling.

"Sip it slowly," he said.

"You're crazy for helping me," I said.

"I already checked you for weapons when you were passed out. I learned my lesson when the last one tried to steal my kidneys."

I tried to get off the desk.

"Hold on," the electrician said. "You better slow down unless you want to have a heatstroke. Just sit tight and don't make any trouble for me."

I sighed and lay back down.

"You're the one who brought me here."

"Would you rather be dead?"

"Okay," I said. "No trouble."

The electrician turned to his work desk, which was cluttered with wires, busted light boxes, gutted out appliances. He picked up a screwdriver and unscrewed the plate off the back of a television.

"What's your name?" I asked.

"The electrician," he said.

I closed my eyes and passed in and out of unconscious several times. The electrician brought me more water to drink, then some of his dry rations. I took slow bites and chewed a long time before swallowing.

A large calico cat and a brown kitten walked into the room. They wrestled each other beside the desk, mewling and spitting. The electrician tossed them a small mechanical toy resembling a horse. The mechanical horse fell on its side and its legs whirred. It moved in circles on the floor. The cats batted the toy until it ceased moving.

Maybe I was too dehydrated, too malnourished, but I thought the mechanical horse might be kicking me in the teeth. Something about the way the cats slunk around the toy, as if it was a stranger, a monster, made me think that a fundamental rule of physics in the universe had been suddenly and inexplicably altered. The mechanical horse seemed enormous and everything else small.

I got off the desk and left the electrician's office. While I was walking down the steps, the electrician caught the front door before it closed.

"Where are you going?"

"That horse is scaring the shit out of me."

"What?"

"Forget it. It doesn't matter," I said.

"Why don't you stay for a while?" he asked me.

I looked back at the electrician. He stood in the doorway touching a white scar on his throat.

"You remind me too much of my father," I

said.

"I remind everyone of their father," the electrician said. "You shouldn't leave so soon. Come home and have dinner with my family. I'll see you make it onto the bus tomorrow. To the ocean."

I wanted to protest. I wanted to tell him I wasn't falling for his tricks, I may look young but I wasn't born yesterday, oh no sir. I knew he probably wanted to take me home so his family could murder me and store my body with a bunch of other young idiots in his attic

Instead, I collapsed again in the streets and hit my head against the dirt. The electrician picked me up and took me back into his office. I lay on the desk underneath the fan while he wrapped a bandage around my bleeding head. I was shaking and weak and overheated.

"I'll stay," I said, my voice a murmur. "I'll stay. Just put that horse where I can't see it."

He picked up the horse toy and shut it into a closet. He went back to his workbench. I stayed on the desk until he closed his office for the day.

As we walked to this home I clutched his shoulder to keep from falling. We approached his porch and I let go for a moment, wobbled, trying not to fall.

When we got to his front door, he stopped.

"I should tell you something," he said.

"What?"

"Just don't be surprised by anything that

happens next."

He swung the front door open. His daughter and his wife sat at a candlelit dining table, waiting in front of a meal of breaded catfish, jelly, fried bread, and wedding cake. They folded their arms in front themselves on the table, the silverware in perfect alignment with their fingertips. The wife wore a black smock and animal red shoes. Around her neck hung an eye sized, pale green jewel.

The daughter wore a wedding dress.

"Where did you get all this food?" was all I could think to say.

"We're so glad you're here," the wife said. "Ever since my daughter's fiancé died we haven't had much company. Would you like to see his ghost picture? We purchased it from a psychic."

On the wall behind her there was a framed picture of an almost indiscernible figure floating in a black space. Brilliant light of all different colors swelled on the figure's body. Thin filaments of hair splayed out from the figure's head in all directions. Hair colored orange and blue.

"It's fake," I said.

"No, I'm positive he was a real psychic. Won't you sit down?" the wife said.

"What is this?" I asked the electrician.

"Sit down for a while and have something to eat," he said.

The electrician touched my shoulder. Then he touched the white scar on his throat.

"I'm sure you're hungry."

I sat down in the chair opposite the daughter in the wedding dress.

"What's your name?" I asked.

"Call me Mrs. Fredrick," the daughter said in a scarred, scratched voice.

I couldn't see her face hidden behind the veil.

I grabbed a biscuit, trying to hide the fact that my fingers were shaking, that the blood swelled in my ears like a swarm of bees.

"So where are you from?" the electrician's wife asked me.

"Edgewater," I said.

"I've never heard of it," she said.

"Mother," Mrs. Frederick said, and she shook her head. "We've been through this before. You know where he's from."

The wife touched the jewel on her necklace with her needle thin fingers.

"Don't ask questions like that, " the daughter said. "Not when you know the answers."

"Settle down," the electrician said. "Let's try to enjoy our dinner, shall we?"

We ate for a while in silence. I couldn't remember the last time ate a full meal, but I felt like I couldn't swallow the food in front of me. I couldn't drink the water, as if I was dying of rabies and the sight of it sunk me with fear.

I turned to the electrician.

"How did Mr. Fredrick die?" I asked.

"The shuttles took him."

"I think it was all the pre-marital sex," the wife whispered to me.

She cut up her fish in precise, triangular shapes. She watched her food as if it might attack her.

"Would you like some wine?" the daughter asked me.

"No thank you," I said.

As if she hadn't heard me, she uncorked a bottle of wine and poured a glass. I watched her take a capsule from her sleeve and pour a white, powdery substance into the glance. She pushed the glass toward me, chunks of powder still floating on top of the wine.

"What is that?" I asked.

Of course, no one asked me.

"Aren't you hungry?" she said. "You've barely touched your food."

"I don't think I can eat anymore."

"It's a special occasion."

She glanced at my untouched glass of wine. In her wedding dress she appeared less of a person and more like a dolled up broken light bulb.

"I should be going," I said.

"You must stay the night," the daughter said. "It's too dangerous out there for you to leave right now."

"Where am I going to sleep?" I asked.

"In my room, of course. It's too cold to sleep

out on the couch."

"Is this why you brought me here?" I asked the electrician.

"Come upstairs," the daughter said. "You can get undressed and I'll make the bed for you."

"I don't think this is necessary," I said, my voice quiet.

"I have everything prepared," she said.

"You don't need me to do this."

"There is no one left," she said.

I stood up abruptly.

"You brought me here so that your daughter could play dress up?" I asked the electrician. "A wedding dinner followed by a wedding night?"

"Mr. Frederick," the daughter called me.

"Is that who I am to you?" I asked, "Your dead fiancé?"

"You're so silly," Mrs. Fredrick said. "Come on upstairs. I'll undress you myself."

"This isn't the first time you've done this, is it?" I asked. "And you two, you just help her continue her delusion."

The electrician and his wife looked down at their dinner plates.

"Listen to me. You still have your father. And your mother. Most people don't even have that. You think you can't love again, but you will, if only you stop these stupid games."

"But we have all this wedding cake," she said.

"I'm leaving," I said.

The electrician stood up.

"Please don't go," he said.

"Don't you see what you're doing?" I asked.

"Why don't we all just calm down," the wife said. "Have you tried the jelly? Have another piece of bread."

"We're all making this world worse than it needs to be," I said. "God hates us. He even hates his own prophets. He sends plague machines to kill us and hell shuttles to take us away. And what do we do? We become serial killers and madmen. We turn each other into slaves. We cut ourselves off from love. We destroy each other better than God ever could."

"Mr. Fredrick, you're obviously not feeling well," the daughter said.

"That was a nice speech," the electrician said to me. "But it's obvious you're as mad as any of us."

"Probably, but I'm still going to the ocean. The person I'm searching for is probably gone forever, but I'm going to keep searching until I'm dead."

I headed for the front door. The daughter ran after me and grabbed my arm. She pushed her veil away, revealing her blank, white face, her electric eyes, her pouting mouth - the unmovable, eternal bride.

"Please don't go," she said.

"Can't you see what you're doing to yourself?"

"It's dangerous out there."

"It's dangerous everywhere."

I pried her fingers off my arm and went outside. She cried out and it was a bloody, hollow sound. As I took off down the path someone turned on the television in the living room of the house.

"These are the ends times, ladies and gentlemen," Teddy said. "A time when the faith of the people will be tested. Slim Sarah is not the only one who has been put on trial, but her exemplary submission should be applauded. Only those who prove their obedience and purify themselves in God's name, will be spared."

I heard the electrician walking behind me.

"The blood of the sinners will flow through the streets. There shall be no mercy for those who oppose me."

Not Teddy speaking anymore, but God.

I stopped.

“Don’t follow me,” I told the electrician.

"I came to give you this. To get to the ocean."

He held money out towards me. I wanted to refuse it, but then I thought of Leda, and I took it from his hands.

"I'm a heretic," I said. “Did you know that?"

"I hope you get where you need to be," he said, "Nobody does, but I still hope you do."

We stood facing each other outside in the dark, with television noise rushing past us.

"You were brave in there. With my daughter," the electrician said.

"You wanted me to refuse her?"

"She needed that."

Television static invaded my body. It picked me up and rattled me. I stumbled forward and stones caught in my shoes.

"I'm so scared," I whispered.

"Let that fear push you forward. Let it take you to the very end."

"I am the beginning and the end. I am all powerful and all knowing," God said, "and I will bring destruction to this cursed land."

"Where can I find the bus stop?" I asked the electrician.

He told me.

"Thank you," I said.

I left him on the path and headed in the direction of the bus stop. I got lost in the dark and ended up roaming the woods for a few hours searching for the way back to the path.

In a small clearing, under the glare of the black moon, a girl thrashed in the weeds.

"Hello?" I called out. "Are you okay?"

The girl continued thrashing, her body rigid with convulsions. I reached out to touch her, but then I realized she wasn't a girl at all.

She was a monster. A small, wiry monster with tusks jutting from her chin and ragged black claws on her hands. Her protruding teeth dripped with poison. She whined and snarled, seemingly oblivious to my presence.

I thought of the mechanical horse toy in the

electrician's office. I thought of how it landed on its back but continued to move its legs, turning itself into a circle. That horse moved just like the monster on the ground.

The dread I felt watching the toy horse returned. Stronger this time. I couldn't move for a long time. I could only watch the monster kicking its legs, turning in circles on the ground. A monster seemingly unharmed except for some sort of sickness. I thought if nobody stopped it, then the monster might be trapped in this clearing forever in painful, perpetual motion.

. Turning as if from the beginning of time, it had been in this clearing, trapped forever in perpetual motion. Unable to touch or be touched.

Then the monster stopped moving, and its limbs dissolved into dust and blew away.

I found my way out of the woods and to the bus stop, but the image of the thrashing monster and the mechanical horse toy stayed with me. I coughed up dust. I coughed and coughed.

Nine

THE BUS DROVE FROM the desert to the mountains, and down toward the remnants of the coastal town. The ocean resembled a gray block of stone. Empty buildings lay across the landscape like bleached whalebones. Only as the bus neared the water did the ocean came to life. The early morning sun stirred the stone into waves and churned the gray into blue.

"I've never seen the ocean before," I told the bus driver.

I was the only passenger left on the bus.

"It's where everyone goes to die," he said. "My cousin dug himself an oubliette in the sand. Nobody ever did find him."

When I got off at the final bus stop, I couldn't think of Jeanine or Leda, Sissy or Momma. I thought only of the ocean.

I took my bloodied shoes off in the sand and peeled the last remnants of my shirt away. As I approached the water, I saw objects bobbing in the waves, others half-buried in the sand or encrusted in salt and seaweed.

They were deadhead corpses. Even with burst lungs and broken fingers and nerves turning to glue, the hot wire spiders inside their heads still clicked inside their heads. I was about to turn back, nauseated.

Then a voice spoke to me from the water. The waves drowned out the syllables, made the words unintelligible, but I heard it. There was a voice out there.

I waded out into the ocean and the water drank at my cuts and bruises. The water breathed with me, in and out. A deadhead child's hair brushed against my ankles before the current swept her body away.

I swam to a giant metal structure laid on its side, half-jutting out of the ocean. I grasped its side and struggled to keep hold of it while the waves beat against my arms and face. I bent my head down and curled my entire body against the structure.

The voice spoke to me, and this time I could make out the words.

"Hello? Hello? Is anyone there? We haven't heard from anyone out there in a long time. We can't access any of the regular communication devices. It seems something has disabled most of the broadcasting towers. We're not even sure this message will reach anyone. If anyone can hear this, we want you to know that we're sending help. Don't be afraid. Help is coming soon. Don't be afraid. Hello? Hello? Is anyone there?"

The voice repeated itself over and over again. As I clung to the structure, numb and gasping for breath and being beat on all sides by the waves, I realized the voice was not coming out of the ocean. It was coming out of the metal structure and the structure was a broadcasting tower. It was another thing forgotten like the temples and the pictograms.

"Hello? Hello? Is anyone there? We haven't heard from anyone out there in a long time."

I didn't want to let go of the tower and the thousand miles voice. I struggled to hold on as long as I could.

"Don't be afraid. Help is coming soon. Don't be afraid."

I kept my head above the water and kicked the churning water underneath me. The water rushed over my head. I held my breath. The waves receded. I breathed.

"Help is coming soon. Don't be afraid."

I couldn't hold on any longer. I let go of the tower and the waves carried me away. My body washed up onto the shore. I heard the echo of the words repeating themselves over and over again.

"Don't be afraid."

I lay trembling, facedown in the sand. The waves washed over my bare feet I tried to hold onto the message of the voice underneath the ocean's roar. Maybe if I concentrated long enough I could trap the words inside my limbs and never be afraid again.

Someone grabbed my arm and tried to pull me out of the water.

"No," I said. "Let go!"

I thrashed, trying to get away. I tried to open my eyes and see who had grabbed me, but the saltwater stung too badly.

I grabbed fistfuls of woman's hair. I dragged her down into the sand with me and held her head under the water. Her body convulsed. She grasped at the sand and her body bristled electric. A whisper from the tower passed through her hair.

"Don't be afraid."

She reared her head out of the water and busted my lip. The saltwater burned on my cut mouth. She shook me until my head rattled. I tried to grab her neck. I scratched her collarbone with my fingernails.

"Stop it," she said, still shaking me. "Please stop. I thought you were dead."

"Okay, I'm stopping," I said, each word a gasp.

She released me. I clambered to my feet, only to collapse a few feet away from the surf. Deadhead arms reached for my hair, and the furious clicking of the hot wire spiders beat against my ears. My attacker stood in my shadow. I coughed up water and bits of seaweed.

"Someone who was dead once asked me where the road goes," I said, "and I didn't know. But I know now. It goes here."

She leaned over me as a lay in the sand and pressed her wet hands against my forehead.

"I know you," she said.

"I'm sure you do," I said, still coughing. "I'm

a popular dead husband these days."

"Charles," she whispered.

I opened my burning eyes. The first thing I saw was the sea of her hair spilling over me, her hair wine dark and frayed at the ends. I saw her thin mouth and her stretched, yellow skin.

"Leda?"

I parted the dripping hair from her eyes. They were just as I remembered them, dark eyes flecked with spots like stars, eyes nearly too big for her head.

"Leda."

The ocean spray and the sun sent a halo down on her head.

"The voice spoke to you," she said.

"What is it?" I asked. "Where does it come from?"

I kissed her before she could speak. Her mouth was wet and scorched with heat. She took my head in her hands and I held her in my arms. I pressed my lips against her nose, her chin, her throat.

She rocked against me. I clutched at her frayed hair. She kissed every finger of my hand. She pressed my palm against her cheek.

"Why did you leave me?" I found myself asking her.

"Come with me," she said.

She pulled me off the ground. She brushed the sand from my arms and face and led me across the beach toward a house that sat on the cliffs above the water. I nearly collapsed halfway to the house. I would have fallen into the sand if she didn't catch me. We stopped walking for a few minutes. I folded against her body and she held me, silent, as she stroked my hair. I lay my face against her collarbone and clutched at her skeletal back. I felt small and weak against her. She seemed like a house about to slide down and crush me.

"You're so tall and strong," I said. "You were always the strong one."

"I missed you," she said.

"You were dead," I said, "but now you're alive again."

Leda touched my busted lip. My body seized up and I clung to the fabric of her dress. I stumbled and fell to my knees. I couldn't get up. All of my bones curled inward like spiders. They bit into my skin and locked me down into the sand.

I kept clinging to Leda's dress, her white-weave dress, fringed with lace and doused in ocean spray. My Leda, the avatar of the ocean. I expected for her to flee from her dress at any moment, dissolve into the ocean, and leave me alone again. I'd kneel there forever, with nothing left but lace and her scent haunting me.

But she remained with me.

Leda traced the outline of my face, as if unlocking me from a spell. My bones uncurled from their fetal paralysis. I pulled myself to my feet.

We walked up to the house on the cliffs. It stood on a platform that raised itself above the rocks. It was built out of stones the color of smoker's lungs.

Leda opened the door and we went inside. At first I couldn't see in the dark. Leda closed the door behind us. The air inside the house smelled musky and wet.

When my eyes adjusted to the light, I made out a figure sitting in a rocking chair in a corner of the room, her body dripping wet, skin shining like insect eyes, her hair a nest of moss and thorns and bone.

"Charles," Jolene said, and she smiled to show me her bloodstained teeth.

Ten

JOLENE HELD HER HAND out towards me. Her sharp fingers seemed poised to penetrate my skull.

Her body sucked the air out of the room and flattened the objects around her down into two-dimensional space. She smeared the table and the rocking chair like tar against the wall. I smelled burnished feathers and rotting fish scales on her breath.

"We've been waiting for you," Jolene said.

"He doesn't know what this means yet," Leda said.

"I know," I said, my voice quiet. "It means every moment comes back to the first moment."

"Isn't that so?" Jolene said.

Leda tried to get me to sit down in a nearby chair, but I couldn't. I felt my wrists peeling away and my body melting into my ribcage. I imagined the bones of children in the dark corners of the house, the bones of my baby brother, gnawed and chewed and cracked.

I saw myself at the bottom of Jolene's pool, looking up through the green water as Edgewater burned. I saw Momma and Sissy smoking cigarettes and watching television in our dark-creak house as their skin crackled in the flames Every time I tried to emerge from the bottom of the pool to save them, Jolene pinned me underwater with her tiny white feet.

"She's a friend," Leda said to me.

"She's a monster," I said. "She ate my baby brother. She took his enzymes."

I fumbled for the doorknob.

Leda grabbed my shoulder, but I shrugged her off and wrenched the door open. I ran out into the daylight. Leda ran after me.

When I got to the ocean, I fell down in the sand near the tide line.

"I'm not going back in there," I told Leda when she caught up with me.

"There's nowhere else to go," Leda said, "If you didn't think otherwise, you wouldn't have come here."

"You brought Jolene here," I said.

The voice whispered through me once more.

"Don't be afraid."

Spit ran down my chin and in-between my fingers. It coated the sand on my arms.

"She's going to help us," Leda said.

"You're a servant of the monsters," I said. "This is all a ruse, to prove that I'm a heretic."

"Charles—"

"Now you're going to send me to the hell shuttles. Is that it? Is this is what this has been about?"

Leda crouched beside me and touched my forehead. Her black hair covered my eyes. The curve of her nose and mouth fit into the space of my forehead.

"Hush, Charles," she said.

I hushed. Her smell overwhelmed me, calmed me. She smelled like the strange creature that used to crawl into bed with me.

"You know none of that is true," she said. "You've heard the voice."

"But what does it mean?" I asked. "And what does this mean?"

I lifted my head and reached for her hair. I brushed it back to reveal the number six tattooed on her head. The same tattooed number I saw on Smarts' armband the night he died.

She grabbed my hands and pressed them to her waist. Underneath her dress I felt the contours of her dead flower chain. Her body went rigid. I pulled my hands away, and the chain broke. Flowers fell around her bare feet.

"You can't hide this from me anymore," I said.

I released Leda and started sobbing like a child, as I'd never allowed myself to as a child. The surf bowled me over into the sand and grit stuck in my teeth. I crawled away from the water as if it had claws. The sun beat me over the head as if it was a rowdy drunk. The corpses of deadheads bobbed in the water.

Leda ran to me and pulled me again into her embrace, and I thought that all women must come from the ocean, that Leda's heart was made of anemone and her skin was sealskin, slippery and dissolving into the ocean depths.

"Hide this from me and I swear I'll leave," I

said, spitting up chunks of sand and plastic.

"I lied before, when I told you I moved away from the ocean," Leda whispered, her breath quickening.

"I know," I said.

"Why didn't you say anything?" she asked.

"Would you have told the truth if I did?"

"The hell shuttles took me away," Leda said.

"How is that possible? Nobody comes back from hell."

"It's just like in the stories when they take you to the hell shuttles. The guards come in the night, any way they can. They come through the doors and the windows, almost like ghosts, without making a sound except for their shoes. Their shoes sound like piano keys. They wake you up like in a dream, like every nightmare you've ever had, and they pull you out of bed and spin you down the street. And when they march behind you, their piano shoes play gospel hymns.

"It doesn't matter what you say, what you ask, or what you promise, there is no escape. They pull you into the line at the end of the block. There you wait with the other prisoners, your neighbors and childhood friends, for the hell shuttles to arrive. I waited for hours in the cold dark. There was no light except for the flare of the guard's cigarettes. When a guard pinched a girl's arm and she cried out, all the neighbors closed their curtains with a crack."

“Then what happened?” I asked.

“I was a good girl,” Leda said. “I never cussed or made people angry or went after the neighbor’s dog with a hunting bow. I prayed around the television with my family. But none of that mattered. When the hell shuttles came the guards shoved us in like cattle and they drove us down into the earth, down into the place where we could never come back. The guards stripped me of my clothes and shaved my head. They told me I was filthy and worthless. I was the gutter trash scraped up from the bottom of the world. They told they crossed my name out of the book of life, and I would be cast into the lake of fire for all eternity."

"It doesn't mean a damn thing, no matter what you do," I said. "Ezekiel told me. It's completely random, who goes to hell. Who lives and who dies."

“They read out a list of my sins” Leda said. “Everything I ever did wrong. I don’t even remember if they were true or not, but I couldn’t think. Down there, you don’t own your thoughts. I tried to imagine the ocean and the flowers in the floral shop, something good and untainted. I tried to remember what it felt like to be rocked in my mother’s arms. I wanted a cocoon memory that I could crawl in. But there was nothing. That place stripped all goodness away until there was nothing left.”

“They always warn us about hell,” I said.

"But they never tell us what it means."

"When I saw the tattooing needles they laid out for me I tried to run away, run straight through the concrete wall. They held my arms to the floor and one guard pinned my neck underneath his boot. He said I had a bird neck, a broken bird body, that the problem with birds was that they were always trying to fly away, breaking themselves against windowpanes. He said he wanted to make love to me if only he could remember how to do it. Then they tattooed the number six onto me. It's an identification number. Block six. Where they put the heretics.

"In hell there are big rows of gleaming machines, a faceless army of machines. These machines have only one purpose. To torture us. They made us freezing cold one day, burning hot the next. They made the air prick us like pins and sear our skin. Some of them the machines had jaws like animals, mouths full of steel fangs. Others repeated words all day and night so we couldn't sleep, things like, 'There is no hope. You deserve this pain. There is no hope.'

Leda's hands shook as she held onto me. She bowed her head so I couldn't see her face, only the black strands of her hair, the dark tattoo of the number six.

"Don't stop talking, please," I said.

"This woman named Hadley found me trying to kill myself by ramming my head into the concrete wall. Except I couldn't do it, because my bare feet kept slipping on the frozen floor.

"Hadley pressed her fingers into my temples. She said, 'You know you're the bravest person in here?' I spit up blood on her fingers, but she didn't pull away. 'I can see you with my eyes closed,' she said. 'You glow like an atomic bomb.'

"'Does this seem brave to you?' I asked Hadley, 'standing in the corner like a dog, trying to kill myself? I've forgotten what it's like to be human.'

"Her body was small and straight like it hung off a clothesline, her skin like talcum powder.

"Hadley looked at me and I saw iron weapons in her eyes. If she wanted to, she could have killed me with those eyes.

"She said, 'Most people here don't believe in death. They think dying is like falling asleep and waking up the next morning in the same hell. But you believe, and that's brave. How do you do it?'

"I tried to tell her about the voice that I'd heard since I was a child, a voice calling out to me through the waves, but at that moment the machines rained down on us. They slammed our ribs with noise until we couldn't breathe. They churned out a blizzard. The other prisoners moaned and cried. Their skin blew away in the snow. We lost each other in the storm for days and I hunkered down in the corner, shivering, chewing on my fists. I tore off chunks of my fingernails and ate them; I would have eaten my hair if I had any left.

"The entire time I sat alone in the blizzard and the snow, all I could think of was the sand plum cake my mother baked for me on my 18th birthday. She decorated it with sepia colored caramel frosting and violet flowers. It was the only cake my mother ever baked for me. The priests said there was a sugar shortage. When my mother gave me my slice I trembled because I felt my stomach protruding underneath my dress. I had a 17 flower waist at the time, 8 flowers too large. I licked the caramel frosting off my fork and fed the rest of my slice to the dogs. If only I could have that cake now, I would never go hungry again. That cake was the only thing I could think of. God dredged it up as a special memory to torment me. I started to think I was in hell because I didn't eat my mother's cake. I tore off chunks of my fingernails and ate them. I would have eaten my hair if I had any left.

"After the machines turned off the blizzard, the guards forced the heretics of block six to dispose of the dead. We dragged them to the end of the final hallway, all the way through the ice, and threw the dead down into a chute. There I found Hadley, leaning over the chute, peering down into the darkness. I assumed the bodies were incinerated, disposed of somehow. But

Hadley said the bodies weren't destroyed, but stored for a time before they were re-animated for God's army.

"'How do you know this?' I asked her, and she said she'd seen it herself, armies of our dead emerging from the earth. It might possible to jump through the chute and emerge out the other side, but she didn't know for sure."

I thought of the night long ago when Ezekiel took Chicory and me out to the machine fields and he raised the dead.

Leda scratched a figure into the sand. The number six.

"When I met Hadley I realized I had never loved anyone before. Good took me away from the ocean and my family and all human warmth. He had to send me down into the place without hope for me to realize what love meant.

"Hell makes peoples' minds shrink into rigid and small things. The starvation and pain turned people into selfish demons. They would kill each other friend, or step on their friend's skull to keep their feet from burning on the floor. Hadley was different. She was our guardian mother our night watch. She held us and kissed us and rocked us, even as we were pitched across the floor and forced to crawl through burning mazes searching for a place to rest. She said I was the bravest one in there, but it was she. Throughout the endless nights I rested my head in her lap, too weak to cry, and she stroked my forehead, my cheeks, my tattoo. She asked me, 'Why do strangers no longer kiss?' and kissed me full on my bleeding mouth. She said, 'This is all we have left.'

"I told her sometimes, 'I don't deserve to be held. I didn't eat my birthday cake.'

"She only held me tighter, although she was so thin and starved her bones shook with the strain.

"I knew I was going to die soon. My eyes felt like dim-lit pinholes. My head felt too big and swollen for my neck to lift. I was no longer in control of my arms or my legs. They seemed to disappear right into the floor. I spent most of my time catatonic, slumped on the floor, but then something happened.

"Another prisoner stole Hadley's food. It was only a little bit of soup in a stone bowl, but he wanted it so he kicked her and scraped her face and tore her scalp. That was the first time I ever saw Hadley cry. We were all so tired. We were all so sick. I thought Hadley would never break down but she was human just like the rest of us.

"I dragged Hadley to the corner of our cell and I told her about the voice. I said 'Do not be afraid. They are coming to save us. I don't know when, but we still have a chance. Do not be afraid.'

I kept holding onto Hadley and I thought of the voice from the ocean washing through me. It blocked out the noise of the plague machines. It blocked out the cold and the hunger. I curled around that voice and held it to my stomach like a little glowing seed until all other thoughts disappeared. And I think that's what saved me. That's why I didn't die.

"The next time the guards forced block six to dispose of the dead, fourteen of us jumped down into the chute with the corpses."

"We fell several feet down and landed on a pile of bodies. I thought I felt them grasping me in the dark. Their fetid smell stained my skin and burned my throat. How strange I was afraid, because you'd think I'd be desensitized to death by then. Someone started yelling that we were trapped in there, that the walls were closing in on us, and I began to believe him. I felt the darkness squeezing my bones.

"Hadley found the way out through a shaft. She talked to us until we found our way to her through the blackness, groping and blind. I reached out and she took my hand. She pressed my fingers against the cool metal of the shaft.

"She said to me, 'We're almost home, darling.'

"We crawled up the shaft and into daylight. The first thing I saw was a crooked sign with the word "Edgewater" scrawled across it in yellow paint. Then I saw the field of machines. They slept as if paralyzed by sunlight. I went into hell knowing I'd never see daylight again, but here it was bursting off my fingertips, laying in lazy ropes around the trees, falling like golden flakes on my tongue. I stepped out into the field of sleeping machines and the smell of the grass and the woodlands, seedy pine and fennel and sap, gushed out, and hit me like an explosion. Hadley caught me before I fell. When I laughed I thought it might crack my ribcage.

"All together, we ran into the woods out of sight. Some of us embraced each other. Others lay stunned in the grass. Hadley took my hands like leading me into a waltz and we spun each other around until we were dizzy. Hadley and I devoured the heads of yellow flowers and collapsed underneath the trees. Hadley and I lay together, limbs entwined.

"I'd forgotten what it was like to be warm. She touched my shaved head, my paper translucent skin, and told me she never really saw my skin before, that I had skin like honey.

"I called her my vanilla girl, ice-cream girl. Hell didn't whiten her skin. As a child she must've flown into clouds that stuck on her limbs.

"We talked about our future together. We would run away from the towns and the plague machines to a meadow of yellow flowers, and build our home out of saplings and conifer leaves. We could grow a vegetable garden and make clothes from butterfly cocoons. At night we'd write philosophy by candlelight. We'd write about things we'd seen and things we wanted to see.

"Some about going back into hell and rescuing the others. We could break into the Prophet Headquarters and steal the hell shuttle records, rescue people about to be rounded up. But we didn't have the power to do any of that. You could tell that hell warped some of them, made their spines crushed and angry forever. One woman broke her legs trying to fly away from the top of a tree. And there was this man, a bald man with holes where his eyes should have been, like someone gouged them out. He told me he would kill everyone who ever wronged him. He kept rambling about a kidnapping and a ransom nobody would pay."

"That was Smarts," I said. "I used to know him. When we were children. He came to Edgewater the night you disappeared."

"I never asked his name. Eventually everyone went his or her separate ways, except for Hadley and I. We lay underneath the trees until nightfall, and then held each other until we fell asleep.

"I dreamed of hell. I dreamed of the machines with their proboscises sparkling like glaciers. Their steel teeth tore my skin away. Hadley shook me awake. I thought I was still in hell but then the sun splattered on my face, my hair. All morning I murmured, 'This isn't real, this isn't real.' Hadley pressed her lips into my hair. She just repeated, 'We're never going to go back there.'

"We snuck into an abandoned home and stole clothes to wear. I felt like I slipped into someone else's body. Whoever I used to be died in hell, and my ghost emerged from the ruins."

"A monster killed her, didn't it?" I said.

Leda's hands tightened against mine.

"How did you know?" she asked.

"Because that's how all stories end."

"Out in the woods, we passed a pagan temple. Kali came out of the ruins, out of nowhere, like she peeled herself off a pictogram. Her blue powdered skin was dull as paint, her tongue cracked and crumbling. She moved so fast. She saw Hadley's tattoo, so she broke her neck and flung her against the temple's stone steps. I ran away while Kali drank Hadley's blood, into Edgewater, and that's when the flower shopkeeper found me, huddled on her porch steps. She took me inside, fed me, and gave me a place to stay.

"That's why you came to Edgewater. You were looking for a place to hide," I said.

"Yes," Leda said. "But I found you."

"Why did you leave?"

"I didn't want to. But then the night you were gone with Ezekiel, Jolene came to me. She knew who I was. She told me the prophets and the high priests all talked about the people who escaped from block six. She said she could help us. She told me some of the other escapees of block six were gathering down at the ocean.

Someone would meet me at the bus that night and if I wanted to go, but there was no time to wait."

"Why would Jolene help you? And with what?"

She brought my ear close to her mouth and whispered.

"We're going to kill God."

The distant mountains seemed to scuttle close and crush my limbs against the ocean. The tower from where the voice emanated seemed to rise like a reanimated corpse from the water. When I closed my eyes I saw my family's rickety, dark-creak house sliding into the swamp, my father's hands clutching a slick jar of formaldehyde.

"Don't say things like that," I said.

"Listen to me, Charles," Leda said. "You've heard the voice. I know you saw the tower out there in the water. As a child, I used to swim out there and hold onto the tower as long as I could, because it was the only thing I could hold onto. Our whole lives have been constructed from fear. Our families are engineers of terror, because they too were constructed from fear, made brittle by fear. The tower was the only place that felt different. Hope was a forbidden word in our family, but hope sprung from the tower, from the voice, as if from some eternal — from a place that couldn't be destroyed, that existed beyond fear. It's real."

She pressed her fingers against my heart.

"Somewhere out there is a place that exists beyond God's control. I know it's real because that's where the voice came from."

"And where is this place?" I asked.

I choked on a tight knot of anxiety. The memory of Jolene crawled up my knuckles.

"Home," Leda said. "Can't you feel that this isn't where we're supposed to be? Doesn't the wrongness of this place rise up in you like a sickness? The monsters and the killings, does that seem normal to you? The slip implants and always being afraid and the hell shuttles and hell itself? But when you hear the voice, you know it comes from a good place. It's the place where we should be. Our home."

"But where?" I asked.

"I don't know. I don't think anybody knows. Maybe it doesn't even exist anymore. But God wants us to believe that the Black Planet is our home, that he is eternal and this place he created is all that exists in the universe, but anyone can look around and see that's a lie. There are other worlds. You can see the abandoned temples. The toppled tower. And we escaped from hell, which God said couldn't be done. There was something before God, and there will be something after he is gone.

"Someone took us from our home. They took us so far that maybe we can never go back, but we have a chance to change things. There's hope inside of us, the voice speaks to the hope inside of us. We can kill God."

"Why do you trust what Jolene says?" I asked.

"You felt it, didn't you?" Leda asked. "You heard the voice and you felt the same way as I did."

"Yes," I said quietly.

"Can I tell you something?" Leda said.

"Of course"

"After I left Edgewater, I kept having this dream we're sitting out in the desert together. You cradled a cow skull like a baby. It was so hot in that desert. I knew we hadn't had food or water for days. I panicked. I said, 'We're going to die, Charles. We're going to die out here.' You looked up at me calmly, serenely, still cradling the cow skull. You said, 'Everything dies. But not us. Not today.'

"'I'm so thirsty, Charles, I know I'm going to die' I said. I kept saying your name like I would forget it. In the dream your name was the strangest sound I'd ever heard. And then you said, 'We're going to get out of here, and I'm going to find us a lake. A cool, glittering lake. We'll forget this horrible heat. We'll jump into the water and swim out so far we can't touch the bottom. I know we need to get to that lake, so we're not going to die.' Then I wake up."

"What do you think it means?" I asked.

"I'm not sure; I think it means life isn't as strange as we were taught. Or that it's right to want this. To want to find the place where we can swim out," Leda said, "or maybe it means I missed you."

I looked out into the water, and though I couldn't see it from where I sat, I knew the tower was out there in the waves, broadcasting the eternal voice.

"Will you help me?" Leda asked. "Will you help us?"

Three figures walked across the beach toward us.

They wore gas masks and crusted military boots and armbands bearing the number six. One of them carried a rifle slung over his shoulder. Another, a woman wearing a purple taffeta dress with a butterfly bow, carried a bottle of vodka.

The man with the rifle called out to us, "Sorry we're late. You wouldn't believe what we've had to deal with out there."

He pulled off his mask and revealed his wounded face, his cheeks slashed and sutured together with white thread. The woman took off her mask and stared me down with a mother bear scowl. When the last man took off his mask, I saw he had one mechanical eye and one real eye. The mechanical eye contracted in the sunlight. He pulled it out of the socket, the eye tethered to a thin cable, and tossed it from hand to hand.

The man with the rifle said to me, "I know

you. We met out in the desert."

"I should've known," the man with the mechanical eye said. "Nina bet a thousand to one you were going to fall into a sinkhole and die out in the desert. But I said you had crazy eyes, and no man with crazy eyes like you ever died without getting where he needed to go."

I looked to Leda.

"I'm here to help," I said. "Just tell me what needs to be done."

Eleven

NINA TOOK ME to the cliffs above the ocean, and taught me how to shoot a gun.

"It doesn't matter if this is our home or not. It wouldn't make a damn difference if we found it or not."

"Why is that?" I asked.

"Keep your eye on the target."

Nina steadied my shoulders and oriented my body toward the red bull's-eye target she'd painted on cloth and propped up with a wooden frame. The gun felt like an oiled membrane in my hands. Leda and the others stood a distance off, talking and drinking from the bottle of vodka. I learned the man who carried the rifle was named Camp. The man with the mechanical eye called himself Shooter.

"Because we'd still be unhappy," Nina said. "Try to breathe," Nina said. "Steady yourself and squeeze."

I squeezed the trigger. The gun shot off and blew a hole in the corner of the cloth fabric, splintering one side of the wooden frame. I took several steps back.

"If you think it doesn't matter then why are you here?"

"Where else would I be?" Nina said. "Shoot again."

"I've never shot a gun before."

"Point the barrels down when you're facing

me. That's a great way to blow someone's ear off."

I pointed the gun down and turned toward to the cliff side. The corpse of a deadhead with his split head and fingers his licked away to the bone by crabs was dashed on the rocks below.

"Did you know my sister and mother are deadheads?" I asked.

I raised the gun, steadied my shoulders, and fired. The bullet tore through the center of the bull's-eye.

"I see now," Nina said. "You're one of those kinds of people who have to get angry before they can act. Well, not to worry, there are plenty of things to be angry about."

Nina walked back to where the others waited. I shot at the target a few more times, unloading the clip, before I joined them.

"We're meeting the others in the desert later," Camp said to Leda as I approached.

"How many do we have now?" Leda asked.

"About eighty. We've been recruiting the prisoners we free from slave camps in the desert."

"That's not nearly enough," Leda said.

"It'll have to be," Camp said.

"And what about ammunition and rations?"

"We raided a warehouse a few weeks back. We should have enough to last us."

Shooter held the vodka toward me. The mechanical eye in his head clicked as it focused on my face and my stomach churned. I declined the bottle.

"I thought we would have more people by now," Leda said.

"We're not going to get any more. Not after Slim Sarah's celebration festival or the increasing hell shuttle raids. People are more scared than ever."

"I need to show you something," Leda said. "Let's go talk to Jolene."

Nina and Camp headed toward the house. Shooter drained the rest of the vodka and then tossed the bottle over the side of the cliff, then followed after.

I felt as if I was shrinking back into the skin of a small boy at the bottom of Jolene's pool.

Jolene sat in the corner of the room in her rocking chair. Her nails scratched grooves into the chair's arms. The air bristled around her. Camp, Nina, and Shooter stood on the opposite side of the room, facing Jolene, their bodies tensed. They'd probably never been this close to a monster before.

Leda approached Jolene.

"You need to hear this," Leda said to us. "Jolene, how do we kill God?"

"I've told you already. You're not a very good listener. If you wish to kill God, you must activate the defenses."

"And how do we do that?" Camp asked.

"At the beginning of time protective agents

were installed on the Black Planet should the creator ever become dangerous to humanity's survival. When God became destructive long ago, the protective agents were activated. But they were defeated, and now lay dormant."

This was not the same Jolene from the swamp that spoke to me in subterranean threats, the Jolene that once that pulled me into the sick, wet folds of her rotting dress. This Jolene spoke in a blank monotone, as if reciting a speech left festering for years in the back of her head.

"In order to activate the protective agents, you must get into God's castle. There you will find the guardian spirits of wind and fire, which hold the secrets to His power. They reside in a black room, asleep and waiting for someone to activate them. When you step into the room, it will activate and the agent will speak to you through the fire. You must know the right words to speak to the agent. When it says 'Stand on your feet and I will speak to you,' you will respond 'I stand on my feet and I listen.' This will allow you to access its secrets and awaken the protective agents."

"You see why eighty isn't enough?" Leda said to Camp. "We could have five hundred, a thousand, and it still wouldn't be enough."

Jolene looked at me and smiled. I turned my face away.

"Is that the only way to activate the protective agents?" Camp asked. "Getting inside of God's castle?"

"There were once ancient temples that housed guardians, but I know of none that still exist," Jolene said.

I thought of the pagan temple in the desert, and the room that lit up with a storm when I walked into it. I thought of the voices that issued forth from an electric cloud, but I said nothing.

"Then we need more time," Leda said. "If we go into God's castle now we'll be slaughtered by monsters and plague machines."

"Time isn't going to wait for us," Shooter said.

"So we're just going to go get killed, then?" Nina asked. "I didn't crawl out of hell to turn around and offer my head to God on a fucking platter."

"If we don't try, nobody will," Camp said.

"You've heard the rumors, you've watched the television," Shooter said, "We've been threatened for as long as we can remember, but the prophets aren't just blowing smoke anymore. Slim Sarah's celebration festival, whole populations sent into the hell shuttles. Plague machines are dissolving whole cities into dust. It isn't just to make people afraid. We're not talking about your standard plagues. We know this. We've talked about this before. This is the beginning of the obliteration of the human race."

Nina turned the television on.

"Do you know what the chronic problem

facing our society is, folks?" Teddy asked. "It isn't the rising death rates or the chronic unemployment. It isn't the fact that one out of every six citizens has disappeared in the last few years, or that more and more sinners are being sent to the hell shuttles every month."

The camera pulled back. Delilah slumped at Teddy's feet, clinging to his knees in a soporific stupor.

"It's apathy, ladies and gentlemen," Teddy said, his hands clasped together. "The problem in our society is pure, unadulterated, reckless apathy. Apathy to the wonderful force of God working in our lives, apathy to the desires of the creator. You are destroyed by your addiction to inertia, by the gravitational pull toward frozen matter. God can instill you with purpose and bring you away from the brink of your useless nihilism."

Teddy opened his hands and they were full of bloodied slip implants. The implants were dirtied and rusted red, as if they'd been used before, maybe torn out of people's heads and spilled into Teddy's waiting arms to be used again.

"What's wrong with you, Nina? Turn the damn television off," Shooter said.

Nina didn't move. Leda turned the television off and the screen snapped black. For a long moment, nobody moved or breathed in the silence that followed.

"I know what to do," I said.

"I'm sure you do, Charles," Jolene said.

I clenched my fists and my eyes rocked in my head, trying to ignore her presence in the room.

"I've found a room like you've described," I said. "Out in the desert, there's a pagan temple with such an agent and the spirits of wind and fire. And I know how to get there."

"Are you sure?" Leda asked, "Charles, if you're sure—"

"I'm sure," I said. "It said just what Jolene described, only at the time I didn't know what it meant."

"Why didn't you speak up earlier?" Nina asked.

I didn't know how to explain that I hadn't really known how bad things had gotten until I'd seen Delilah quivering on the floor at Teddy's feet. I hadn't known if I should help them, not really, until I'd seen Teddy holding up those bloody slip implants.

"Where did you find this man?" Nina asked Leda. "He must've been a pretty good fuck, because he obviously isn't that bright."

"That's enough out of you," Camp said.

"You'll take us there?" Leda asked me.

"Yes," I said.

Nina shoved past me, nearly knocking me into the wall, and went out the door. I gripped the striped wallpaper to steady myself but it tore away in one great sheet to reveal the ribbed plaster beneath. It was just like the wallpaper that once covered my baby brother's room. When I looked at Jolene, her smile ate at me like acid.

***

That night Camp and Leda built a campfire on the beach.

"Won't someone see us?" I asked.

"Isn't it sick?" Camp asked, as if he hadn't heard me, looking around at the deadheads washed up on the beach. "Every time I see a deadhead I always think it's my sister. We've gotten so used to looking for people we love among the dead; it doesn't even feel strange anymore."

Camp took a beaten up, silver harmonica out of his coat and played while Shooter kept time by tapping on his mechanical eye. Nina sat a ways off, drinking. Leda sat cross-legged next to the fire and I lay my head in her lap. When she bent down her hair enshrined me. I fell asleep with her breath expanding into my chest.

I awoke a few hours later to Leda gently shaking me. The fire was nearly dead, the burning driftwood melting into a grimace, and everyone else lay in the sand, asleep. Leda put a finger to her lips for silence, and looked out toward the ocean. A figure moved toward the tide line. Leda and I got up and walked away from the fire.

We found Jolene facing the ocean with her arms outstretched. The wind whipped at her hair and dress.

"Jolene?" Leda called out.

It was as if the nighttime intensified the roar of the ocean. It swallowed Leda's voice and withdrew back into the water.

"What's going on?" Leda asked Jolene, as we got closer.

I pressed my fingers into Leda's shoulders. Jolene lowered her hands and looked back. Jolene's hair, snarled and alive, reached out for Leda in the wind.

"I wanted to see the ocean," Jolene said. "I see you've brought Charles with you. How's Sissy? How have you been treating your mother?"

"They're dead," I said.

"A more confident man would dream about being a hero," Jolene said. "Someone who could save everyone they ever loved. Mount up on a white horse and ride into battle. But the most you could ever do was try to hold on while the world fell apart around you."

Jolene appeared to grow impossibly tall.

"You ate my baby brother," I said. "Why are you here now?"

"That time is over," Jolene said. "We were created by God to fill specific roles. A plan for each and every one of us. For an eternity I guarded the swamp, watched Edgewater fall and be rebuilt a thousand times over. I watched that dark house become home to family after family and then become empty again. I ate the dead children to teach each new generation that hope did not exist."

As I often had over the last few days, I felt myself weakening, my limbs losing feeling.

"The longer we're trapped in our systems the easier it becomes for us to see their intrinsic flaws," Jolene continued. "We reach dangerous conclusions about ourselves and our world that others may try to kill us for. Even monsters like me."

She turned back to the ocean. She cocked her head and outstretched her arms. The wind and the spray tore against her clothes.

"I've always wondered. If I was meant to stay in the swamp forever, then why have I always wanted to go to the ocean?"

"I don't understand any of this."

"Charles, those are going to be your dying words," Jolene said.

She closed her eyes and smiled.

"If you truly want to know why I'm helping you, you won't get any easy answers. It's not because I believe in the goodness of humankind. It's not because I believe God and his monsters are evil. I only wish to have the capacity to change. I wish to know that we have the ability to take a different direction than the one presented to us. That is more important than good and evil. Than life or death."

Jolene fell silent, and stood transposed against the ocean, her back bent, arms open, as if she could take the waves inside herself.

"I think I know what you are," I said.

"Finally, some conviction," Jolene said.

"It had something to do with a mechanical horse. And a monster I saw shortly afterwards. I don't remember much of that night, but I do remember that. I think you're something like the plague machines. Something like the slip implants."

"It is possible," Jolene said.

"Then is God something like you as well?" I asked. "A machine that can be broken?"

"What does it matter if he is or not?" Jolene asked. "You know what to do next."

"And you?" I asked. "What are you going to do next?"

Jolene looked back at me, her eyes placid, mouth dripping with insect wings. Then she turned back toward the water.

Jolene lowered her arms and walked into the ocean waves. The dark water reflected her back at us, a mirror of clouds and stars. She kept walking until the ocean completely submerged her. Leda and I stood together in the silence for a long time after that, embracing each other in the cold. The black moon rippled on the surface of the water in the place where she disappeared, like a locked gate that kept us from following her down.

Twelve

WE PACKED WHAT LITTLE supplies we had and headed toward the desert, back the way I came.

A few days before arriving at the temple we met up with more heretics in the desert. They sat on top of an overturned bus eating paste rations from tin cans while taking bets on how long it'd take for a slaver's corpse to stop kicking. They'd just finished raiding another underground slave trader operation, and the kicking corpse lay on top of sandstone steps descending down into the earth. The corpse was hamstrung and torn open with bullets. When I saw him, I reached for the gun on my hip to make sure it was still there.

One man sitting on top of the bus saw us approaching and waved. He jumped down and embraced Leda.

"They call me Wires," he said. "I forget my real name a long time ago. I don't remember why they call me Wires.

Wires took Leda's hand and kissed her on the cheek. "Leda is a good girl. She's polite to old men. A real good girl."

"This is Charles," Leda said.

"Yes, I heard." Wires said. "We're finishing up here. Been recruiting wherever we can, getting prepared to go to The First City. Killing God would almost make forgetting my name worth it."

I heard the plague machines groaning from miles away. The clouds above churned with black dust.

"You think they know what we're doing?" I asked.

"They do, champ," Wires said. "When the original fourteen broke through from hell, you can bet the people in charge took note of it. And we've been recruiting people for months now, destroying slaving operations. For sure they know."

"We should break into two groups," Nina said. "One goes toward the temple while the other heads to The First City. More of our people are waiting there. We'll have a better chance of succeeding if we all don't rush headfirst into the temple where they're expecting us."

"That's the best idea you've ever had," said Shooter.

"We better go fast then," Camp said.

"Charles, you'll take half of us to the temple," Leda said, "And we'll meet the others in The First City city."

Leda and Wires continued speaking, but I could no longer hear them over the blistering noise of the machines. I pressed my hands over my ears. I thought I saw Wires mouth, "You're a good girl." to Leda before patting her on the shoulder and heading toward the city.

Several people joined Leda and me before we headed off for the temple, including a hard-mouthed man named TJ, or Tommy Jones, depending on what he felt like being called that day, and Sunray, a woman with arms a latticework of rope burns and black bird tattoos. Her blond hair caught the sun and seemed to swallow her face whole.

The first time I walked through the desert, it took me weeks to reach the ocean. The desert stretched through my mind, vast, rolling, endless. But this time the pounding noise and the black storm grit of the machines chased us.

***

It only took a few days to arrive at the temple entrance. When we arrived, the plague machines were waiting for us.

They sat near the horizon line, with hard eyes and swollen nests full of breeding insects. The machines extended their necks and reached up into the sky to pull the storm closer to the ground. A prophet wracked with seizure stood beside them.

Underneath the machines God's dead army stirred their feet in the dirt. Some were newly dead, their skin only bloated with a tinge of gray. Most were in further stages of decomposition. Their skin flaked away at the blue bones hung together as if by strings. Their heads were obscured by swarms of insects that hovered around their skulls.

"Where did they come from?" I asked.

"What does it matter?" Nina asked. "See anyone you know?"

The machines lurched toward us. The prophet, twitching and hacking blood, shouted at us through a loudspeaker.

"God has found you unworthy of life! You have rejected the gifts of The Trinity and will pay eternally for your crimes!"

"Let's be quick," Camp said.

We went down into the temple.

The machines came quickly. The prophet's voice barreled its way into the ruins after us, and the machines smashed against the temple's foundation. We heard the dead army surging behind us.

"How is that even possible?" TJ asked. "How do they move the bones without any muscle?"

"With God all things are possible," Shooter said. "Unfortunately."

We went down a flight of stairs, further into sprawling expanse of the temple ruins. A thought hit me in a panic. I couldn't remember where the room was. The first time inside the temple, a girl dragged me through its rooms as I was half unconscious, and I couldn't orient myself.

"Where's the room?" Leda asked.

"I'll find it."

"What did he say?" TJ shouted.

No one responded.

We wandered through rooms I couldn't remember from before, rooms containing bloodstained baths and broken computers, rooms with words written on the wall in spider languages and others with empty pools full of coins and statues with their faces smashed in.

In my absence, the temple must have shifted its rooms and erased all familiar markings.

The prophet's voice smashed through the temple ceiling.

"There is no escape from the almighty God! You shall be punished for your transgressions and burn for all eternity in hell!"

I stumbled and almost fell to the floor.

"Come on!" TJ said. "We don't have much time."

We turned a corner into a hallway full of the dead. They held makeshift weapons and scratched the walls with their nails and teeth. Their bones shifted to the rhythm of the machines above.

The prophet stood among them. He was a bow-backed, dark haired man with eyes the color of warm spit. When he smiled blood spilled from his mouth. He was too old to be a prophet for much longer. The shiny sphere in the back of his head sucked out his life and spit back cerebral palsy.

"Hello, motherfuckers," he said.

"And looks like we're out of time," TJ said.

We ran back the way we came and the dead

ran after us. Nina took her rifle off her shoulder and fired a few shots. A dead man killed her with a sledgehammer blow to the side of her head. Sunray screamed and tried to pull Nina's body away from the oncoming horde, but a dead woman grabbed her sunlit hair, dragged her down onto the floor, and broke her neck.

I ran without looking behind me, through the ever-rotating channel of rooms, through claustrophobic hallways and tilting chambers. I reached out for Leda, thinking she was still behind me, only to find no one there. I went into a room full of insects with lion's faces and red teeth. They stung my arms and face. I cried out, ran out of the room, and fell in the hallway.

I got to my feet. I passed the familiar sandstone pictograms of once-glittering machine shells surrounding the black moon, and the monsters with pumice red nails waiting on the black planet below. I passed pictograms of the monsters growing tails of fire as they were hurtled to the planet. After that I saw the machines fighting the monsters and tearing them apart.

At the end of the hallway, I came to pictograms I'd never seen before. Even with the army behind me, I couldn't help but notice the pictogram of a field of yellow poppies where the monsters lay down to die and decompose. Above them shone the black moon, and from its rays sprang more flowers, cities, people.

A plague machine stuck its fist through the ceilings. Its clenched fingers, caked with plaster, unfurled against the floor and a cloud of locusts streamed forth.

I escaped into an adjacent room. The remains of the dead girl in the black vellum dress lay on the floor, her faced in face strewn in pieces. Something shifted behind the pagan altar where the girl once slept and ate from clay cups.

"Charles!"

Leda crouched in the corner of the room behind the altar. She'd lost her gun and her clothes were torn and stained with blood, hanging off her body like strips of skin. She tried to stand.

"Don't move. Please. Where's Camp?" I asked. "Where are the others?"

"I don't know," Leda said.

I reached for her. She smelled of plaster and paint flakes and black ichor. Insects crawled into my ears and burrowed into my skin.

"This is what happens when you defy the almighty God!" the prophet shouted. "This is what it feels like to watch everyone you love be destroyed. How does it feel? Is not God a beautifully just god?"

Leda pressed her bloodied hands to her ears. I pulled my gun from its hip holster.

"Charles," Leda said, her lips swollen purple, insect wings spilling out of her open mouth. "You need to find the room."

"It's gone," I said.

But I didn't mean the room was gone. I meant the floor and the walls. My fingers and feet, the rupturing earth. All of it, gone, my body no longer belonging to me. In another part of the temple, someone screamed. I pulled stingers out of my skin. Insects hissed at me in the walls, clacking their red teeth.

When I ran back down the hallway I found the pictograms defaced and the sandstone eaten away by tiny insect mouths. God's voice slithered through the ceiling.

"You should have known better! Did you think I wouldn't find you and destroy you? Did you think you could get away with rebelling against me? Those on the side of God are always triumphant."

I ran past God's voice snaking toward me, into the swarm of locusts poison and beating their brains against my head. On the other side of the wall the prophet hacked and coughed. He laughed like a garbage disposal.

Around the corner a dead woman reached out for me with her hands transforming into a buzzing swarm. Human fingers sprouted out of the stone. I slipped down into a pool of dark hair and hands.

She grabbed my neck and her nails scratched at my arteries.

"Where's the pretty dark haired girl?" the prophet spoke from the other side of the wall.

"Where is she hiding? I can hear her crying."

The prophet spoke in a singsong melody, and as the woman pulled back my head, I imagined his words splattering red against the walls like engorged butterflies. Like frozen meat.

I stuck my gun muzzle into the rictus of the dead woman's mouth and squeezed the trigger.

Her head snapped back. I reared up. Her fingers left an angry slash across my face and I watched her fall, silent, down into hair below.

"Where are the rest of you motherfuckers?" the prophet yelled.

I followed his voice. He coughed again and I gripped the gun tight. It throbbed in my hands like a headache. The walls seemed to close in on me and the storm kicked my head like a bad baby. The ceiling's belly scraped against my forehead. The end of the hallway opened its jaws to let me through its honeycomb colored stone.

The dead burst through the walls.

Even through all that, I felt the heat emanating from the prophet's shiny sphere, and I ran towards it.

"Come on out lost little lambs," the prophet said. "I'll take good care of you."

I turned another corner and then I was on top of him. Together we hit the ground. I slammed my knee into his ribcage. Before he could make a noise, I smashed the butt of my gun into his temple. The dead army surrounded me. They grabbed my hair and my throat but they couldn't pry me away as I hit the prophet again and again. His shiny sphere cracked. Black fluid seeped out of the back of his head.

When the prophet died, the dead army collapsed and they didn't get up again.

The plague machines continued rocking the temple from side to side. I headed back toward Leda.

I found Camp crouched over Leda. A swarm of insects obscured his head from view. Somehow he still managed to clutch his rifle, even though his arms were swollen purple with bites and venom bulged in his veins. The temple lurched and I slid across the floor toward them. Camp caught me before I hit the wall.

"What happened?" Camp asked, looking down at my hands.

They were covered in black fluid.

"I killed the prophet."

"You what?" Leda said.

I lifted Leda off the ground. I pulled stingers out of her cheeks. Her eyes were swollen shut.

"We have to find the room," I said. "Can you walk?"

"We can't go. The others are dead," Camp said.

"But we're not," I said.

Camp followed Leda and I out of the room. I kept one hand on her shoulder, the other on the gun. I knew where to go. The black fluid on the back of my hands seemed to shock my system into remembering. It was as if the hallways were the passageways of my brain.

I found the black room.

I stepped inside and it burst into a storm of light and fire. The white cloud spun down from the ceiling. Camp stumbled and went down on one knee before it.

"Stand on your feet and I will speak to you," spoke the shifting figures within the cloud.

"I stand on my feet and I listen," I said.

Fire rolled through us. An enormous, translucent fist shot through the storm cloud and hovered in front of us. It held a scroll, which it unrolled in front of us like a glowing wall. Glowing white words flowed on the scroll in a constant, indecipherable stream.

"What do you wish to access?" the voice spoke, cool and toneless.

Behind the scroll the shifting figures coiled in and out of the cloud.

"The defenses," Leda said. "We wish to access the defenses."

"My apologies. That registry no longer exists."

"Registry?" I said. "This is a computer?"

"We are the living creatures. We have been here with God since the beginning of time," the voice said. "What do you wish to access?"

"Someone's destroyed the defenses. Got rid of them." Leda said.

"What do you wish to access?"

"We need to access the defenses," I said. "The protective agent."

"My apologies. That registry no longer exists."

"Do you have history records?"

"My apologies. That registry no longer exists."

The words continued flowing through the glowing scroll.

"If this is a computer, then it's been wiped," Leda said.

She pressed herself against the wall on her tiptoes, trying to avoid the flames rolling through the floor. Her face was pale; her eyes reflected fire back at me.

I gripped Leda's hand and our fingers were sticky with blood.

This couldn't be what we came for.

"Who is God?" I asked.

"He is the creator of the universe. He is the alpha and the omega. The savior of the world, and the destroyer of evil."

"No," I said, "I mean, what is God? Where did he come from?"

"I do not understand the questions."

Somewhere in a distant part of the temple, God's voice shouted through the plague machines.

"There is no escape from the almighty God! You shall be punished for your transgressions and burn for all eternity in hell!"

"What do you wish to access?" the voice asked again.

"The protective agent gone. The history records are gone. Who's been here before us?"

"Before humanity there was only God."

"Yes, but where did God come from?"

"I do not understand the question. What do you wish to access?"

Above us, the ceiling shook. Leda gripped her head as if it might burst.

"Forget this," Camp said. "We're not going to last another minute once those plague machines crash through here."

"The plague machines!" I called out to the room. "We wish to access the plague machines."

"Earlier in this conversation, I identified your language as 21st century Earth English. However, I am not familiar with the term plague machines. Did you mean the splicers? Nano-machine factories?"

"Who the hell made this thing?" Leda asked.

"Nano-machine factories," I said, taking a guess at the computer's question.

"Nano-machine factories register accessed. What is your input?"

"Disconnect them. Shut them down," I said.

"Request confirmed."

The plagues machines above sputtered and died. After a moment's pause, their limbs thudded and collapsed. Some crashed through the temple ceiling and the walls. The voice of

God, mid-sentence in a damning condemnation, stopped.

"Disconnection successful."

We walked out of the glowing room and it fell back into darkness. Out in the hallway the corpses of God's army shone with locust skins. We had to crawl over the bodies to get to the stairs. Leda crawled ahead of us, head down.

"Leda?" Camp called.

She didn't respond. She crawled beneath the toppled pillars at the entrance and out into the open air.

Camp and I followed her outside. As I went, I pulled the locust stingers out of my skin.

Leda crouched underneath an immobile plague machine.

"It's over," she said. "If we can't access the protective agent there's nothing left for us to do."

***

We slept in the desert among the battered hulls of the plague machines. In a dream, Teddy floated down from heaven on a static wave.

"You're going to throw away your chance at salvation because of a woman?" he asked me. "Your father taught you better than that."

"I know what happens to the people who search for salvation," I said. "The same thing that happens to everyone else."

"Why didn't you marry a nice girl like Chicory instead of chasing after a tramp?"

"This isn't about Leda."

"Of course it is. She was never anything more to you than a symbol of the unattainable."

"I didn't ask God for much. I only wanted the noise to stop."

"You want to know what I think?" Teddy said. "You clearly have mother issues."

He opened his hands and showed me faded photographs of my house. He flicked his hands, and the photographs revealed Momma and Sissy. They sat in front of the television with swollen limbs and emaciated bodies. The hot wire spiders inside of them shone an angry red.

"You left your family behind to die. And don't forget about sweet Jeanine," Teddy said. "Remember her? The girl you abandoned? The girl that loved you?"

He held out another photograph. This one of Jeanine. She was stripped of clothing and head shaved. She curled up on the floor of a dank cell, shivering. On her head someone tattooed the number six.

"What were you planning to do again? Prevent the apocalypse? Kill God? Your family's already dead, son. There's no home for you anymore. If you think about it, your death would be a blessing."

"Earth," I said. "The computer said we were speaking 21st century Earth English. What is

Earth English?"

"It's nothing but words. If God dies, you and the rest of humanity will float through this black universe alone. There's no going back to what you once were."

"Is that what you think we want?" I asked. "To go back? The further we go back, the darker it gets. I've seen the pictograms. I've seen the pictures of the plague machines fighting the monsters and the machines being thrown down from space."

"You have no idea what you saw."

"Why are you even speaking to me? It's over now. There's nothing left we can do, right? So why don't you just come and kill us?"

Teddy said nothing.

"Unless I'm wrong," I said. "Maybe you know something I don't. That there's still a chance."

Teddy said nothing.

"It's in the pictograms. There's the proof God wasn't always in control, isn't it? That's why you're talking to me. You're trying to scare me away. You know his own creations rebelled against him, and they can do it again"

"Oh, Charles," Teddy said. "You should've listened to me when I was sticking my fingers down your mother's throat and dragging her across your bedroom floor. It would've ended up so much better for you."

The wind blew through the desert and Teddy

blew away on a beam of the black moon.

***

When I awoke, I found Leda perched on top of the arm of a plague machine, muttering prayers none of us got out of the habit of reciting. She spoke the sort of panicked, hopeless prayers I heard from people on their way to hell.

"I know what to do," I said.

She pulled her tattered dress around her shoulders like a coat.

"There's nothing left to do," she said.

"Teddy came down to speak to me," I said. "Or maybe I was speaking to myself. I don't know. But I know it's not too late."

For a long time Leda wouldn't meet my eyes.

"If we turned the plague machines off, we can turn them back on. Isn't that right?" I asked. "We can still kill God, and He knows it. Why else would he send his army after us? Because we're powerful and he's terrified."

Leda trembled. Slow and hesitant, she smiled.

"I'll wake up Camp," I said.

In the early hours, the three of us went back into the temple and down into the dark room with its ancient computer.

"Stand on your feet and I will speak to you."

"I stand on my feet and I listen," I said in response.

We turned the plague machines back on. We

told them to make it cold.

Thirteen

THE AWAKENED PLAGUE machines froze The First City. The sky split open and poured out cold grain. A storm of sleet and snow fell upon the gray city. Leda held me as the city turned into a sheet of ice. For a long time none of us spoke. I expected another prophet to lurch out of the city, wheeling an undead army behind him.

But no one came.

We entered The First City. Wires and the rest of the heretics were waiting for us, silent and shivering in the cold. The streets were empty in the white haze. The buildings loomed up like frozen statues. It didn't seem like the same place that had once held Slim Sarah's celebration parade. There were no guards or people or monsters outside, no streamers and corpse painted smeared infants. I saw no prophets preaching the end times or hell shuttles herding away moony-eyed girls with skewed lipstick asking for cigarettes.

Leda was the first to ask, "Where is everyone?"

When we passed the Prophet Headquarters, the televisions on the side of the building flickered on. God appeared on the television, his head bulbous and mask melting.

"Heretics!"

Then just as quickly as they turned on, the

televisions shut off. A few seconds later I heard an electrical snap, the sound of the city shutting down.

"The machines," I said. "They must've shut off the power."

"So we're just going to be able to walk to God's castle?" Wires asked. "I really wasn't expecting that."

Leda held her gun in one hand. She pressed her other hand against her side.

"Are you okay?" I asked.

"I must've torn something," she said, "reaching for my gun."

Her blood dripped onto the frozen ground. I reached for her hand. She pulled away.

"I'm fine," she said, rasping, squeezing her arm. "I'm fine."

We ascended the mountain toward God's castle. Up high the air grew thin, and the castle shimmered like a water illusion. Its turrets became animal limbs. Its windows melted into teeth.

On the side of the mountain a prophet preached the end of days as he dangled a butcher knife over his hog-tied son, who lay in the dirt with a red apple in his mouth.

"Repent for the end is near!" the prophet said, and outstretched his arms.

The butcher knife in his hand reflected the grainy sky above like a mirror.

"Hey, can you tell us where everyone's

gone?" I asked.

"God is no longer speaking to us, my child," the prophet said. "Our spheres have gone blank so that even the prophets can no longer hear his voice. God demands sacrifice. He demands justice."

The group filed past him. When I got close to him he grabbed my shoulders and pulled me toward him.

"You look like the gentle sort, not like all these other ruffians and mad men. What do you hope to accomplish by going up this mountain?"

"Let go of me," I said.

"We have good reason to be afraid," the prophet said. "The end times are approaching! Can't you hear it?"

I pulled myself out of his grasp, and ran up the mountain path toward the others. The prophet's son gagged on the apple jammed in his mouth.

"I wouldn't advise going up there!" the prophet called after me.

We kept going.

At the end of the path we came to a cave, surrounded by a sheer cliff face.

Inside the cave rows of televisions flickered to life. The walls inside the cave were not made of rock, but of steel. God faced towards us on every television screen, motionless except for the breath that stirred in his black chest.

"There must be a backup electrical generator

in here," Camp said. "Of course God should be comfy up in his creepy cave castle while everyone else freezes to death."

At the end of the cave we came to a dead plague machine. Its stomach bulged with dead insects. Its arms lay outstretched on the ground, winding around a spiral staircase.

"Have we come the right way?" someone asked.

"This is the only way," Leda said. "What I'm wondering is where are the guards? The servants?"

She ascended the stairs first, and the rest of us followed.

We entered God's castle.

The walls inside resembled trembled, exposed muscle. The transparent ceiling, like a filmy mucous membrane, revealed the dark sky above.

When the last heretic stepped off the staircase, the plague machine below whirred to life. The cave echoed with the sounds of a brewing storm.

"Keep going." Wires said when some looked behind them, hesitating. "Nothing we can do about that."

We found a television bolstered above a closed iron door.

"This is a broadcast to the citizens of The First City," God said from the television. "And particularly to those who have blatantly disobeyed my commandments that were decreed since the beginning of time. No one who disobeys me will go unpunished. No one will escape..."

Camp headed toward the door.

"Wait," Leda said. "We don't know what's behind there."

"You're right. Everyone get out of the way."

Camp raised his gun. Several others drew their guns and got into position for opening fire. Camp opened the door with a soft click and pushed it open.

Whatever Camp saw inside the chamber beyond the door made him lower his gun and start breathing hard.

"Camp?"

"I found out what happened to everyone," he said.

Inside the chamber hundreds of people were dead.

Servants and guards lay on the ground, slumped in chairs, collapsed against tables and walls. Others were stacked on top of each other, or holding hands, biting into their arms. Glass cups littered the floor and the tables. Some still clutched cups in their blood-drained hands.

Through the transparent ceiling I saw the black moon rise. Its light shone down on the dead faces and transformed them into the color of stone.

We walked through the chamber, stepping over bodies without speaking. The only sound came from the television and the plague machine churning in the cave below the castle.

I only spoke when we left the chamber and went into an adjacent hallway.

"They killed themselves, didn't they?"

Leda ground her teeth together, her jaw shaking.

"You saw the cups. They drank poison."

"Someone must've told them to do it," I said.

We approached another door.

"Stop talking," Camp said.

He raised his gun and moved in to position once more to open the door. Before Camp could act, the door swung open. A hot light shone in our faces. I threw my hands up to shield my eyes from the glare.

"Come in, come in!" spoke a familiar voice. "Ladies and gentlemen, it's been a rough last couple of hours here in The First City, but soon you'll be returned to your normal broadcasting schedule."

I lowered my hands and followed Camp and Leda into the room.

In the center of the room, Teddy sat on his gray bed beneath the hot light, directly in front of a camera bolted to the wall. Delilah lay on the bed next to Teddy. She stirred in a bad dream and her arm hung limp across the side of the bed, almost touching the floor.

Teddy lifted up his arms as if to embrace us. Hot wire spiders spilled from his hands.

"I'd like to introduce to you the

troublemakers that have been responsible for all of this mayhem," Teddy said to the camera. "Say hello to the heretics from block six!"

Fourteen

ALL THOSE YEARS I watched Teddy and Delilah on the television I pictured them as terrifying demi-gods, larger than life, sequestered away in a version of reality that was brighter, bigger, and more real than mine could ever be. Teddy and Delilah were as flat and pale as bad watercolors. Only then did I realize how small they were.

"You're really quite clever, you know," Teddy said, staring at me. "Turning the plague machines against the monsters? Shutting down the city's entire power grid? It took me a while to realize what you'd done so I could reverse the damage. But now the city's up and running and the plague machines are working properly again."

Teddy's head snapped back toward the camera.

"Which just goes to show you, folks, you can't ever defeat those who are on the side of God."

Camp pressed the muzzle of his rifle against Teddy's chest.

"You're wrinkling my suit," Teddy said.

In about a second, he ripped the rifle out of Camp's hands, broke his arm, and crushed the gun into powder.

"You know my viewers expect a certain level of professionalism. Do you want to be responsible for their disappointment?"

Camp stumbled backwards as Teddy wiped the remnants of the gun from his suit. Wires caught him before he fell.

"I assume you came here to find God." Teddy said. "You'll see him soon enough. We are going to do such great things. You should be very excited."

Teddy turned back to the camera, even as he kept talking to us.

"I think you'll find I have a very tempting offer for you. All of you out in the hallway come in here. You're a part of this as well."

The rest of the heretics filed into the room. Some with guns raised, but most with their weapons at their side, their eyes like empty televisions. They all looked at Camp, with the wet bone poking out of his elbow.

"Wouldn't you agree that these sinners should be destroyed?" he asked the camera. "But even though God is powerful and swift in his justice, he is also merciful."

"What happened to those people in the chamber then? The ones who drank the poison?" I asked.

"Cut that question out of the footage," Teddy said.

He spoke to someone who must've been behind the wall, controlling the broadcast.

"These miserable heretics, the lowest of the low, who have committed the worst type of sin and attempted to defy God himself, will be given a second chance. Right here, right now, on live television for all to witness."

"What is this?" Camp whispered.

I thought Teddy's widening smile might kill us.

"Beg for forgiveness, heretics," Teddy said. "Show God that you are repentant and you shall be spared."

No one spoke.

"Come on! I was expecting a little more enthusiasm than that. Don't be shy. Just turn to the camera right there and ask God to forgive you. He will ensure your immortality in paradise at his side. That's all! No catch!"

Wires spoke.

"So what you're saying is all we do is say that we're sorry and we get to walk out of here?"

"Walk out of here?" Teddy said. "Of course not. You misunderstood me. "

Teddy produced a small vial of blood, dry and crusted black, from his inner jacket pocket and held it out in front of us and then toward the camera.

"Your body will be destroyed, but we will forever preserve a small amount of your blood in God's coolant storage system."

"That's insane," I heard myself saying.

Teddy snapped toward me.

"Tell me your name."

"Charles," I whispered.

"Charles," Teddy repeated. "Is not the parts

equal to its sum, Charles? Did you know that one human cell contains the genetic code for creating a complete replication of an individual? In a single drop of blood lies the essence of a human being. Don't you see what I'm offering you here? There are only 144,000 spots in heaven, and through God's benevolent will, you can achieve salvation. Right here. Right now. And the whole planet will witness your ascension."

"A drop of blood is not the same as a human being," I said. "You can't just kill us, store our blood in a freezer, and call it salvation."

"My dear boy," Teddy said, "what did you think heaven is?"

"This is bullshit," Camp said.

"Did you think salvation meant we would allow you to retain your individuality, your disgusting, sinful, earthly bodies? Did you think we would let you into heaven with your sex and bile and sickness? You betray God by simply existing. Your bodies rejected the very thing that would have made you worthy of salvation. Your bodies received a glimpse of eternity, and in response they withered and died."

"The slip implants?" I said.

"There were attempts before that. Even the prophet's bodies eventually reject their spheres. They grow sick and die young because a human always rejects God's gifts. And despite God's blessings upon them, the prophets are still human. And there is no place for humanity in heaven."

Teddy ran his hands through his slicked black hair.

"So what's it going to be, folks? Salvation or hell?"

Teddy paced up and down the room.

"No one? Come on!"

Teddy grabbed my arm. His hand was cold.

"Just look in the camera and smile," he said. "The whole world is watching. Tell them you beg for God's forgiveness. Tell them!"

His hand was not a human hand but a calcified, bent organ of glass.

"Let go of me," I whispered in a dry voice.

His hand bulged. The veins collapsed and his skin turned black, and then gray. His knuckles stretched out like animal claws, rearing and spitting. He tightened his grip and I gasped.

Leda raised her gun and shot Teddy in the chest.

His head slammed into the light above the bed. Delilah squealed and turned her face away.

There was no blood.

"I'm very disappointed in you all," Teddy said.

He headed toward the door. Several of the heretics rushed out of the way to let him pass. His footsteps resounded down the hallway.

"What is wrong with all of you?" Camp said.

He pulled himself away from Wires and

stepped in front of the camera. Delilah hissed and writhed in the bed.

"Listen up," Camp said. "I don't know if anyone can hear me, or if this camera is even broadcasting anymore, but if it is you need to listen to me. We're the heretics from block six, and I'm going to tell you everything that God's been hiding from you. We escaped from hell several years ago..."

I went down the hallway after Teddy. Leda, Wires and several others followed after me.

Teddy crossed the hallway through an open door, which led to an antechamber. Past the antechamber, I followed him onto an exterior bridge toward a large, domed chamber I recognized from television. God's throne room

Televisions on the walls and floor of the bridge broadcast Camp in front of the gray bed. He held his broken arm as he talked about he horrors he'd seen down in hell.

"Listen to me carefully! God is not on our side!"

I heard a loud pop. Wind and freezing water rushed through the antechamber and onto the bridge. The water spilled down the sides of the bridge into the chasm below. In the city below the plague machines churned. Black angry clouds descended down on The First City.

Teddy headed toward the black gilt throne in the center of the chamber.

"You think you can kill God?" He said with

his back turned to us. "You think this world would be better without us here to protect you from yourselves?"

He reached the throne and reached for an object resting on one of its arms. God's black mask.

Teddy placed the black mask over his face.

"Your defiance has convinced us to start our purge sooner than expected, but it's better this way. Without you on this planet, we will create paradise. Unchanging, clean. Perfect."

Cold water rushed into the sanctuary at our feet. Down the hallway, people shouted, and then gunfire rang out.

"It doesn't have to be this way," I said.

"Spare me the trite sentiment."

Teddy spoke like the black water that carried Jeanine's butchered swans across its glassy surface.

"Who would you be if you killed the creator of the universe? Without God you would die alone chained to this planet."

"I saw the pictograms in the old temples. I know there was a world before this one. The monsters used to be equals of God. I think once the machines protected us instead of destroying us with plagues. Do you expect us to ignore our history, when its remains are buried around us?"

"There were those who once rose up in defiance against the almighty God," Teddy said, "but they were hurled to the earth and destroyed."

"You actually believe what you're saying, don't you?" I asked. "You really believe things are better now."

"Did you expect to kill God, go home, and make utopia out of nothing? You already ruined one world with your ignorance. Will you have to ruin another before you realize you deserve your annihilation?"

"I don't believe you," I said. "I've been to the ocean. I heard the voice. It said help was coming. Someone, or something, is coming to save us."

"It's not a voice, Charles," he said. "It's a signal over a thousand years old. By the time help came for you, you would have eaten yourselves alive."

Wires choked and spit blood into his hand.

"You may be God but you sure are a terrible salesman, and that's the truth."

Teddy's head snapped toward Wires.

"You think I'm God?" he asked.

The storm whipped through the chamber and tore the heat from my body. The shouting and gunfire continued in the hallway behind us. I held onto Leda and we pressed into each other for warmth.

The membranous ceiling opened and stars rushed into the chamber.

Teddy stood.

"It's been a great run," Teddy said, "but it's time for me to go see my Father."

He disintegrated into gray dust.

Teddy's pale skin cracked and broke into gray pieces. His snappy gray suit fell to the ground and he rose up as swirling dust toward the sky.

"If he's not God then who is?" Wired asked.

Leda's gripped my arm until it hurt.

"The moon," she said. "Charles, look at the moon."

The black moon lit up, illuminating the sky.

The black moon wasn't a solid ball of mass, but a platform of metal rings that formed interconnected circles, a geometric apparition of living machinery. Each ring seamlessly moved within the complex maze of the platform, like ribbons of sinew folding in and out of each other.

If it wanted to, I thought, the moon could reach down and grab me by the throat. It could lift me up into the air and turn my brain into a television screen.

On the television, a guard shot Camp in the head. He collapsed out of view. Delilah writhed and laughed, then began to choke. She turned her head to one side, and vomited gray sand.

The black moon pulled my head away from the television and forced me back into the center of its geometry.

"Charles," Leda said. "What do we do?"

I wanted to look at her, to reassure her, but I couldn't look away from the black moon.

"Charles—"

"There's nothing left to do," I said.

Guards from the city arrived. My wrists grew limp and my jaw soft. I dropped my gun in the rising water and pressed my hands to the back of my head. Leda and Wires did the same. I trembled with the black moon full in my eyes.

They arrested us. They took us outside where the hell shuttles and the rest of the heretics waited. Everywhere the black moon shone its colorless shadow upon us, darkening the face of the black planet, cool, and silent as always.

Fifteen

THE HELL SHUTTLES LEFT The First City and crossed a vast machine field. I pressed my face to the iron slats of the window. Plague machines and monsters stood in the field, unmoving, looking upwards.

They disintegrate into dust and rose up to meet the black moon.

When they were gone, lightning struck the grass dead and set the flowers and trees on fire.

"Do you see this?" I asked Leda.

Leda slumped to the bottom of the shuttle. She wouldn't look at me.

"That's why they poisoned themselves," she said. "Those people in the chamber, they found out what God was, so Teddy forced them to kill themselves."

"Greetings, prisoners," spoke a cheerful female voice from loudspeakers inside the hell shuttle. "Soon we will be arriving to our final destination. But first, let's have a little trivia. Can you guess why all of humanity must be consigned to the eternal fires of hell?"

People pressed me further into the iron-slatted window. Wires stood on my left, breathing heavy through his clenched teeth. In the darkness of the hell shuttle, everything was gray.

"That's correct!" the female voice said. "Humanity must be destroyed because of the inherent imperfection of the human form, its unmanageable decay and inability for adaptation."

The gray dust in the sky blocked out all light and shape except for the glowing black moon.

"Form follows function, isn't that so?" the voice said. "That's what every child was taught in Biology 101, but what happens when technological advancements exceed the evolutionary rate of humanity? Function can no longer benefit from the weak and slow human form. This is the future, and there is no need for you to be in it."

The hell shuttles approached a dark tunnel.

"Have a nice trip down."

We went into hell.

The shuttle traveled through miles of gray cellblocks. We passed the first cellblock. Hundreds of naked prisoners pressed against bars and huddled together on the floor. In the distance the silhouettes of angry machines extended a dozen arms outward and heated the floor and the walls until the prisoners' skin ruptured with blisters.

In the next cell block a blizzard screamed through the walls. Prisoners clung to each other in six feet of snow, growing lethargic and blue, their fingers black with frostbite.

So it passed this way from one cellblock to the next. Heat and cold, heat and cold, until the difference no longer mattered.

"This is really hell?" I whispered to Leda.

Leda said nothing.

Our hell shuttle ground to a stop. The door slid open and masked guards grabbed several prisoners and hauled them out of the shuttle.

"Don't let go of me," Leda said. "Don't let go. Don't let go."

She repeated the words even as a guard grabbed fistfuls of her hair and tore her out of my arms. I cried out her name, but the machines grinding away into the walls, the screams of gray-faced, metallic boned ex-humans, drained my cry away. I ran after her, and a guard slammed his elbow into my face, knocking me to the ground. He grabbed the back of my shirt and hauled me up with my nose bleeding.

We were ushered out of the hell shuttle toward gray, box-like chambers at the end of the row. Behind us waited an endless line of hell shuttles, their lights doused with snow and shimmer heat.

The guards stripped us naked in the chamber and threw our clothes into a pile for burning. They forced us against a concrete wall.

"Don't touch me!" Wires said like a wounded bus.

Nozzles snaked out of the walls and doused us with chemical spray. I bared my back to the spray and it burned my skin. I clenched my teeth and my knees buckled.

"Leda!" I called out.

A guard grabbed the back of a neck and threw me to the concrete floor. His boot crushed the back of my head. I spit blood and it flowed across the concrete floor and formed a pool around my mouth. He shaved my head as I wallowed in my blood.

He pressed the tattooing needles to the back of my neck.

"Am I a heretic?" I asked.

"Sure thing," he said.

"After you're done with me they'll do the same to you."

"You bet," he said.

"Leda!" I screamed, "Leda, help me!"

He held me down with his boot as I squirmed.

This couldn't be real. I'd waited for this moment for my whole life but it couldn't be real.

He tattooed the number six.

He shoved me out into a hallway with the others. We were ushered down to block six. I called out for Led again and again, but the machines answered instead.

They gripped my hands with their blinding heat. They stung my fingers with eyes like poison nets. I stumbled against the other prisoners. A guard shoved me against a wall.

"Follow them!" he ordered, and slapped me across the face.

We marched away from the line of hell shuttles and into the place where light couldn't follow.

Maybe this was where the deadheads ended up when doctors punched the slip inside their heads. Maybe if I looked long enough I would find my mother and sister, Jeanine's ghost, the last vanishing shade of my father.

The guards opened the gates of block six and ushered us into our new home.

Wires grabbed my shoulder.

"We're so good at doing this to each other," he said. "That's the terrifying part."

The guards dragged him away from me. Someone grasped my fingers and pulled my cheek against the cold metal bars. It was a girl with a sharp, emaciated face with and eyes wide enough to walk through. She edged her hand through the bars and brushed my cheek. In the center of her head was a torn hole where her slip implant used to be.

"Charles," she whispered.

Jeanine.

I turned back. The storm nearly blinded me. Pink dots of blood lined my vision, and from all sides gray limbs reached out to block my way.

I pushed my way through the crowd and the open cell gate toward Jeanine. She leaned against the cell bars, shaking. All her bones jutted blue underneath her skin. Snow lay crystalline on her face and shoulders and would not melt.

"I never got to tell you that I loved you," she said.

"Your brother told me."

I tried to warm her body, only to realize we were both frozen. I couldn't give her warmth because there was none left.

I pulled her out of the cell. From all sides machines bared their teeth and shuddered. People screamed and fell down. Others remained silent with their naked backs bared like offerings. I bit down on my tongue. I thought I'd never stop bleeding.

In the last cell of block six, I found Leda, naked and huddled on the frozen floor. They'd shaved away her locks of black hair and tattooed over her fading six with a bigger, bleeding six.

"Leda," I said.

She didn't look up. Jeanine shivered against me.

"Leda, it's okay. We've heard the voice," I said. "Don't be afraid."

"I've heard that voice for thirty years," she said. "You know what Teddy said. Help may be coming. But not for us. It's too late for us."

I knelt beside Leda and tried to pull her into my arms. She resisted at first, and her arms stiffened.

"Please don't. We failed," she said.

"It's the end of the goddamn world. Let me fucking hold you."

Gently, slowly, I pulled her into me as and snow and sleet fell down from the ceiling. I kissed the back of her neck and rubbed her arms.

I couldn't feel my limbs anymore.

"This is a fucked up planet you know that?" I said. "All of my life I just wanted love, to be loved. I didn't know we'd have to change the composition of the universe to do so."

"I love you. I'm so sorry," Leda said.

Televisions on the ceiling and walls flickered on.

"Hello humanity," God said. "Good news. The rebellion has been crushed and those who would attempt to defy me have been banished to hell. With this final purge of the black planet my supreme rule shall never be challenged again."

Leda's breath hitched. Jeanine convulsed with cold. They turned away from the television and buried their faces in my back.

"Life is a strange and flawed phenomenon," God said, "After you are gone, the universe can return to its state of equilibrium."

The television screens switched to a live stream of the black moon and its interconnected machinery as its living geometry spun faster and faster.

The screens cut to several different live streams of the empty planet's surface. The skies boiled. The black moon shone its face on the earth. There were empty cities, empty machine fields, empty houses. The only things that still moved on the face of the planet were the hell shuttles as they headed down into the earth.

The black moon opened its core, and fire

rained down on the earth. It was shining fire, shining like the black moon, and it obliterated everything it touched. Leda tried to lift her head, but I pushed her face into my shoulder.

"Please don't watch," I said, even though I couldn't look away.

She curled into me. I rocked her, and hell stood still.

The shining fire burned the towns. It destroyed the fields and the trees. It evaporated rivers. It burned the pagan temple. It obliterated the abandoned tower in the sea and the sea itself, everything that told us of a world before God. The fire destroyed the ancient, bristle thumbed trees and the swamp where Jolene once dragged away my dead baby brother. It destroyed everything that once stood between the black moon and us.

Even as we froze in hell I felt the fire's heat. It reached for me through the television and passed, smoldering, through my bones.

It burned fast, and burned clean. Who we used to be burned, and I burned with it. Soon there would be nothing but the ash that hovered in the sky, the glowing crook of the black moon, this invisible prison below.

"In my perfect world we'd have night flowers that sang lullabies," Jeanine whispered in my ear. "Every book and marriage would have a happy ending."

"Please," I said. "Not this game. Not now."

The three of us clung to each other on the frozen floor. The fire rained on and on, beating over our heads, creating God's paradise. I tried to imagine the lake Leda dreamed of, that cool, sparking lake. I tried to delve down into the waters and disappear in their depths, but even my thoughts froze over.

"I want to go back home," Jeanine said. "Take us back home."

"This is home now," I said. "I'm so sorry."

Help was coming, but not soon enough. Help was coming, but not for us.

Author's Note

I became friends with a newly minted atheist, a recent graduate of Religious Studies from a Christian university. He told me he was schizophrenic. He used to see God sitting in the corner of his room like the angry cloud that wrapped itself around the shoulders of Moses. He saw angels taunting him from heaven, demanding his penance. This wasn't the fluffy God of protestant Christianity: Let's all hold hands, God is love, Jesus forgives you; this was the angry and demanding god of the Old Testament.

"God stole my life. He stole my family, and I feel so alone," he said.

We sat in the parking lot of a Wal-Mart. I sat curled in the passenger seat of his car. Both of us were crying.

"Do you ever find your way out of the dark?" I asked.

"I think it just stays with you."

It may not make much sense to anyone who hasn't grown up in a religious community - but to many people, leaving religion is leaving their identity. Especially for someone who'd just spent the last four years training for the seminary, reading religious texts and exegesis. Your family is Christian. Your friends are Christian. Your books. Your jewelry. Your shirts. Your past. Here, rip my skin off. I know why he cried for weeks, unable to come out of his room. The family doesn't understand. The friends abandon you. The church that was once a place of comfort and solace is now a beacon to your terror and your fear. And you can't shake the feeling, months after making the choice to abandon your religion, that you made a mistake. That you're going to hell. That god is following you in the night, like a cannibal, a Great Destroyer, ready to tear your heart out for being a coward. A betrayer.

There's a reason that in Dante's Inferno the ninth of hell is reserved for traitors. The traitors of god reside in Judecca, after Judas Iscariot the betrayer of Jesus Christ. Here the traitors to their masters are punished by being submerged completely in ice, unable to speak. Unable to move. Those who commit minor sins have the ability to at least be distracted from their sins by their exteriors, such as the lustful blown about in the wind. But the further you get to the center of hell, the less you can move, until we get to Judecca, where you'll never breathe properly again.

Nothing to distract you from the consequences of your betrayal.

I'd stopped believing in God by the time I was fourteen, but meeting my new friend brought back painful memories. My disillusion came mainly from rereading the bible and realizing that God was a petty, angry, mean, cruel god.

That I found no connection between the "loving god" of church and the smoldering monster I found in the bible. He routinely killed and punished his own people, set them up to fail, raped a virgin, and condemned people to eternal suffering for perceived petty slights. The God of the bible was the Bad Father, a raging Borderline with an ego complex.

"But what if God exists?" people asked me, "what if you're wrong, and God exists?"

My answer was The Crooked God Machine.

In a world where god was irrefutably real, but cruel and disregarded human concerns, what would you do? To me the question of religion is not one about belief versus disbelief. Any coward can bow down to an unjust god, real or not, but if a great humanitarian can go to hell because he didn't say "I believe," then we all suffer as a human race. So do you go to heaven quietly, or do you destroy yourself in protest against injustice? In a world that seems immeasurably cruel, do you fight for the chance at a better world?

The Crooked God Machine is not only a story about god and the danger a world would be put in where he existed. It's about a family falling apart. It's about finding, and losing, friends. It's about finding love among ruin and chaos. It's about not having an identity because of the demands suffocating you, and learning how to rebuild yourself years later. It's about the strength and resilience needed to exist in a cruel world. It's about losing everything - your home, your status, your clothes, and your life - but still managing to keep your love for others and your defiance against injustice.

I first started writing this book when I was 19 years old, and published it at 22. Now, two years later, I've learned a lot about the process of self-publishing and writing. In the 2nd edition, the book is more polished, with much-needed edits and revisions. I tried to stay true to the original book and not change any plot points or structure, because a book is a piece of history, a captured moment of emotion and belief. I was an angry nineteen-year-old kid, a big fan of Naked Lunch, and typing out revisions of this book in a basement while I worked on a dairy farm in Oklahoma. Revisiting this book pierced me with old emotions. The wound is newly scarred, and I hope I've maintained the rawness and anger I felt during that age in these revisions.

Read on for a science fiction short story I've added exclusively for the 2nd edition.

Honeycomb Heads: A Short Story

ONE NIGHT THE Residents carried our children away while we slept. We searched for them on the frozen surface of the planet with our satellite and snowmobiles. We found no traces of them left on the ice, no scraps of hair or clothing, not a drop of blood squeezed from a finger, no footprints of either Resident or child. The Residents stole several of our security cameras, so we couldn't trace the direction they'd disappeared. Even our omniscient satellite remained silent about their whereabouts.

"Maybe they never even existed," said one of our childless professors.

Late at night I sent a message to Central Station near Earth:

Why the fuck did you send a philosopher with our colony?

Of course, I never received a response.

It was our biologist Anja who found the grid-like entrances to the underground reserve where The Residents lived, camouflaged in ice and unlocked only by body heat. Our colony governor advised we shouldn't go in. Our central satellite couldn't map the tunnels underground. There could be new species with new diseases. We could carry viruses with us back to the colony that would teach us nothing except new and unusual kinds of pain. I've been talking to the professors, and maybe our children never even existed?

Central Station overruled her and authorized investigation into the reserve.

Several of us went underground in hazard suits with supplies to last for two weeks. We travelled down a network of dark, warm tunnels. We had no directions, except down. In two days our communication devices stopped working. We lost contact with the colony. We couldn't even talk to each other behind our thick hazard suits, and communicated by turning our flashlights on and off, by tugging on each other's shoulders, pointing at our feet when it was either collapse or sleep.

In a week we reached the substrate, where walls glowed, flecked with warm, golden dust. We sweat underneath our hazard suits. My eyes burned with sweat I couldn't wipe away. Before I arrived at the colony I spent my entire life in southern California, possibly the last desert on Earth, and once went to the hospital for 2nd degree burns from the sun. And yet I couldn't even remember being this hot.

I thought of turning back, but then I thought of Tammy.

In a week and a half, weak from our liquid diets, our heads buzzing and red skin on our faces peeling away, we arrived at a long, lit hallway. Amber-liquid cells honeycombed the walls. We found our children in stasis inside of them.

They regained consciousness when we pulled

them out of the liquid, but they were sleepy and slow, barely able to move.

I found my daughter Tammy in the last cell, her dark eyes open but unseeing, her blond hair a nest for her wrists. She kicked her feet, languid little sleepwalker's kicks. I plunged my arms into her liquid cell and pulled her out. I tore the helmet off my hazard suit.

"Mommy?" I said, gasping in fetid underground air. "Can you say Mommy?"

She spit bubbles.

"Can you say Elle?" I whispered, trying to clean her wet face with my sweat-soaked shirt.

The others pulled off their helmets and stripping away their hazard suits. They shook their waking children, trying to force them to speak. One of the scientists started yelling about toxicity and viral possibilities, but it was difficult to listen to him when my daughter was coughing on my hands as I cupped her chin, as she tried to open her eyes with fluid stuck to her lashes.

She vomited amber liquid on my arms.

"Where are they?" someone asked.

"Where are the Residents?"

In the center chamber past the honeycombed hallway we found the Residents, sloughing off their chitin and dying in piles of quivering muscle. The queen sat on a throne of glittering dirt. She was gorged on honey, her stomach bloated, her lips glistening.

"Why did you take our children?" I wanted to ask.

I wanted to stick my hands through the warm dust brushed onto her stomach, to pull out her viscous blood and smear it across her face. I wanted to break her fingers and see if she, this creature undiscovered and under researched, light years away from earth, knew how to scream.

The seven eyes rolling in her head snapped toward us. Her mandibles clicked, echoing through the large chamber. She held an arm out toward us, stretching it so far it dislocated from her shoulder with a loud pop. Glittering blood poured from her wrist, and she died.

We travelled back through the maze. Though we abandoned our heavy hazard suits in the hallway of cells, it took us longer to get to the surface than it had to go down. We carried the emaciated children on our backs, in our arms. There legs atrophied and they could only walk a few minutes before collapsing. Their skin stuck to our skin with sweat, but they were cold.

Back home at the compound, we cleaned the crystallizing amber off the children in the showers. We wrapped them in warm towels and lay them down to sleep. As night came, the temperature-regulating shields went up. The beasts out in the dark, beasts with ice-colored fur and ridged, protruding teeth, came out of their dens and wrestled each other and hunted and wailed. The children shivered and rolled in their beds at the noise.

We were beginning to think that moving here was a mistake.

Earth had been dying for a long time, no surprise there. Overpopulation, over-pollution, war, and a failing economic system. It's a story that the Vikings were singing thousands of years ago. We poisoned the rivers and obliterated mountains because the human brain is physically incapable of understanding long-term consequences. Good thing we discovered space travel before we all went bankrupt.

Several planets had been found and colonized in the last fifty years by private organizations searching for the promised land, some sweet milk and oil that would make them rich enough to live in private galaxies after Earth collapsed. We could've gone to Indica where the blue dust of the planet that swept across the plains was a sweet, mild hallucinogen that seeped into the pores of skin. Or we could've chosen to go to Enslia, where colonists breathed cold fresh air that smelled of flowers, and bathed in hot springs so pure that the water cured their arthritis and closed up old scars. We could've even gone to Mars, where residents lived in domes built from nanite machines and were coddled by robots. The best literature and movies came from Mars, produced from a society that never forced its people to die on factory lines or mines.

Instead we ended up on Frigg, where ice dunes ridged the surface of the planet. At night when the sun plunged down behind the polar mountains the temperature could fuse our organs together with cold.

"It's not so bad here," our architect Taylor said once. "Things have gone horribly wrong on other planets. In some places, the habitation process was corrupted, or halted, or the machinery malfunctioned. You heard what happened to the people on Deus, didn't you? Apparently the government got involved and everything. "

Taylor pointed toward the sky.

"Good thing she's kept us safe so far."

Only at night could we see our satellite, big as a moon, hovering over our planet. Its gears worked in silent space, but sometimes I thought I heard it talking to me. In my dreams I sat on top of a curved hill, freezing to death, unable to speak. Yet the satellite extracted my thoughts. They traveled to her through space on a silver thread.

"I don't trust you to keep us safe," I said.

"You don't trust yourself," the satellite responded.

"What have you done with my daughter?"

"You blame me?"

"You could have warned us. "

"Why would I?"

She rearranged the stars to smile.

"Why would I?"

The doctors administered nutrition to the children through IVs. Their stomachs couldn't hold down food. The children screamed in pain as they slept. The doctors injected them with antibiotics and painkillers. They kept screaming. The children shivered and clenched their teeth as they slept throughout the day.

In the morning before the sun rose, the children awoke for an hour or two. They stretched and stirred, pressing their emaciated spines to the bed, rocking from side to side.

Throughout the barracks parents cried, "Can you say 'Mommy'? Can you say 'Daddy'?"

The children didn't speak. Their blood pooled in their veins. Their hearts beat at half speed. Before noon, they'd slipped back into sleep. This continued for a week.

A second week.

By the third week their bodies resembled pieces of gray furniture. When they opened their eyes their pupils did not shrink in light. They were dilated, broken into fractals, swirled in red. I thought they'd collapse underneath the weight of their bones.

Before all of this, I once asked Tammy where she thought her soul lived. She laughed at me. She had her father's laugh, the kind of laugh that made you want to sink down through your own skin.

"You're silly," she said. "You know it doesn't matter."

We were beginning to think they'd never fully wake. The doctors came and went every few hours. Parents stood by their child's bedsides, piling on blankets, taking off blankets, adjusting the lights, smoothing foreheads, trying not to break their own fingernails against their cheeks.

"What was it like underground?" someone asked, clutching at locks of her child's colorless hair.

"Warm."

While everyone else shivered in the cold, those who went underground were heated and red. I pressed my face against the cold barracks wall, trying to cool myself. My stomach felt ready to rupture. When I took a shower my top layer of skin cracked and peeled away.

And as our children continued to sleep, we became insomniacs. We couldn't close our eyes, because maybe our children would walk over our eyelid and disappear.

Our scientists had taken vials of the amber substance from the tunnels to study. In our lab they found the amber was a sort of prenatal fluid. The cells were like amniotic sacs, filled with proteins and carbohydrates.

We traveled millions of light years across the universe to get away from earth, only to find creatures with the same protein structure we possessed, molecules once spit out of a star factory that bloomed into single-celled organisms on the surface of a desert world. Life was not an anomaly. Only a bad joke.

Taking samples of the children's blood revealed their veins flowed with Resident DNA.

Anja invited me into the communal kitchen to talk. Anja used to smile in a way rare for scientists, blushing up to her eyes. On earth she'd become the department head of her research lab, yet on weekend nights still performed at the Venus Lounge, a chanteuse who dipped her skin in gold and sung forties jazz songs.

I was told she would've made Billie Holiday rip her hair out in jealousy.

She hadn't sung in years. Not since she came to Frigg.

"What's happening to our children?" I asked.

"Isn't it obvious?"

Anja poured me a cup of coffee. I hadn't drunk coffee since we came back from the tunnels, and looking at it made my insides squirm with heat. I set the cup down on the counter

"Let me guess," I said. "When The Residents kidnapped the children breathed the prenatal fluid, they mixed their DNA together."

"Elle, has anyone ever said you should be a scientist?" Anja said.

"This is me rolling my eyes at you."

"But that's not everything," she said.

"Do I want to know everything?"

Anja looked down, tracing her finger around the rim of her coffee cup. When she flexed her fingers, the skin on the back of her hand cracked and bled.

"No," she said. "This is why I never had kids."

"Because you thought they'd be captured by aliens and their genetic code restructured? That's a stretch."

"Because I get too attached. It's a poor trait for a scientist."

"Not for a parent."

It was difficult to believe that the thinning, sleepy thing sinking into dirty sheets could be my daughter.

Tammy had her father's tousled blonde hair, his energy. Everyone used to say standing in the same room with her father was like being struck by lightning, and Tammy was no different; touching her was a static shock. She wanted to be president. A model. A writer. A veterinarian. She wanted to create a machine that would build for us a new dimension where we could hide when we wanted to be alone. Somewhere we could walk in the forests and not run into a thousand other people walking the same path.

She seemed to defy the laws of space-time. All at once she could be jumping on the couch and running through the kitchen, breaking cups, smashing cabinets.

The camera her father gave her before he walked out on us never left her wrist. When she wasn't singing and dancing and screaming, she sat on her computer and cycled through photographs of her eyes.

"I'm trying to find myself," she said.

"I thought you said it didn't matter."

At that Tammy sighed, like I'd never understand.

Why, no matter how fast our computers ran, no matter how far we extended our fingers in space, could we not ever get back to the origin? In my eyes, I would not find myself. Forget the soul, forget God, forget essence; even if I tore open the zygote that fused to form me, I would not find myself. If I travelled to the loneliest planet in the universe and set up shelter there, deprived of all unnecessary accouterments of society, I would not find myself. I would find only the face of a cold mountain, an underground honeycombed hive, my reflection fading in the bronze mirror of a metal lake.

I'd find my daughter, floating in a cell breathing amber fluid that'd make her forget those eyes belonged to her.

***

One night, the children woke up.

***

The children tried to leave their beds. They kicked and screamed when we held them down. I hit the alarms, and doctors rushed into the barracks. The sedatives did not calm the children. The painkillers didn't keep them from screaming loud enough so we couldn't hear each other speak.

Tammy's eyes were wild and filled with adrenaline.

"Do you remember who I am?" I asked as I held her down by her shoulders.

She said "Mommy" like being kicked by a horse. "Mommy" like the last spitting spark of output from a machine being destroyed by a virus.

The other children spoke.

"Mommy," they said, their voices blurring into each other.

Mommy.

They screamed and screamed. The doctors examined their bodies searching for pain points, bruises, infections. They pried open the children's mouths and checked for swollen tonsils, red throats. They checked their hearts, beating fast but to be expected. The scientists filtered in and took more blood samples. Some of the children flushed yellow. Some started vomiting. They strapped a gangly, writhing boy to a stretcher, but not before one of his flailing arms struck a young doctor in the mouth. They wheeled him off to the lab for x-rays. The doctor stopped for a few moments, her hands over her face, her body rigid.

"He drew me flowers once," she whispered, and then fled.

"We need more straps," a parent called out.

His child pushed him, and he fell. When our children stopped eating, many of the parents did as well. How easy it was, to dissolve underneath stress. When he hit the floor he broke his bones. His child reared up from the bed. I chased after him. I caught him by his skinny arm and pulled him into my embrace. He screamed louder. Tammy jumped up from her bed. I screamed louder. She'd send a lightning bolt down on our heads. She'd tear the walls down with a sideways glance. So many weeks without movement, comatose and thinning, I thought her heart might burst.

Tammy ran toward me. An old part of my brain thought she wanted to touch me.

Instead she touched the boy convulsing in my arms. They grew still. They clasped hands and touched foreheads. She breathed cool breath into his mouth, he breathed warm back.

I released him. They nuzzled each other's necks and sank onto the floor, the color returning to their faces.

We let the children go. They rose from the beds and met in the center of the room. They interlocked hands and huddled together, thrumming, rubbing shoulders. The doctors carried off the man with the broken bones. The children huddled closer. Breathing in. Breathing out. Their screaming, now subdued, still rang in my ears.

They slept together like a Rat King, whose tails have been matted and tied together underground in darkness, the bones fused. Several organisms fused into one. I could not see Tammy in the pile of children, so tightly they held each other. The only visible part of her was the ends of her blonde hair.

Whenever anyone tried to pull them apart, they cried out as one, a throbbing, swelling insect noise. We couldn't inject lullabies into their brain stems. We couldn't cradle them to our chests and administer medicine that would teach them how to be human again.

The professor of philosophy speculated they were a new evolutionary step of the human race, but he didn't know a goddamn thing. The head of the biology department, Doctor Einsler, suspected the Resident DNA acted as a virus that would override the human parts of their brains.

"And do what?" I asked.

That, he didn't know.

Their bodies gave off a new kind of heat, their skin drenched in cooling sweat. Their eyes grew a film across them and they no longer used them to see. They saw with their fingers, grasping and studying objects they once found familiar, reaching out for each other and keening if they ever found themselves alone. Maybe they were like insects, searching each other out with pheromones buzzing on their noses and lips.

They sat outside in longs rows touching each other's backs. Tap. Tap. They relearned words with fingers encrusted in powdered snow.

Maybe "Love" meant a thumbprint of ice on the lips.

"Feed me," a brush of powder underneath the chin.

Hannah Pash, six years old, once wanted to be the first president of Frigg. Now she stripped the skin off her fingers and dug into the ice with her toes, hissing at any adult who touched her.

Little Ben used to be obsessed with time. He drew diagrams of a clock tower he wanted to build in the center of our colony, even though we were all synced to the master clock. When his mother tried to give him his grandfather's antique watch, he smashed it on the ground and picked through the tiny gears searching for food.

They fed each other droplets of artificial honey and reconstituted packages of dried ice cream and powdered strawberry. They sucked on their fingers until they bled. They keened like coyotes as they grabbed at their growling, shrinking stomachs. What did The Residents eat? We didn't know.

Why did they steal our children in the first place, and why did we enter their inner chamber to find them in ritualistic death, their queen holding her wrist out toward us? We didn't know.

"Why don't we know?" I asked Anja.

"We didn't think we needed to," she said.

Anja went to the Doctor Einsler and requested permission to study The Residents. Not so fast, he said. There was red tape to go through, papers that needed to be signed. Requests for armed guards to accompany the expedition. Funding to be acquired. And anyways, they would send someone else. They needed her to continue study on the cross pollination of new GMOs.

"Fuck that," Anja said.

She set off on a snowmobile one morning through the temperature-regulating shields. She carried a tranquilizer gun and what rudimentary examination tools she snuck out of the lab.

At night I imagined her trying to sleep and cook dinner outside in the freezing cold. Every time a beast wailed, I imagined her being trampled underneath him. At daybreak, I climbed to the top of the barracks and searched the horizon line for her, waiting for her to return.

She didn't even have any children of her own, yet she was the only one who ever went out to search for answers.

I didn't cry like the others at first. I found parents weeping in bathroom stalls, weeping behind refrigerators. Schoolteacher Miss

Madison lay curled up in my bed after the children refused to come to class anymore, a mask of blankets over her face. The doctors dragged her into the medical center where she stayed for a week.

While the children chittered and played with each other and clawed at the frozen dirt searching for a way into the earth, the parents formed a wailing wall. They hugged each other while the children interlocked arms and legs in a Gordian knot of skin. They talked of abandoning Frigg. There were planets where people could drink the dirt like rich coffee, planets where the sun healed disease.

And besides, we didn't have it so bad on earth. Sure, it was crowded. Sure, only the rich could afford oxygen masks and the rest of us had to cross our fingers that cancer didn't metastasize in our brains, but we killed all the animals that could kill us back. We never had to worry about freezing to death or being trampled by iced-back beasts. Tammy and I had our own apartment and a tiny kitchen table that we couldn't eat at without bumping elbows. We had warm food and coffee that didn't make my stomach want to crawl inside out.

I had Tammy.

I signed up for the waiting list to leave Earth before Tammy was born, and when we had the opportunity to leave I thought for once Tammy would be able to stretch her legs and not hit another human being with her feet. She could see mountains and breathe pure air. Several of her classmates were already coughing up polluted black blood, others on multiple medications for stress and anxiety and ADHD and depression and fatigue.

We came to Frigg four years ago. Central had not sent anyone else since. Communications had come infrequently and brief. Four years, and we had yet to discover resources that would churn a profit or even how to take care of ourselves.

The only time Tammy still let me touch her was when I brushed her hair. She sat quiet in her tiny pink chair, staring at herself in the mirror. It was the stare of meeting someone you've only known in a dream, of trying to remember.

"Tammy," I said. "That's you."

Her eyes never blinked.

I brushed her hair until it turned the color of powdered snow and fell out. I collected the hair from the floor and tied it in a ribbon, hid it in my pillowcase. It was only hair, I told myself, and hair doesn't mean anything. Yet I couldn't deny the way losing her hair changed the shape of her face.

After all the children lost their hair, we started finding teeth embedded in the snow. They spit teeth out into their hands as if trying to get rid of a bad taste.

Anja still hadn't come back. Nobody suggested sending out a search party, we were too busy crying on X-ray sheets.

I couldn't cry. If I cried then the monsters would come out of the walls and the snow. If I cried, all the water would drain out of my body and I'd be a husk to be swept under the carpet, or a skin blanket for hospital patients. I'd have to cry for every terrible thing that happened to me – in chronological order – for the death of my parents from the blood-congealing cancer, for Tammy's father leaving me, for the last time I ever looked at earth on the shuttle out. How earth resembled a tiny ball in space, like a marble on black velvet, its waters poisoned and brown. How I felt skinless in that moment. Gutless. You only get one origin, and we'd ruined ours. Soon the earth would die, and we'd never get to dive down into the pools that we crawled from millennia ago.

Please, don't make me cry.

The children dug into the ice until their fingers bled.

Then, as if they'd been waiting for this tragedy, news from the colonization program came. Our colony was being dismantled. Frigg had been declared inhospitable and unprofitable, like we'd known all along. It was time to find a new home.

We didn't have to say it out loud to know. The children wouldn't be coming with us. We'd been mourning them since the night The Residents came and stole them away. The doctors stopped treating them, their parents turned away, brushing away the tears frozen on their cheeks. By the time we were ready to board the ship, they'd have mandibles where their mouths used to be.

I found Tammy in my bed with three other children. They tapped out symbols on the backs of their heads. Most of their teeth were gone. Their flushed skin cracked and peeled away. They wriggled out of their skin like The Residents in the tunnels, leaving shells of themselves behind. Underneath they were translucent, their organs dark and crystallized.

"Do you want to go home?" I asked her.

She did not blink when she reached up and removed the eyes from her head.

I grabbed her hands. Her eyes, those dark, all seeing eyes, fell onto the ground. The earth started to shake. No, it was me who was shaking. My hands seized up. My tongue curled to the back of my throat.

"Help," I whispered, but nobody heard me. The other children fled.

The lab was empty. The kitchen was empty. The dormitory was empty. Darkness fell. The temperature dropped. It had been daylight only a moment ago, hadn't it? Difficult to tell, how long I'd been on the floor searching for eyeballs. Maybe I'd lost my sight as well. Maybe the darkness was blindness; the children infected me with their fingernails, the soft seductive hush of their hearts collapsing into dust.

Scrabbling on the floor, for the first time in years, I cried. I fell to my elbows, choking, shuddering.

My daughter climbed onto my back.

"Mommy," she said.

"Please," I said.

Though I didn't know what I begged for.

The colony was packing up, taking what they could. They were probably talking about going to Enslia, somewhere with warm air, someplace where they wouldn't risk waking up in the middle of the night with their limbs turning black from frostbite.

The industrial buildings we built would degrade. The temperature-regulating shields would use the last of the battery cells, and power down forever. The signals would go quiet.

The satellite would continue to hover over the planet, watching the empty spaces, waiting for instructions that never came. On self-regenerating cells, it would wait forever.

Mommy.

She shivered and I lay her down in bed. I kissed her forehead. I kissed her decaying mouth. She touched the spaces where her eyes used to be. I wanted to tell her, "You could have been a photographer. You could have been a ballerina." I wanted to tell her, "Life isn't fair, but this, this is beyond unfairness."

For the first time since I pulled her out of the

amber fluid in the tunnels below, we slept together.

And I dreamed.

I dreamed of a tapping against my stomach, a tapping against the back of my head. It first seemed random, but then I realized there was a rhythm, like a complex piece of music. Children surrounded me. They breathed soft against me, their eyeless faces pressed into my back and throat. Tap. Tap. Tap.

I dreamed their touches streaked rich colors against my skin. They painted geometric shapes across my mouth. This was not the mad, frenzied dance of insects. Food. Fuck. Fight. This was an ancient language, of cosmic and astral beauty. It was a language of emotions, embedded deep into the skin. Through their taps they showed me the history of the universe. Stars burst into life and exploded in death. Planets bloomed like flowers. They took me to the birth of Frigg, the ice on the surface so hard and thick it could not be penetrated.

They took me deep underneath the surface, into the reserve where The Residents lived. Their touches traced a network of tunnels, no longer a pointless maze built by mindless insects, but a neural network made of synapses rubbed off fingers, a structure made from the memories left on decomposing shed skins.

There were palaces down there built out of crystal. There were underground fields that went on for miles. Bright jewels grew on the ceilings like suns. They took me to meadows of lush grass past the amber cells. They took me into libraries of touch. Resident librarians passed their knowledge through fine fingerprints. History and physics and fiction were told through impressions of bodies.

With a touch they showed me we made a mistake.

I woke up with a start. The children surrounded me in bed, reaching out to touch me. Their eyes fell out of their head. They spit out the last of their teeth. I could hardly differentiate between them anymore. They were all soft-shelled insects, caught in collective ecdysis.

I went out into the dark. The creatures in the distance howled. It had taken years to prepare this colony, but it was as if only in preparation to leave it. I found the scientists and engineers in the ship's central station, running through the protocol of tests before takeoff. People were stowing away what little belongings they had left. They, like the children, had grown film across their eyes.

"We need to go underground." I said.

"Where the hell have you been?" Doctor Einsler asked me.

"Why did we never go further underground? All those years we searched and suffered, and we never thought to look below us?"

"There's nothing down there except the

Residents and the tunnels."

"You're wrong," I said.

"How do you know?"

"The children told me."

"The project has been cancelled. We aren't getting any more funding."

"What about the children?" I asked. "What about Anja?"

"Forget about Anja. She went AWOL and knew the consequences. And the children, they're not ours anymore."

The ship rocketed out of the planet's gravity as I curled on cold ice. I was alone with the children.

They tapped on my back.

Come on.

They're waiting.

I crawled to my hands and knees and struggled to my feet. I hadn't been eating. I hadn't been sleeping. I couldn't feel my fingers or my toes. I seemed to not be in my body, but hovering above it.

Come on. They're waiting.

I took the last vehicle left behind, a rover with half a tank of gas.

Come on.

The children piled into the vehicle. My hands were so cold I could barely work the controls. The children touched my face. My spine. My body seemed to extend out past into theirs. I drove the rover past the heat regulating shields.

The temperature dropped even further.

Their hands drew a map on my body with dripping honey and fingers and spit. They guided me across the ice, through herds of snarling, fighting creatures, through forests of frozen trees, dead for thousands of years. They forgot how to speak with their mouths but the language of their fingers dripped colors into my brain.

Keep going. Come on.

They're waiting.

Tammy's breath was sweet in my ear.

The gas ran out and the rover shuddered and stopped. We climbed out and walked across the frozen landscape on foot. I thought we would freeze to death, but they created a barrier for me with their tiny bodies. We were warm together. They urged me forward when my legs wanted to give out. Not much further. Not much further.

We came to an underground entrance and climbed down into the tunnels. We no longer needed hazard suits or flashlights. The way had been laid out for us in the trails of glittering dust. We touched the walls, leaving behind red streaks. The children's organs, black and crusted on the surface of the planet, glowed underground.

They were luminescent.

Underground we came to a golden field. We were warm for what seemed the first time in years. Heat flowed back into my blood.

Creatures like fireflies danced in the dark. The children dug through the dirt and grass and unearthed translucent fruit.

Tammy held one out to me, cupped in the palms of her hands. I took her gift. It tasted like spiced honey.

I found Anja in the field, wrapped in white sheets, her skin dipped in gold. She no longer had a mouth. She talked to me with her fingers.

The shapes told me a story.

We can remake ourselves. We don't have to yearn for who we used to be. Nostalgia is a lie, and this can be your home.

Deeper into the reserve, Residents were being reborn, shining, from the husks they once crawled out of.

Tammy touched my face.

My name is not Tammy, she said. My name is fingers dipping into cold dust, a warm fingerprint. Step into the amber. You too will have a new name. A beautiful name. Feel the liquid wash over you. You never knew your brain could think thoughts like this, geometric puzzles. You never knew that it could remember a history older than earth.

The amber pulled me in. It cooled my bones.

Welcome home.

About The Author

Autumn Christian is a game designer by day and speculative fiction writer by night. She is the author of The Crooked God Machine and A Gentle Hell All love letters, blackmail, and inquiries should be sent to her email address at **axtian@gmail.com**. She's been a freelance writer, a game developer, a cheese producer, a haunted house actor, and a video game tester. She considers Philip K. Dick, Ray Bradbury, Katie Jane Garside, the southern gothic, and dubstep, as main sources of inspiration. She is waiting for the day when she hits her head on the cabinet searching for the popcorn bowl and all consensus reality dissolves.

Other Books by Autumn Christian

A Gentle Hell (2012)

We are Wormwood (2013)

Printed in Dunstable, United Kingdom

80522240R00228